Erien Tales Book Two: FaeBorn

Terri Pray

He had a beautiful fae blood woman for his bride, his best friend was a dragon and the most feared pirate in the land had his back, so just what could possibly go wrong?

So maybe he'd forgotten about the minor detail where his cousin wanted him dead.

And there was that small matter of a God trying to interfere with his life.

But these were minor matters in the grand scale of things.

In a world where magic, court politics, demons, gods and romance could merge at a moment's notice it sometimes didn't pay for a prince to fall in love.

Dedication

What started as a short story has given birth to a world, and without those who believed in the wonders of Erien it simply wouldn't have been possible.

To my Fred and Margaret McCann, my parents who though they are 4000 miles away still manage to cheer me on. Mum's been waiting on Fae Born with baited breath ever since she finished reading Dragon Prince.

Meg, for being both friend, editor and proof reader.

For Sarah, who rejoices in telling her school friends and teachers that 'Mommy writes about Dragons', and for her brother, Jack who never became grouchy when cuddle time had to be juggled with writing time.

And to my Sam, my love, life and heart. My own Cluiun, a knight with tarnished armor who never stopped believing in me.

Cover art: Meridth Dillman http://www.meredithdillman.com/
Layout and interior illustration: Sam Pray
Editor: Meg Linehan
Sales agent: Schar Niebling, elfinlady@aol.com

About the Author

Originally from England, Terri Pray now lives in IA with her husband and their two children. Her work ranges from sweet romance to erotica, horror through to fantasy. She currently has 11 books in print, 30 ebooks with various publishers, and two fantasy novels that has become the basis of a d6 fantasy rpg launching late 2005 from Final Sword Productions. For more information about her feel free to stop by www.terripray.com, www.worldoferien.com and coming soon www.underthemoon.org.

Prologue

There could be nothing else in existence that was quite as annoying or grating on the nerves as the sound of bird song, at least not to Kaleb's ears. It was bright, cheerful and full of life. That infernal noise irritated him beyond anything else he had experienced over the countless years. Not even the laughter of a child sent a twitch through his body the way that collection of mindless chirps and squeaks called music somehow managed to.

Still, it shouldn't have really surprised him.

She'd had more than a passing hand in creating those songs. Adding those special little touches that she would have known caused his jaw to clench. The bright chirrups triggered images of him wringing the life out of every bird on the planet one by one. Worse still had to be the affect they had on others. Another little gift she had added to the make up of those creatures. Weaving in their ability to help cast away the darkness and offer hope to those that walked Erien with each new dawn chorus, and all thanks to the Immortal Ellora.

As if those of Erien truly needed such encouragement.

Fae, human, dragon kin and sea born, it didn't matter. Offer them a glimpse of light in the darkest circumstances and they would grasp it without thinking. Taking the thread or offer of a chance rather than stare fully into the darkness they claimed belonged to him.

Inspiration they called it, but it wouldn't have mattered to him if they had named it chocolate pudding. It still boiled down to the same thing.

Hope, and that he could corrupt.

The darkness wasn't solely his domain. No part of the world belonged only to him or her, but that would change soon enough. The balance would tip.

He'd been patient, far more so than those who spoke his name in hushed whispers would ever give him credit for. He'd waited longer than mortal born could ever guess for his chance to tip the balance.

Their turn.

That's what would be screamed when the others found out what he had been doing. They'd demand that it was their turn to rule, have the strength and hold the key to Erien. Already more than a few of his kin pushed to topple him from the position of power he had begun to achieve.

It wouldn't matter, he was ready for them. All those years plotting, waiting, searching for the key, the right souls to grovel at his feet had finally paid off. It was finally his turn. Vengeance, destruction and desolation, those would become the ruling force on Erien. Power would be his once and for all. Just as soon as he destroyed that irritating dawn chorus. Nothing could come close to matching the sound of those creatures, though the cry that escaped the woman tried.

"Mine, he was supposed to be mine!" Dark flames burst forth from the finger tips of the slender woman, crawling their way along the floor in search of food to sustain their blaze. The flames consumed everything in their wake until they reached his feet. There alone was their hunger denied, snuffed out with little effort on his behalf. "You promised him to me, Kaleb. You swore he would be mine. I gave you my oath, my soul in exchange for his presence in my bed!"

Dark pits where eyes should have been met the fury of the young woman's words that had been enough to break through his own musing. "And so he shall be, Arinnana. I never said you would be the first in his bed, nor stated when he would come to you." How easily these creatures angered ever thinking things through before letting themselves be claimed by their emotions.

The charred remains of what had been a human being fell to the ground as nothing more than ashes, unnoticed and near forgotten by both human and god alike within the throne room. Less than two days ago the room had been decorated with symbols of order, peace and the bonds the land shared with Dragon kind. Now ashes, death and dried blood remained as the only memory of those who had once called this place home.

All destroyed, sacrificed to the Lord of Vengeance, except for Arinnana and her unstable mother. Did she not understand her place under his power came solely at his whim? She would soon enough. Such lessons were amongst the few real pleasures his existence offered.

"My sister sleeps next to Rhodan as his bride and you expect me to simply accept that?" The slender fingers clenched in rage, her feet marking a path across the room to the shadows of his being. "You lied to me!"

"You expected differently, child? I am called the Lord of Lies by some." Full lips twisted into a sensual and dark smile. His fingers curling slowly into the shadow formed robes that adorned his body his body. One near perfect in human eyes, a chest bare to the waist left open to Arinnana's gaze, his loins barely concealed by the suggestion of a cloth and legs that rippled with taut cords of defined muscles. But a single look into his eyes would have torn the desire from any sane woman and turned it into fear.

Had sanity ceased to be a part of Arinnana's life when she and her mother had abandoned safer paths upon swearing to Kaleb's service?

For a moment he saw the rage fade, leaving fear and confusion to take its place. Once the woman before him had been a loyal daughter to the Dragon Throne and her Father until Rhodan had denied her proffered love. Now his power claimed her through an oath freely made.

Oh, he knew the arguments that even now would surface in her mind. How if anyone should take the blame for the oath to him it should be the Prince, Rhodan. All he would have had to do was fall in love with her, but no he had fallen for another instead. How it was his fault and no one else's, but that she would forgive him eventually. That was the nature of women such as Arinnana.

After a few nights with Rhodan begging for her touch, Arinnana's rage would fade and when it did Kaleb would grant her the power to meld the Prince to her being.

Then would Rhodan would know such pleasure at the woman's touch such as he had never felt before from a living soul. She would embrace him into the service of the Lord Kaleb, teach him of the power, the wealth and then bring him to his knees to swear to Kaleb.

"He will be yours, when the time is right and together you will spawn a race loyal only to me." His gaze never left her face, taking in each subtle change in emotion. Confusion shifting into a moments fear before anger reclaimed control.

Arinnana screamed, the fire she still struggled to control erupting through the air failing once more at the edge of his being. "I want him now! Give him to me now!"

His hand snapped out, closing on her throat with talon bedecked fingers that threatened to cut off her air. "Never again presume to give me orders, human. I rule here, not you. Do not think that my favor will save you from my anger. You are mine, a thing, a toy to serve my amusement and if you please me a vessel for my glory."

Arinnana clawed at the hold on her neck, feet kicking frantically as he pulled her further from the floor. Didn't she know how futile it was to struggle within his grasp? She made an amusing toy, a willing convert to his calling and still she didn't understand just
how far he would go, or how easy it would be for him to snuff out her pathetic life force. All it would take would be a single hint. A glimpse that she could not longer serve some purpose with him.

Blood beaded under his talons, marring her smooth neck.

"Please don't." Light flickered within the pits of his eyes, a fire he could feel without ever needing to see it.

"You can beg better than that, pet." Kaleb's tongue slithered out from behind his lips, far longer than anything a mortal might lay claim to. "I know you can, you've seen servants crawl on the floor for just spilling a drink and now you offer me a simple 'please don't'?" There it was, that first real glimpse of understanding, fear, hope, giving way to terror. Did she now feel how rapid her heart beat, how easy it would be for him to snuff out her life with a single twist of his hand.

Not that he would have wasted her death in such a manner. Far better to drink in the suffering of hours. Days. Weeks if he remained interested for that length of time. The screams would echo along the stone walls, sinking into the heart of the castle, tainting its structure until the end of time.

Such a delicious idea.

"Don't kill me, My Lord, please." The woman's hands dropped down to her sides, her breath coming in short gulps and he saw the fear push away the last of her rage.

He could taste the fear on the air and drink it from her liquid eyes. "Oh you can beg better than that, Arinnana, much better than that I am sure." His lips touched Arinnana's in a kiss that stole the heat from her body.

Her body hit the cold stone floor, knocking what little was left of the woman's breath from her already chilled form. The fire, darkness, the power within her would refuse to answer her call. Yet, no matter how hard she reached within, it would linger just out of her reach and leave her staring at the bare feet of her God in human form. Did she think he would allow her the chance to strike back at him?

Mortals. Foolish, small minded creatures. How they ever came to hold any importance on Erien he would never understand.

"Show me how well you beg, pet."...

Chapter One

Light filtered in through the thick curtains that lay in thick ripples of rich cloth across the leaded windows. Noiselessly they caressed her body with warm fingers seeking to tease her from the bed as they had done so often before. Except her world had changed in ways Riana never would have dreamed until days before the wonder that this morning had brought into her life.

A wonder?

The dream held smile slipped as her lips turned into a wry grin.

Calling Rhodan that to his face would be asking for trouble, already he laid claim to a level of pride that left him walking a line close to arrogance. He was a strong, proud and bold man who had walked into her life without ever knowing the devastation his presence would cause. Oh, being in love with him did not leave her blind to the faults of her husband. He'd either preen at the thought of being a wonder, or laugh the comment off, but right now his only comment came in the form of a low snoring sound that he might well deny ever making should she face him with the knowledge of the racket he now made.

Heat claimed her skin at the memory of their first night together. How his hands had touched her in places no one else had ever even tried. Lips that had left searing kisses in their wake, drifting from one part of her body to another, lingering on her breasts before moving slowly down her stomach to the heat between her thighs.

She shivered with the memory. Candle marks had passed in their love making. Each time the flame within her had risen to meet the challenge of his own need until they had both collapsed to his bed in a sated and dreamless sleep. Not since the darkness spawned by her sister had Riana enjoyed such a welcomed sleep and now Rhodan remained in the bed next to her.

His eyes were still closed, mind wrapped by sleep as she pulled back her hand from his hair, the temptation to tease through the dark locks almost overpowering.

Would he object to being woken by her touch?

Her fingers caught on the bedding, ready to tug them from his form and a wicked need touched her lips that she had not known until the night before. The door that opened up without warning pushed away Riana's thoughts of exploring her new found husband and desires both.

"Wakey wakey sleepyhead. It does no good to stay in bed all day though I must admit I am a touch disappointed with you. You did it again didn't you? Went wandering off to new adventures without as much as a word. I could have tried out a whole new wardrobe, but no, you had to go off on that great beast without me." The smell of fresh bread followed the entrance of a man dressed in clothing that would have put a courtesan to shame with his choice of rich silks, satins and brocades. "Inconsiderate boy. I should slap you silly for breaking your promise to me. I'll have you know I ruined a perfectly good silk doublet crying over you this time."

Riana's hands clutched the edge of the coverlet, raising it high in a quick attempt to regain some of her modesty as a pair of pale green eyes washed over her form. "Well out you go lass. I'm sure he'll call for you later if he found your company of enjoyment. Go on then or are you claiming modesty now."

One slender eyebrow rose, threatening to disappear into Riana's silver hair. "I think you have me confused with someone else."

He set the tray down by the side of the bed, slender hands that might have been the
envy of many a woman with the care he gave them, rested on his hips. "Airs and graces are better suited for those with the position to carry them off. Off with you wench, I have some matters to discuss with my Rhodan."

A coldness seeped into her words, stiffening graceful shoulders as Riana straightened her body before the new comer with every ounce of dignity she could muster. The coverlet half slipping from her body, only to be replaced by a soft mist her body formed of its own accord. A mist that draped its way about her body, caressing at her skin before settling in place, barely covering her nipples from the view of the man whose name she didn't even know. "Your Rhodan? I would think twice, Sir, before laying claim to my husband in such a manner."

"Husband? Now there's a line I haven't heard in some years. If the prince had a wife the entire court would be a buzz with the news." He rolled his eyes. "Rhodan, tell the wench with the ideas above her station to be gone, I really am not in the mood for this after your little stunt earlier this week."

She could feel it, the anger simmering to life more with each passing moment. It didn't matter if this new comer was just here trying to play a joke or was deadly serious, the reaction was the same. Calm, breathe, focus, don't let it loose just yet.

"Enough of this, both of you. Simon, this is my wife Xantriana. Riana, meet Simon, Senior Squire of the house of Leyfiana." Rhodan grumbled his way through the introduction punctuated by yawns, the sheet slipping down to his waist as he sat up.

"Your wife! She was telling the truth? You ungrateful swine. After everything we've been through together you went and did this? You married and didn't even bother to invite me?" Simon tugged a lace trimmed handkerchief from a bloused sleeve, dabbing it at his eyes in quick jabs and sharp sobs. "I'm hurt,

hurt beyond all accounting."

"It was a quick wedding and you're on the invitation list for the formal affair once things have settled enough for one." Rhodan grumbled, pushing up to sit against the head of the bed.

Riana's gaze moved from the sleepy form of her still awakening husband to the pink and purple satin clad Simon, then back again. The comments sitting uneasily with her and combined with the looks the new arrival kept shooting Rhodan left her with a feeling of uncertainty. Just what was the relationship between the two men? Surely her husband didn't...

"Wonderful indeed. I've always wanted to be a bridesmaid." Simon plopped himself down on the edge of the bed, reaching past Riana to pat Rhodan on the leg. "What do you think about me in shell pink or would that leave me washed out? It's so hard to find colors that work with my skin tone."

"That would be something you'd need to discuss with Riana. That would be her province, not mine." Rhodan grunted, reaching over to the tray. "No sweet rolls this morning, you're slipping."

"That's all the thanks I get for bringing you a tray each morning?"

Rhodan snagged a slice of bread from the tray. "You'd make a good fish wife at times, Simon."

Her doubt grew and sought a voice. "Is there something I don't know about between the two of you?"

The pout that claimed Simon's lips might have been humorous if it were not for the doubt that already rested in Riana's heart. "Rhodan, you promised me you would not tell a soul about us."

Riana's heart dropped like a stone into her stomach. She'd heard some odd tales coming from the court but never anything to suggest that Rhodan's interest lay anywhere other than in women.

"Simon, that's enough of your games for today. Riana has not had the easiest of times and Jeriah has already tried to prevent the marriage from taking place." Rhodan slipped out from under the covers fully, tugging a robe over the body she had come to know well only the night before.

"I always said your cousin needed to be quietly kicked over the edge of a cliff at high tide." Simon buffed his nails with a soft cloth. "I know just the gentlemen to take care of that matter for you as well. Nice folk, even if their dress taste leaves something to be desired. I'm sure they could handle it all in a nice discreet manner."

Her confusion grew with each new word, and even Rhodan's insistence that the new comer cease his games did not lift the doubt from her mind.

"Simon is an old and dear friend, though I swear he has caused me more trouble than anyone else ever could." Rhodan pressed a hand to Riana's shoulder. "I know what it can look like, but that's exactly one of the shields I have used to hide behind in the past."

Sobs resounded through the room, a fresh kerchief appearing from his sleeve only to be dabbed at suspiciously dry eyes. "He's such a cad, a bounder, used me and tossed me aside. Perhaps we could discuss this over a glass of wine later? We could pick out your wedding dress. With your coloring you'd look stunning in midnight blue my dear, with silver lace to match with your hair."

"Someone mind filling me in on what's going on?" Cluiun leaned against the door frame, his smile tugging at the edges of his scar. "Or is this the morning entertainment?"

Riana's fingers curled into the nearest pillow, nails threatening to burst through the covering in the moment before she threw it at his smiling face. The gossamer thin gown pulled taut across her body with her growing fury. "If this goes on any longer I swear I'm going to kill someone!"

"Well my love you certainly have an interesting temper under that delightful exterior." Rhodan cupped her cheek, brushing a soft kiss over her lips.

"Just you remember that, Rhodan. You married her which means you get to deal with the wicked end of her spirit." Cluiun dodged the pillow and smirked at everyone in the room. "Though looking at that outfit..."

Riana's face turned into living flame as she dove under the covers to the sound of the three men laughing...

"Married, what do you mean they married last night?" Jeriah snarled into the mirror, his hands clenching into tight fists. "That's not possible. The entire court would have been in attendance. Formal announcements would have been made. Nothing of the sort has occurred."

"Possible or not they wed last night in front of that damn flying lizard." Shadows threatened to block out his view of the woman, but even they failed to shut out the vivid marks on her face. "You should have been watching them more closely. He wed her without a full service by sneaking their vows in before the Dragon."

Punching the mirror would have offered no help, but the desire to smash it into a thousand pieces grew with each snapped word from the woman. Dragon, he'd never even considered that option. How had Rhodan known? He'd not been the most diligent of students. Damn flying lizard must have told him what to do.

"And just how was I supposed to prevent that marriage from taking place if I didn't even know about it?" His teeth gritted, jaw clenched tight as Jeriah fought to control his fury.

What did the woman expect? Miracles? Of course, she was obsessed with Rhodan, in claming him as her husband and toy. Well she would be welcome to him though dead it would be far easier for him to lay claim to the throne once Justin had died.

"Then you should use your spies more affectively. Did you not set people to watch Rhodan and that creature? You know the ties that bind Dragon Kin to your family, what rank they hold in the eyes of your people. How could you not be aware that he could take vows in front of the beast and it would be as binding as if he had stood in the center of the court?" Flecks of spit glistened on her lips, dismissing any lingering thoughts Jeriah had retained about bedding the wench. "I seem to know the ways of this court better than you do. Do your job Jeriah, or I will find someone else to replace you. Because as sure as you wish to seize the crown there will be others waiting in the shadows who would serve me just as well."

"I misjudged the knowledge Rhodan had. I never took him for one that paid attention to how important the ties between Dragons and his line might be. You have no idea how tightly the King has clamped down since Rhodan's arrival. Any power I had, any ability to sway him, vanished with Rhodan's arrival and announcement to wed." Years of work had vanished in an instant. Quiet suggestions had become more forceful ones, but still Justin had refused to act. The box with his crown sat within plain view of the mirror and Jeriah both, yet it might as well have been sat in the fire pits of the north.

A darker shadow moved across the surface of the mirror, eyes appearing within the circling darkness. "You will not fail me, Jeriah."

"What..." Cold, naked fear gripped his heart.

"You know who I am, or must I take full form? Perhaps it would be best if I reach through this mirror to rip out that piece of flesh you call a heart?" The words snarled through the silvered surface.

"Kaleb... Lord Kaleb?" He knew the legends surrounding that creature. All the dark tales. Creatures like him were held to be myth by some, worshiped as Gods by others. Did he believe Kaleb to be a God, perhaps not, but he had enough power to destroy every hard won plan Jeriah had put in place. If protecting his life work meant cow-towing to the demon spawn being then so be it.

"Who did you think held final say here? Obey my servant or feed her with your still beating heart!" Flames in the shape of eyes burned from the mirror then vanished as quickly as they had appeared.

"Kaleb." His voice had become little more than a whisper. What excuses did you offer a being that could kill you without ever entering your room?

"Your control is slipping away from you, Jeriah. Get it back before I replace you." The woman snarled through the rippling glass. "Or perhaps you crave to find yourself bound and stripped for my pleasure. Does a part of you crave the pain? The delights I might offer you in those long hours before death claimed you? I can give you that, welcome you into the realms of torment, should that truly be your desire." Darkness claimed the surface of the mirror, shutting off the conversation before he could offer a new protest.

"Bitch." It would have been so easy to swipe that thing off the table, send it crashing to the ground but what good would it have done, except loose him the last edge he had. Unless. The marriage, if Justin didn't know of his son's actions then maybe, just maybe there was a chance yet to sneak back into the Kings favor. If he phrased it correctly, played on the chance this could be seen as an insult, or perhaps a way to dishonor the woman. Rhodan's well known habits of lifting the skirts of any willing woman would work in his favor. Riana was noble born, protected by law. Such a deceit by Rhodan, even hinted at could destroy any faith Justin still had in his wayward son.

"It's a long shot, very long. But only if he already knows." Well tailored boots covered the ground towards his door, fingers plucking the half cloak from the waiting hook. "Still, it has to be tried. What do I loose by trying?"

The cloak sat easily about his shoulders, though Jeriah tugged it into place, draping it until it matched the court fashions. He turned, checking his appearance within the long, polished silver mirror, slender fingers plucking at a loose thread that only he could see. Perfect appearance, the dutiful family member, concerned member of the court. He could play the role well. "Yes, yes that will work. Just a word in the right place, enough concern to ease Justin's tension."

It would work, as long as he timed it just right.

"So, did the children enjoy themselves last night?" Orent stretched out her wings in the morning sun, arching her neck as she spoke. He'd never seen a more beautiful creature, each time he saw her she was enough to take his breath away, now was no different. "Or are they still engaged in whatever mating practices you humans involve yourselves in?"

"You still haven't taken a look for yourself?" Cluiun picked out a warm spot on the low wall to sit, grinning at the memory of Riana and her barely covered body. That was one comely looking woman. Maybe if they had met under different circumstances, or Rhodan hadn't taken a fancy to her so quickly, he might have tried his luck a little there himself.

"No, I made Rhodan a promise never to look in on his activities without permission." Orent fluttered her eyelashes at him, her large head tipping to one side and for a moment he almost forgot she was twenty times his size and covered in scales. "You could always let me take a peek at what you get up to, Cluiun dear."

"Orent, you are incorrigible, did anyone ever tell you that?"

"Not any one who could ever pronounce the word correctly at least." Orent's tongue snaked across her lips. "So are they planning on making an appearance today, or have they camped out in his room for the duration?"

"When I left Rhodan was explaining who Simon was to a very distressed and confused Riana." His fingers rested on the hilt of the sword Rhodan had left in his care the night before. Cluiun had tried to convince himself that there simply hadn't been the moment to return it to his friend as yet, but he knew better. The sword felt right, as if he were the one meant to carry it and not Rhodan.

A dangerous feeling, he was the first to admit that.

"Simon, ah yes. He can be a little difficult for some people to accept. Not sure what it is about you humans, always so ready to judge on the outside of the person instead of what lies within." Orent folded her wings back in against her body. "But he is a good man and one loyal to Rhodan unto death. Someone you might all need in the coming weeks."

"No long honeymoon? Pity I was looking forward to helping relieve the King of some of his mead supplies. I hear he has one of the finest stoked cellars on all of Erien." Cluiun chuckled, trying to ignore the call of the sword. It didn't matter how hard he tried to push the weapon from his mind it kept trying to tempt him to touch it, draw it from the leather and find something or someone to strike.

Such a weapon as this belonged in the hands of one prepared to use it. Not in the grasp of a prince who would toss it aside, or put it in the safe keeping of another. All it would take would be a simple tug to pull the blade free of its leather and...

No. He wasn't going to let his mind wander down that path.

Once he had returned the blade to Rhodan he'd seek out that drink after all. He'd

need it if the prickling feelings in his hands were anything to go by.

"I doubt Justin even knows about the wedding vows yet so the mead will not have been thought of." Her eyes narrowed on Cluiun. "The sword is causing a few problems for you?"

"No point denying it, is there?" Cluiun smiled, but he could feel the tension building across his shoulders. Each time his mind wandered towards the presence of the blade the urge to draw it, find a reason to use it, increased. "Yes it is, never been around a weapon like this before. How come Rhodan never mentioned the down side of looking after the bloody thing?"

"Because it's not really supposed to be awake right now."

"Awake? Now why does that sound like bad thing?"

"That might well be because it is a bad thing, a lot more than a 'bad' thing if the truth be known. Swords like that one are not supposed to awaken unless trouble of the Immortal kind is about to show up." The black scaled dragon gave a near imperceptible shrug.

"Immortal? As in a God?" Great, that was all he needed. What ever happened to living happily ever after once people married? Wasn't that how all the stories went. Hero weds the maid of his choice, they tumble into bed and then the bards always wanted to skip what happened next. Cluiun could never understand that, they'd have played to much bigger audiences if they just went into a few extra details.

"Either that or a goddess. You're not afraid of a Goddess are you, Cluiun A big, strong man like you?" Impossibly long eyelashes fluttered delicately in his direction. "You could handle any woman that tried to cross your path."

"Women are far more dangerous than most give them credit for," he wasn't going to fall into that trap. The last time he'd underestimated a woman he'd nearly ended up with a dagger in his gut.

"Well well, aren't you proving to me more unusual by the day." Orent's tongue snaked out, licking over her lips in a slow, near provocative manner.

Just what was going on? Had he stumbled into a mead tainted dream and had yet to awaken? Or found himself in a bards first attempt at an epic? Swords that woke up, dragons flirting with him, and a woman now wed to a man he considered a friend that he still wouldn't tip out of his own bed if she turned up there.

"I've just got one small question for you Orent?"

"Fire away." A small trail of smoke curled upwards from her nostrils.

"You are flirting with me, aren't you?"

"Why my dear sweet boy, I thought you'd never notice."...

Chapter Two

Rhodan's gaze moved from Riana to Simon and back again as he tried to remember just why he had agreed to a quick marriage? It wasn't that he minded waking up next to Riana, or even the idea of spending the rest of his life with her, but Simon's performance was enough to send him reaching for a travel sack and send him dashing off in search of Orent.

"Would it have been so hard to tell me what was going on, after all we've been through?" Simon dabbed at his eyes with a lace trimmed hankie, blissfully ignoring the wild glances Riana kept throwing his way.

"Simon, no one knows about the marriage, outside of those within this room." His head pounded. This would have been so much simpler if he'd bothered to find Simon in the first place.

"You didn't tell Orent? She'll be devastated!" Simon shrieked. "I don't want to be the one to have to tell her. I know she doesn't eat human's too often but she'd be tempted to with that news."

"Well Orent knows…and Cluiun." He'd need a large sack, three week trip, perhaps a little longer. He'd heard that the Chasm of Dracor was rather attractive this time of year. So it got a little hairy trying to navigate through the razor sharp rocks, and Orent might find a few of the turns a little on the sharp side…

"That brute with the scar and sword knows and Lady Orent and you still didn't think to invite me?" All he'd wanted to do was marry the woman and avoid Jeriah's plans. Was that really such a terrible thing? With the way Simon was carrying on anyone would have thought he'd committed mass murder.

Even after years of friendship Rhodan could feel an itch in his fingers every time Simon glanced his way. "We didn't tell anyone else because we didn't want Jeriah to stop the wedding. You know what he's like. I wasn't about to let him prevent the ceremony from taking place."

"Oh. Well in that case I forgive you of course, but only if you go through the formal wedding later on. I have such a plan for a pink taffeta creation. Riana and I could be in almost matching outfits, we'll be the talk of the court." In less than a heartbeat Simon's tears vanished as if they had never been. "Do you think pink would suit her? I'm not sure with her hair color, but blue washes me out every time. I really will have to sit down and sort all this out. No point going to all the work of planning a wedding if outfits clash."

Would Orent really mind if he packed a travel sack and made a dash for it? The pits of Nimian would have been easier to face than another one of Simon's tirade. "This is enough to drive a man to drink."

"Simon, perhaps Rhodan needs a little space to become accustomed to how things have changed?" A smirk had begun to play along Riana's full lips. He could still remember how they had tasted, the soft sounds they had given life to during the night. "And I believe you and I need to become acquainted, after all I have a lot to learn about my new husband and who better to ask than his long time friend."

"Darling I have more tales than a litter of new puppies it's just a matter of where to start." Simon pounced on the offer.

Rhodan's jaw clenched until his teeth ground down against each other loud enough to draw a curious look from his wife. "Is something the matter my husband?"

A quiet wedding, few days to recover, maybe a small keg of mead, would that really have been so much to hope for? Perhaps it was just as well that a soft tap sounded through from the other side of the closed door, without some sort of distraction he might have been reaching for a weapon.

"Enter." Whoever it was might give him the chance to escape Simon for a bit.

"Your Highness, your father demands your presence in the Great Hall." A black and silver liveried page stood in the doorway, shifting his weight rapidly from foot to foot as he spoke.

"I see, well inform my father that I will be there shortly." Rhodan's heart threatened to turn into a lead weight. Between the way the message had been phrased and the lack of eye contact from the young page only a fool would have assumed the summons could be anything but bad news. A single look at Riana suggested the same thoughts were hurrying through her mind. Only Simon seemed amused by the situation as his lips curled upwards into a cat like grin.

"Your Highness, he said immediately and that I was to make sure you understood that." The page almost swallowed the words, what little color the young boy's face had retained vanished under the stare Rhodan fixed him with.

"And did he at least want me dressed before I appear within the hall? Or is he expecting me to present myself in my current state of undress?" Rhodan scowled as he reached for his nearest tunic. Taking his anger out on the page wouldn't have been right, no matter how tempting the thought was.

"Yes Your Highness. At least I think so." The young and shy eyes finally raised long enough to look about the room. Heat claiming the hairless face in the moment he caught sight of Riana's barely dressed state. "I mean..."

"Never mind, I will be there once I am dressed, lad." The boy opened his mouth to protest, but his lips snapped shut at the look from Rhodan. "Yes, Your Highness."

The door clattered shut, catching on the lock before it shut fully in the boy's efforts to flee the room.

"It's not like my father to send a child to deliver a message that he knows is going to cause problems." Then again how well did he really know his father anymore? So much might have changed since he had all but withdrawn from court that he had no way of knowing until he asked his father directly. Still, it didn't feel right. "Jeriah, this is more his style, probably thought the boy would call the guards to try and drag me down to the hall half naked."

Riana's hand reached out towards his arm, but he had no desire to allow her touch to soften his mood.

"Oh, I don't know, you could make quite the statement arriving in your trews only." Simon smirked from his perch on the edge of the bed. "Think of how the court ladies will swoon and half the men I would guess at the sight of your chest... I must say these adventures have certainly improved your physique."

He tried not to growl at the comments that hit too close to the bone. There were, or had been, a dozen women in the court that would have done almost anything to catch his attention. Appearing half naked would have attracted the wrong sort of attention and no doubt leave him with a lot of questions to answer from Riana. It would be a great way to start off his marriage that would have been, dealing with an irate wife and a couple of hungry women panting at his heels.

"Rhodan, you're letting him get to you. Jeriah wants you angry enough to storm into the hall half dressed and ready for blood." She slipped from the edge of the bed, her fingers curling into his boots a moment before he could reach for them. "If you keep calm and take your time it will back fire on him, trust me on this."

"Well if that is his goal, it won't work. I will not be summoned to my own hall like a
common thief." His fingers tugged the boots into place. She might have been raised in a castle far from the busy aspects of court life, but his new wife appeared to grasp the situation better than one born to the position might have managed. "Riana, have you seen where I put the sword?"

"Cluiun has it." Riana reached for the simple dress she had managed to grab from one of the maids, tugging it over her head as she spoke. "You gave it to him last night to hold, during the service."

"Simon, find Cluiun, tell him to meet me in the Great Hall." If he entered the hall without the sword and Jeriah found out he'd left it in Cluiun's care there would be hell to pay. It would be turned into another dereliction of duty that Jeriah could use against him, even though passing into the Cluiun's care had been warranted at the time. Jeriah would twist the whole event in any way he possibly could.

"That brute? You want him in the Great Hall amongst all those noble born? What are you thinking of, Rhodan?" Simon's voice rose half an octave with each new sentence. "Are you sure you didn't loose your wits entirely when you wed? I've heard of a few strange things happening after a man gets married."

"Now, Simon." His fists clenched. At any other time Simon's babble might have been amusing, but now each new delay added to his growing need to strike out against something. Anything. The wall would have worked well enough, but Jeriah would have been a far better target.

"Well, if you insist. He'll cause quite the stir you know, with his rough dress and manner. It might even start a new fashion trend." He dabbed at a tiny speck of dirt on his upper lip. "Though it's one I will not follow. I much prefer to be a leader in such things. Can you imagine me in such drab garb? I'd really look quite out of place."

"Simon," Rhodan growled a warning.

"But perhaps I might be persuaded to try one in yellow suede," he barely even glanced at Rhodan as his bright gaze moved through the room in search of a second opinion. "Well, what do you think, Riana? Do you think such a color would suit me?"

It took every ounce of self control he had not to reach out and strangle Simon where he stood...

"Don't you think that, well that I'm the wrong... species for you, Orent?" Cluiun coughed, trying not to look the dragon in the eye. "You're a nice enough being, lady, errm dragon... I mean it's just that. Well I don't think we're compatible, physically that is."

"Oh that's nothing that a little magic won't help with, or perhaps you doubt your abilities to..." Her jeweled eyes closed with a demure sigh.

Gods above and below, what had he done to deserve this? All those years of being able to pick and choose from a dozen women any time his ship docked. He'd been fair to them, never forced one against her will. He'd even gone as far as to make sure they didn't feel ill used. Still he had refused to take one of them as a wife. It wasn't that they weren't good women, just, well not the right ones for him.

Had one of them begged for a curse, acted as a jilted lover? Punishment, that's what this was, a punishment from some bored God or worse, a Goddess.

"Do wipe that look off your face, Cluiun. You're a nice enough boy but you are very young. You need another hundred years or so experience on you.

Perhaps then, when you grow up a little, I might be more interested in you." Orent's laughter curled around his body carried on a wisp of smoke.

"You're a wicked woman, Orent." Relief washed through his body. How did one go about turning down a dragon anyway? Well, without ending up as charred meat on the side of the road?

"Why, thank you Cluiun. I do try my best but that best so often goes unappreciated." Scales cracked, her claws biting into the ground as the massive form of the Dragon arched, her tail flicking out in short snaps. Her shoulders pressed to the ground, claws unhooking from the stone paved courtyard, stretching out in the warmth of the mid morning sun.

Cat, dragon, woman, whatever Orent was he couldn't deny the beauty or grace she brought into the world, no more than he could forget the sharp edge of her wit.

"Captain Cluiun! Oh Captain dearie..."

"Dearie?" The very word had him ready to punch something.

Simon smiled from the other side of the low wall, waving a frilled handkerchief at them. "Cluiun, oh Cluiun, ah there you are. You are a naughty boy, running off with Rhodan's sword, just when he needs it."

Just then mention of the sword was enough to prod the images back into life. The hilt in his hand, blood running down its length as bodies piled about his feet. Simon would be the first for calling him dearie. He'd never met such a man as this, had he been born knowing exactly what buttons to press?

'Calm yourself, Cluiun. He's a good man and you'll have to trust me on that.' Orent's voice sounded through his mind as Simon tucked the frilly piece of cloth into his sleeve. What was that anyway? A handkerchief? The man didn't appear to know if he was male, female, or some odd blending half way between them both.

"The prince, darling boy that he is, seems to need that sword he left in your care. He's a sweet boy, really he is, but he'd forget his head at times." Simon offered a long, sweeping bow to Orent before continuing. "Could you be a dear and take it to him, he's been summoned to the Great Hall by his father. Such a terrible tizzy the old dear is in, I can't think what's going on, of course it might have something to do with that Jeriah chappie."

His fingers closed about the hilt for a brief moment before he managed to snatch his grip away. He didn't want to give it up. No, that wasn't quite true the sword wanted him not the other way around. It craved his touch, his hand to wield it through days and nights of battle.

"Go with him, Cluiun. Whilst you still can." Orent's voice nudged him from the depths of the darkened images. Offering him a line Cluiun found himself almost unwilling to take. "You have to give it back to Rhodan he's going to need it soon enough, we both know that."

The urgency in her voice and the slight play of tension moving across her shoulders pushed aside the last of his hesitancy at returning the blade. Whatever the future held for his friend he would not add to the danger that Orent already hinted at.

"Enemies at the gate, or within?"

"Within, court politics that can be as dangerous as any foe you have faced on the sea, Cluiun." Orent nodded slowly towards the waiting Simon. "Hurry, Cluiun."

"As you wish, dear lady." Cluiun smiled, offering a bow to the dragon that almost rivaled that of Simon's in its extravagance.

"Human's, you can be such adorable creatures. I really don't understand why more of my people don't keep human pets."

The heavy wooden double doors opened up into the great hall before Rhodan could even reach out to part them with his own hands. Torches smoked along the walls, one long table still bore the signs of the mid morning meal that had come to replace breakfast in the working court, but what held his attention from the moment he stepped into the room was the stern face of his father. No oil lamps? Normally they were laid out for any formal event. Yet the cushion had been placed before the throne, which only added to the feeling this whole meeting had been hurried along by a hand other than his father's.

If anger simmered within the older man's eyes, Rhodan could not see it. No tension played across his shoulders, nor did his hands grip the arms of the throne as they had done on previous occasions when a summons had brought Rhodan hurrying into his presence. What was going on?

Fifteen measured paces brought him to the worn velvet cushion before the throne. Dropping one knee onto the cushion allowed Rhodan a moment to gather his thoughts before speaking. "You desired my presence, my Liege."

"You have much to explain, Prince Rhodan." Everything, from the cushion to the formal tone his father used spoke of a matter that the King did not dare to handle in any manner except that dictated by generations of monarchs before him. "I see your companions are quick to follow you, despite the fact I summoned you alone to my feet."

A low breeze caught the pennants hanging from the walls, tugging at the long fringes. "I was not aware that they were to keep their distance, my Liege. If I had known I would have requested that they wait. However a public summons suggested that others would be present."

"Perhaps it is best they are here as it will save me from having to summon them into attendance." His father's eyes narrowed at a point behind Rhodan, a deadly cold tone entering his words. "Though I see you forget your sword, perhaps you should be thankful that at least one man within these walls thinks enough of you to care for your weapons. Though I am not certain I care to see the sword of your ancestors belted about the waist of a self proclaimed pirate." That dangerous edge to his words carried a warning he had expected to hear. If he had dared to seek out Cluiun before coming into the Hall that one problem would have been avoided, but perhaps another would have risen to take its place.

"I can explain that, my Liege, if you will but grant me leave to do so?"

"I expect you can, but it remains to be seen if your reasoning falls within the boundaries of what I class as acceptable." A shadow moved at the edge of the dais, just out of line of Rhodan's sight, but he didn't need a clear view to know that the one watching the show would be Jeriah. "We have not often seen eye to eye on that score, more so as you have progressed in years and continued your trips away from court."

Politics. Of all the aspects of court life, the politics that plagued the great hall caused the most grief. Even now, without turning to look across the gathered men and women in the hall he could feel their eyes narrow on his back, waiting for his answer. They'd be expecting lies, denials or quick speeches to distract the King from the matter at hand. The last thing Jeriah would expect was the truth.

"I asked Cluiun to hold the sword for me last night my Liege as I did not think it would be fitting to wear during the swearing of my vows to the Lady Xantriana, nor during our first night together." Did he imagine it, or had a small and carefully hidden smile flickered across his fathers lips?

"And by what right did you wed the lady without a royal witness?" The formal tone never faltered. "You are well aware such a union must be witnessed in order to be binding under the laws of Olain."

"There was such a witness, my Liege, one whose nobility and line cannot be questioned." Rhodan inclined his head before raising his eyes to meet those of his fathers, no matter how he phrased this it would be seen as a challenge by many in the long room. Including Jeriah. So be it, it had been done and nothing could undo their bond but death herself. "The Lady Orent bore witness and accepted our vows."

"My Liege, he expects his actions to be accepted due to the presence of a dragon? Has he forgotten who sits upon the throne?" Jeriah stepped from the side of the dais, his half cloak almost catching on the edge of the steps. "Vows sworn in front of a beast indeed, we had business Prince Rhodan, business to be conducted before he claimed himself falsely married and then defiled that girl."

Riana was close enough that he could hear her small hiss of protest.

"If my wife has a problem with what has occurred between us then I am sure she will voice such. As for the Lady Orent not being a valid witness, are you forgetting what just what throne my father sits upon, Jeriah? The very bonds that have helped keep the throne safe over the centuries?" He struggled to control the anger Jeriah's insult caused. Generations had lived and died whilst bonded to Dragon kind, blood spilt on both sides to protect the land and line.

Bathed in the light of the torches, the oak throne, no one could ignore the runes or the dragon images that made up the throne. From the claws that formed the arm rests to dragon wings spread in flight for the back, every inch of that throne offered a reminder to any present of the oath between dragon and human kind.

If that was not enough then the trumpeting cry of Orent from her place in the courtyard drummed the matter home.

'I can always eat a few courtiers if that doesn't get their attention, but only the ones who haven't bathed in perfume. Last time I ate one like that I couldn't get the taste out of my mouth for a week.'...

Chapter Three

"Well, Jeriah, do you still say that vows taken before the Lady Orent are invalid?" Jeriah's jaw clenched as every fiber of his being screamed with the need to slam a fist or better yet a dagger, through the smiling face of the crown prince. "Or do you require some extra proof? Perhaps the Lady Orent entering the hall, though I would not recommend it, she has been known to step on those who get in her way and I doubt the walls would recover quickly from her having to create her own entrance."

Breathe. As long as he focused on his breathing and not on the glint of triumph in his cousin's eyes then he would be able to keep his rage under control. "You have my apologies, your Highness, but I do now have to wonder what happens with the blood match you demanded only yesterday? Have you decided to bring that small matter to an end through this marriage, or were you thinking of nothing more than delving between the Lady's thighs?"

The woman in question tried to step closer to Rhodan, but the Pirate, what had been his name again, ah yes Cluiun, grabbed Riana's arm keeping her away from the center of the hall. Good, this way he could play the aggrieved noble, one whose honor had been insulted by the actions of Rhodan. "Or did you think I would ignore such an action. How can I now protect the Lady Xantriana against you when you have already forced her into marriage?"

"I was not forced!" Fire flashed in the young woman's eyes as she tried to fight free of Cluiun's grip. "I spoke my vows freely and would do so again if needed."

Such fury and passion, she'd make an interesting bed mate once Rhodan was in the hands of Arinnana. Fae blood held a deeper drive towards the sensual than human blood did, or so the legends said. Sweet hipped, soft lips, a lovely swell to her breasts, she easily matched any of the court beauties present and that was without a touch of makeup or new gown. How would she compare to them when suitably be-decked in a manner befitting the chosen bed mate of the King?

"Yet his friend keeps a firm grip on your arm, Lady. How are we to know if he also has a dagger to you or holds some other threat to your throat?" Jeriah offered a smile as he stepped down from the side of the dais. "It would be no great leap to assume she has been threatened. Perhaps even been told she will service your oaf like friend should she voice any displeasure about this union."

"Jeriah, you accuse my son of forcing a woman into marriage?" The calm voice of the King broke through the tension within the hall. Why couldn't the old man just keep out of it? He'd almost turned the tide in his favor. "Of breaking both the law and the bounds of honor in one fell swoop?"

"Not entirely, my Liege, but I cannot keep the doubts silent. And I am sure that I am not the only one wanting to know why Prince Rhodan could not wait until the match was done. Unless he feared to do so and wanted to sample the Lady's wares before surrendering her unto my care?"

Riana snapped her arm from the grip of the Cluiun, darting forward through the crowd that now filled the hall. Hair longer than any woman had the right to wear, tugged backwards in a living cloak, her eyes turning dark and cold with her words. "I was not forced and I am not a piece of property to be pushed into one marriage or another. You speak of being threatened by the Cluiun? I would rather serve him and his entire crew than spend one night in your bed. Should you and my husband engage in your blood match and by some fluke of nature he looses, I will still not permit your tainted hands to touch me!"

"Peace, Lady Xantriana. There will be no need for such declarations. This is still my court, regardless of what my son and my nephew might think." The soft footsteps marked the path of the King from his throne and down towards his only son.

"My Liege, never did I suggest that this was not your court. I beg forgiveness if, in my haste to protect a woman from harm, I seemed to suggest otherwise." Jeriah smoothed away his concerns behind a well hidden internal wall. "You have my most humble apologies both to your Majesty and your court."

Did they hear the lie tainting his words? No, most of them would accept them without question leaving just Rhodan and his small group of supporters as the only ones he had to watch for. The rest of the court, if he judged the situation correctly, had grown weary of the actions and constant upheaval the Prince brought to the court. There were always new sets of problems each time he returned home after his bold adventures. Only a few months prior to this it had been a claim of theft. Stupid fool had never even guessed Jeriah had been behind that as well.

And there, Rhodan's biggest supporter, the fool Simon stood leaning against one carefully carved column as if the events in the court were nothing more than every day banter. Good, as long as Rhodan could offer nothing more in the way of supporters beyond the prettily dressed fop, his wife and the pirate he would have nothing to fear from them.

"Rhodan, will you withdraw your claim for a blood match with your cousin?" Justin stood two steps down from Jeriah as he spoke to his son. Even now, with the older man's era coming to an end Justin still appeared to be every inch the King. How many apart from him knew about the weakness that rotted away at the old man's core? "I see no reason for the match to take place and I hope Jeriah will, in future, learn to think more clearly before offering his words to you or about you."

A fine line, withdrawing the claim would make Rhodan appear weak following it through would mark him as bloodthirsty and insecure. Either way Rhodan would loose a little more ground in the eyes of the court. The stupid fool probably didn't even know he was trapped no matter what he did. All those years Rhodan had wasted chasing adventures and skirts when his cousin should have been learning court politics would finally come back to haunt him.

"No, Your Majesty. I have no intention of withdrawing my claim for a blood match against Jeriah." Rhodan's hands clenched, his eyes fixed on Jeriah. "I should have settled matters between us years ago, Your Majesty, but I intend to rectify that mistake today."

There seemed little point in keeping the smug grin from his lips, not when Jeriah knew that only a miracle would permit Rhodan to win. Lord Kaleb would see to that even if Rhodan's abilities with the sword might be better than his own. Not even the dragon would be able to save him this time. Perhaps this would work to his advantage in more ways than one? How far could he push the boundaries of Kaleb's rules? He could settle the scores once and for all just as long as he made it look like an accident. A slip of the sword in the middle of the duel. How would Kaleb know any different? He was at most a God, at worst some form of demon that had learned to play on the fears of mankind. But whatever Kaleb actually was he couldn't read minds unless they were under his control, that much he knew about the dark lord and that would work to his advantage. "Then I shall be available at your convenience, Your Highness."

"Tell me something, where you planning on handing him the throne as well as your head, Rhodan? Or had you not bothered to think it that far through?" The heavy doors of the ante chamber had barely closed before his father rounded on him. "Have you any idea just how close you are to loosing everything with this crusade against Jeriah?"

"Father I..."

"You what, Rhodan? You acted without thinking again? How dare you put your pride before your duty to the Throne?" He'd never seen his father so angry, not in all the years of confrontations over women, drinking or jaunts to the far reaches of the Kingdom. "What am I going to do with you... and your bride?"

"You could announce your acceptance of our marriage, my Liege." Riana's hand gently touched Rhodan's as she offered a warm smile to both men. "Wouldn't that solve some of the problems Jeriah has caused?"

Jeriah, if Rhodan had his way that one would be dead before the end of the day. Sly remarks, petty plans. If it wasn't one thing it was another. "I should never have let him live past puberty, all my life he's been there nudging problems my way, laying accusations at my door. I'm well aware of his petty attempts at manipulation."

"Even if I agreed with you, and I am not saying that I don't, Rhodan that is not an action I could have taken. Not without reducing my rule down to being the man that slaughtered his own nephew." Justin, Lord of the Dragon throne, removed the simple crown from his brow and placed it on the oak table before sitting down with a heavy sigh.

The weary look that claimed his father's face was almost enough to silence any further comments from Rhodan. "Father, my apologies, I don't wish to bring you any more trouble. The gods alone know there might be enough heading this way with whatever darkness Arinnana swore to, but Jeriah... I cannot allow him to continue to throw insults my way. Not if I am to keep enough respect within the court to be considered your heir."

"Ah, now you stop to think about the court politics?" A glimmer of a smile creased the older man's face. "Well you are right about that, but killing him won't solve the problem. At best it makes you look the impulsive fool and at worse it turns Jeriah into a martyr for any who even think they have a cause. And what is this about Arinnana swearing to the darkness?"

"She's responsible for the death of my father, your Majesty. I'm not sure of all the details, I just know she was behind it, just as she had me stolen from the castle to try and clear the way between herself and Rhodan." Riana explained quickly. "It's hard to believe, I know, but Castle Valer is no longer under the control of my father. He's dead killed by my sister." She would have continued but the short sharp wave of Justin's hand silenced Rhodan's new wife.

"I see, then that puts me in a very odd position. There is no proof of the problems you speak of and unless I send soldiers to check the situation there will be nothing I can present to the court. However I am willing to send a small guard force there in order to gather information." Justin interlaced his fingers, resting them on his lap before continuing. "I wish I could do more at this time, Lady Xantriana, but I cannot over step matters. Not until I have firm evidence of the death of your father."

"I understand your Majesty, and thank you."

The walls of the ante chamber threatened to close in on Rhodan, his palms coated with a thin film of sweat and the idea of nudging Orent into taking a new flight out across the lands beckoned from the back of his mind. Though this time he would not fly alone. He wouldn't leave either Cluiun or Riana to face the mess that would result. Then he'd come back with the proof his father needed.

'Now now, there are other ways. We won't be taking any sudden trips. You'd only look like the very fool Jeriah is trying to portray you as. You're a stronger man than that, it's time you showed that side of your nature.' Orent's calm words vibrated at the back of his mind.

Politics, he'd done his best to avoid them over the years, now they sought to trap him and could even strip him of his right to the crown if he but took the wrong step. The hair on the back of his neck prickled under the silent gaze of the Cluiun who stood in silence by the door. Riana's hand had fallen away from his arm and even Orent now fell silent within his mind.

Jeriah had been too smug about the match, accepting it without protest or demands that another stand in his stead. He couldn't win, and didn't use magic so would not be able to call upon that during the match. So just what was his cousin up to?

"Then what is it you suggest I do, Father? Continue to let him rain insults down on me whenever he so wishes?" He barely kept hold of his temper, though now his anger slowly turned inwards. He'd walked right into the problem.

"No, Rhodan, you will face him in the match." Justin replied in an all too calm manner. "Having you back out now would only make matters worse, complicating them in ways I cannot even begin to imagine."

"But I thought you said if Rhodan killed Jeriah that would cause problems?" Riana's quiet voice gave life to the confusion that Rhodan shared. "Wouldn't pulling out of the match solve that?"

"Yes I did indeed, but no one ever said a Blood Match had to be to the death." A hint of relief entered his father's words. "Pulling out might imply an act of cowardice on my son's part, that I cannot risk. Rhodan, it will mean you keeping your temper during the fight, and granting the match to Jeriah if he manages to get the first strike in."

His shoulders turned into metal cords. "I will not let him win, Father."

"If he gets the first strike in you can and will grant him the match. There are more important things in life than your pride!" The chair his father had been sitting in danced back across the room as the older man pushed to his feet, clearing the distance in three steps. "I have seldom ordered you to do anything, Rhodan, but for the sake of us all you will fight only to the first blood and will grant the match to Jeriah if he draws blood first."

The blood roared in Rhodan's ears, his hands clenching tight on the air until his knuckles cracked under the pressure. It didn't matter that what his father asked of him was within the law, nor that it was the best for the court and the kingdom as a whole, the very idea turned his stomach.

Soft eyes met his and the concern written across Riana's face only added to Rhodan's growing anger. "And what of Riana if I loose?"

"That is another matter entirely. The law does not allow for him to claim your bride unless you are dead. All he can do is demand a public apology, which, should he win, you will give him."

"I will do no such thing..."

"Yes you will, Rhodan. You are the Prince of the realm and you will act as one, even if that means swallowing your pride."...

Riana hurried down the corridor after her husband as he stalked away from the chamber muttering under his breath. She couldn't blame him for being furious at the situation, she wasn't exactly pleased herself, but at least Jeriah had no claim on her, no matter the outcome of the fight. That is, unless Jeriah's strike, his attempt at first blood, also claimed Rhodan's life.

No, she didn't dare think about that. There had to be something else going on. Justin was a smart man. More than his son perhaps gave him credit for. He'd been King for many years now, and a good one at least until recent years. Even then the complaints most had about him revolved around the normal items, taxes, land grants, who would follow him as heir if something happened to Rhodan. Something was missing from that conversation, an obvious option that had not been spoken of.

"I can't believe he expects me to bow down to that piece of slime." Rhodan turned, striking out with one clenched fist towards a nearby wall. A blow that was barely prevented by Cluiun's firm grip.

"Hitting the wall won't solve problems, even if it might make you feel a little better for a short time. You'll only end up skinning your knuckles or worse, breaking them. So stop and think for a moment here, Rhodan." Cluiun smiled as he spoke, amusement shining within his hazel eyes. A rogue, pirate, perhaps even a murderer if half the stories were to be believed, she still knew he was a man that missed very little. "He said IF Jeriah won. If he managed first blood. He never said you had to allow him that strike."

"No," Rhodan blinked. "No, he didn't. Damnit why do I let the old man get to me. He could have said that instead of letting me think he wanted me to deliberately loose to that bastard."

Men, what was it about some of them that never let them look past the obvious once someone had triggered their temper. If nothing else she'd learned some valuable lessons from her father, and even though she had let herself be caught up in the same fears, the same fury that her husband still tried to fight his way free from she could see what Justin had been trying to do. Or thought she did. "Rhodan, your father wouldn't want to say it because maybe he hoped you'd see it for yourself. It might only be a matter of years before you have to take his place on the throne. You have to learn to see past personal insult for the good of those you will rule."

Fury burned within his eyes for a moment longer and then flickered out of existence. "I know. I know. Orent has been trying to tell me the same thing for the past few years."

'Nicely done, Riana. Very nicely done indeed.'

"I had a good teacher in my father," she murmured, struggling for a moment not to let the pain of his death wash over her again. One day Arinnana would pay for the destruction she had brought down on her family.

'Don't let the need for vengeance cause the same problems for you as they have for Arinnana and others like her. You're better than that. Besides we both know females have far more level heads than our male counterparts. Something to do with the blood not flowing to the wrong head at the wrong time.' Orent's voice warmed the back of her mind. *'There is much I must teach you, but in return you have to help me teach Rhodan what he needs to learn in order to take the throne. I fear we may not have much time.'*

Why would time be running out on them? Justin looked healthy enough, Jeriah's plans couldn't threaten the King as he was sure to have enough loyal guards around him.

'There are others involved in this, as well you know. Be calm, we'll work through this Riana. If luck is on our side we'll have enough defenses in place to handle anything that your step sister throws at us. My main concern is just who else she has sided with.'

The storm that had torn apart the Cluiun's ship, she remembered the fury of it all too well, the sense of magic behind it, a power beyond anything else she had ever experienced. Those self same shadows that had been behind her sister, the violence of her father's death. Had Arinnana sworn allegiance to some power, a deity that now backed her every foul step?

'Now you're thinking the situation through.'

One of the Gods?

'Who else would have the power you witnessed?'

How could she possibly match the power of a God? Even with the gifts she had discovered within her core she had nothing that would match the Gods themselves.

'Don't underestimate your powers, or over estimate theirs.'

"You have a temper that matches the ocean, Rhodan." Cluiun leaned against the stone wall, his quiet chastisement of her husband pulling Riana's attention back to the two men. "Something that you either learn to control or you'll be forever at its whim. Especially with the way that cousin of yours is acting.”

"I know," her Prince shrugged. "I’m going to need that sword back."

"Just as long as you aren’t planning on running the sod through with it."
Cluiun unhooked the sword belt, an odd flicker of emotions played openly across
his face, his fingers clenching about the sheath for a moment longer than was
necessary. "Though I admit I’m not that unhappy at having to give this back."

"Well I guess you’ve been getting a few odd looks carrying it around."
Rhodan collected the sword, fastening it back about his waist. "And no, I won’t
kill Jeriah, no matter how tempting the thought is. I’m not going to promise that I
won’t punch him out though, or leave him with a decent scar from the fight."

"A black eye might be just the lesson he needs," Cluiun agreed, the now
familiar smirk settling back across his lips. "I’ve been restraining myself every
time someone mentions his name. He’s the sort of man I’d happily take out
behind a pub or stables and take a leather strap to. Or a rusty blade."

"I could be persuaded to turn a blind eye if he were to be taken on a walk
somewhere for such a lesson." Rhodan folded his arms across his chest, a cold
glint entering his dark eyes.

"Is that all you two can think about, getting into a fight, or killing
someone?" There they were, leaning against the wall, discussing killing as if it
where the most natural thing in the world. "Don’t either of you realize that there
are more important things in life?"

‘You’re fighting a loosing battle right now, Riana.’

"She’s right you know," Cluiun pushed up away from the cold stone.

"Oh? Like what?" The younger man frowned.

"Like exploring your father’s mead supply."

"Oh you…" Riana bit back a growl.

"Well you did just get married, it would be perfectly natural for your
husband to go and drown his sorrows at no longer being single." Only the teasing
light that danced within the Cluiun’s hazel eyes prevented Riana from screaming
in frustration until the soft voice of the Dragon echoed at the back of her mind.

"You plan on getting drunk the night before you might have to fight your
cousin?"

"Who says the fight will be tomorrow?" Her husband smiled. "Knowing
my cousin he’ll wait until some appropriately dramatic moment, and it will be
late in the day as I doubt he even knows what morning looks like."

"And just what am I supposed to do whilst you two go off and drain a
mead keg?" She fought against the urge to rest her hands on her hips. The last
thing she wanted to do was turn into a fish wife but this was almost too much.

"Well you could find Simon and start planning our wedding. I’m sure he
can help you pick out a decent dress. I know he wants to be your maid of honor."

How much trouble would she get into for smacking her husband across the back of the head with a log? A nice thick, heavy log?

"Don't you want to plan the wedding?"

"That's not the point," Two logs, one wouldn't be enough. She'd need to hit Cluiun as well if only because he was as much to blame as Rhodan for this.

"Well you could always come and explore the cellar with us, I don't mind drinking with a wench. It wouldn't be the first time." Cluiun offered her a sweeping and all too mocking bow.

"Wench? Did you just call me a wench?" The log changed into an iron bar in her mind. And it was no longer aimed at his head. At least not the one on his shoulders.

"Now Riana don't take it that way." Rhodan edged forward, ignoring the warning glints in his wife's gaze. "He's just being friendly."

"Of course, I meant wench in the nicest possible way." Cluiun knew exactly what he was doing, she didn't have to be a mind reader to realize that, though she had no idea just why he wanted to steal her husband away to get drunk when there were more important things to be done.

Orent had been right, this was a loosing battle and she at least knew one when she saw it. Perhaps this is what the two men needed. Some time to ease down after the stress of the past few days?

'Let them have their few moments of fun, to relax Riana of the Silver Hair. The time for fun is fast coming to an end for us all.'...

Chapter Four

Wisp-like shadows wove around his fingers, following the line of the slender chain he held. It glittered with sparks of an energy no mortal would even be able to lay claim to. The barest shred of the most powerful of magics that Erien had ever seen but still nothing more than a hint of what had once been. Alone the pendant offered only a small grain of magic, powerful but a single spell for the one who wore it.

Not enough.

How could they have buried the power, hidden it from mortal and immortal eyes alike? Wasting all those generations of research, the building, forging of weapons, and now all that remained were a few relics like the chain and small silver pendant he held. A weapon or three, a language no one knew how to read. For what?

How dare those creatures declare that he and his kind were unfit to use that power. What right did they have to decide such? Creators of these relics or not they had no right to make that choice for the entire world.

Secrets. He hated them, but this one he loathed most of all. He'd struggled for centuries to find the answer. Not just him, all of his kind. All but one. The youngest of them all hung back from searching. He took no worshippers, no shrines, did he think he was like the old race, that he was better than the rest of them?

Foolish being. So called Master of the Hunt. A master of nothing but beasts of the forest, wolves, the great cats, those creatures that hunted in packs. Why? How much power did that grant him? He'd even turned away those few mortals that had come in search of him, offering the lone god their devotion. No matter how often Kaleb or others tried to bring the Master of the Hunt down they failed. It didn't matter what they threw at him he still existed, still kept himself, and his powers hadn't waned. Did he have access to the ancient rune magic? A way that kept him from being vulnerable to the other deities? There had to be something protecting him.

"I'll find the answer this time," growled words rolled from his lips.

"My Lord?" She'd been curled at his feet on a rug for so long now he'd almost blanked out her presence. Now she peered up at him through a wild mane of long dark hair, the bruise fading across her right cheek. "What is it you seek?"

"Power."

"You have that My Lord," she whispered, pushing up onto her hands and knees. Rags were all that remained of her dress, claw marks visible on her delectable flesh. Yet instead of showing fear at being at his feet her eyes shone with a need he knew well. The need for more. Strange creatures these humans, so many of them took to the delights he offered as if it where the purest of wines.

"Not like this." She was a simple childlike being compared to his kind, she'd never understand the depths of power that hid from him, or the craving he felt burning deep within each time he looked at the pendant.

"No one can stand against you," she wriggled closer, pressing her eager lips to his feet. "I have seen it for myself, your power, your strength."

Seen it, tasted it, craved it. Oh he knew what dark cravings now sat in the pit of her stomach. "Yet you would try, if you thought you had but a chance to take what is mine, wouldn't you my pet?"

"No, my Lord. I swear you are mistaken." Fear touched those dark eyes, words spilling from her lips in her need to please him, pull him from the depths of his thoughts. "I am your faithful servant. Your slave. Do with me as you will. I could not stand against you even should you demand my life as a sign of my devotion."

Faithful until she found a way to be free, to overthrow him, to destroy him or steal the power from him. She wasn't the first, wouldn't be the last, so why did he indulge her? Because this was how it worked. Creatures such as Arinnana amused him. They were so easy to read, a delight to manipulate, but bright enough to actually be of worth to him. But for now she belonged to him, a slave, a well marked piece of property.

She'd screamed so well when he'd carved the brand like scar into her body, screamed and refused to let tears fall even when his nail had glowed white with the magic summoned heat he'd used. Such a strength had become all too rare of late.

Why would he choose weak minded, stupid followers? Where was the challenge, the delight in that? They couldn't follow the plans he laid out. They rarely were able to think on their feet. He needed intelligence, a craving for power, the desire to learn. Those qualities that made his chosen puppets dangerous to control and a part of him enjoyed the challenge they offered.

Anyone could control a fool but only a god could control ones like the woman at his feet.

"Oh I will do exactly that," he brushed his foot under the woman's chin, raising her gaze to meet his. "And we have work to do. No matter how much I would love to spend the time exploring just how well you can scream I need your knowledge of this place."

"My Lord?"

"I need you to find something for me."

"What is it he wants?" Her mother inquired as the older woman followed Arinnana down the wreckage covered stairs. Blood mixed with dust, scraps of armor, the remains of furniture all left over from the night she had claimed the castle along with Guinelia. Until now she'd not been aware of just how much had been destroyed that night, all she could remember clearly were the screams, the splashes of blood, those soft whimpering pleas for mercy that had been ignored. Strange how the rest of it, the destruction of inanimate objects had been blacked from her mind until now. "What would our God want with anything stored in this place?"

"Information," she barely looked back at the older woman. What did she need her mother for now? Kaleb had chosen her, raised her above the woman that had brought her into this world. Who held the power now? The mother or daughter? Guinelia hadn't realized it yet, she had no understanding of how precarious her position had become. All those years of leaning on her mother for advice, for strength, as a way to gain her revenge on Riana had ended. She had become obsolete.

"And there is something here that can grant him more power than he already has? He'd send a slip of a girl to search for something he deems so vital? If you seek not to anger me I suggest you speak the truth or do you really think me such a fool my daughter?" Guinelia grasped her shoulder digging her nails into exposed flesh.

She growled, turning to stare upwards at the stress lined face, a sharp slap freeing her from the cruel grasp. "If you think you can insult me, our Lord's chosen one, in such a manner yes I think you a fool."

"Chosen? You think yourself above me? We are both his chosen." Guinelia's voice dropped into a low hiss, her eyes narrowing, the lines tightening about her thin lips.

"I have worshipped at his feet, seen the power in him, tasted it when he put me to his pleasure. I wear his mark!" Her fingers tore the strands of cloth free from her left breast, baring the living brand he had impressed into her skin. "I am his, fully. Body, mind and soul. If I please him fully then not only will Rhodan be mine, but I will sire a race of true servants for his delight. Children who will be raised to worship him and this land, the throne, the very world will be his as it was meant to be from the start." She hissed, flecks of spit foaming on her lips with her growing anger. She would not be dismissed as a lesser being by her mother, not this time.

"For now you are his chosen. A momentary amusement until he finds someone more suitable." Guinelia shrugged, showing no sign of being affected either by the mark or what had been said. "I am sure you writhed well for our Lord, my daughter, as have I in the past."

"What..."

"He is a god, our god. Did you truly believe he is bound to one vessel for his use?"

"I... but he..."

"He is a god, we are but his servants of the moment, amusements as and when he chooses. Only if we succeed in pleasing him beyond those fleeting times will we gain what we seek." Guinelia slipped past her daughter on the stairs, taking no effort to prevent herself from nearly shoving Arinnana down the steps in the process. "Such a mess, but I can still hear their screams. Do you remember the look of fear in their eyes before I struck? The way they thought themselves safe from a woman such as I? How wrong they were. Appearances can be so very deceptive." The unspoken threat lingered behind those carefully phrased words.

No, it couldn't be true. Fear, uncertainty and distrust all rose as snakes within her belly, curling as they hissed their burning venom against the lining of her stomach. Kaleb had chosen her above her Mother. She would not share the lime light with the old hag, not for too long at least. Like it or not there were still a few things that the older woman could teach her. If she could just swallow her pride and pretend she had been dutifully cowed.

"My apologies Mama, this whole situation with Rhodan and that bitch has me speaking without thought." Play the role of the chastised and now dutiful daughter, not that hard for her to do. The lowering of gaze, a soft quiver in her voice as she clutched her hands before her, fingers intertwining as she spoke. She knew the drill well, after all hadn't she fooled her own father for enough years?

"Now what is it he seeks from down here, gold, silver or a weapon unlike Erien has ever seen before?" The moment had passed, at least for Guinelia or so it seemed. Shrugged off and dismissed the same way she ignored the danger Arinnana offered. Now who thought themselves safe?

"Scrolls, books, things that speak of a rune language no one can read," soon enough she'd be able to choke the life from the wretched creature. Not yet though, no not quite yet. "He believes these things will grant him a power of the likes that Erien has not seen in a thousand years."

"The language of the Titans?" That, it seemed, was enough to cause even her mother to falter.

"Yes, I believe so." What did she know? More than she did that much was obvious.

"Interesting. So our Lord seeks the ancient magic of the runes, but why here?" A question that she didn't appear to expect an answer for as she hurried deeper into the remains of the castle. "There are far better places to seek out signs of that fabled power than a crumbling castle. I doubt my husband had any idea about magic, I would have discovered that years ago if he held power here."

Rune magic. Titans. Words she had heard as a child from the tutors that had despaired at her ever learning. She'd taken in far more than they had ever realized. It had simply amused her to see the looks of sheer frustration on their faces when she'd spouted back the wrong answer. Ah, but how that had backfired when Riana had been taught by those same men and women. Sweet Riana. Bright Riana. The belle of the ball. The delight of Lord Valer's life. So unlike the hard faced older sister. Magic, spells, charms, those had been able to change how they had seen her, at least on the outside, but it hadn't been enough to silence those hateful words.

"What is rune magic, Mama?" Arinnana painted a smile across her lips, adopting a well practiced vacant expression.

"Don't pester me with foolish questions. I know well you had the benefit of tutors fit for royalty." She hesitated for a moment before continuing, a smug tone clear behind her words. "I don't even need to look at you to know what you are trying on me."

"Bitch!" She hissed without thinking.

"Indeed, and your point would be?" Darkness enclosed them, the heavy shadows of the closed wooden door into the far reaches of the cellar lay hidden in the gloom before them.

"I can understand why my father wanted rid of you."

"You step onto dangerous ground with me, dear daughter," Guinelia's words dripped with poisonous warning. "Your father loved me, worshipped the ground I walked on until that Fae creature bewitched him. Before she came along we were happy, blissfully so."

Anger, she could see it, even in the darkness. The tension building across her mothers shoulders. "Yes, of course you were, Mama. That's why the servants would speak of you in hushed voices. Why papa would never even speak your name, only refer to you as that vile woman. Indeed the signs of a man so very much in love." There, just see how her mother felt at the truth being shoved back in her face. No one in the castle but the very daughter she now struck out at had wanted Guinelia back. Fear followed the very mention of her name, rumors of madness and more. Black magic, dark spells, curses, she'd been accused of it all and now Arinnana finally believed them.

"Enough!"

"For now," she agreed, waving her fingers towards the door. A simple spell muttered under her breath.

"Darkness fade

Light I need
Grant the power
Complete the deed"

A basic charm, but it did the job, casting a small ray of light against the door. A ray that grew into a torch bright beacon illuminating the wreckage.

"Ah, so the kitten has learned to use her first claw," the mocking tone set her teeth on edge.

"I see no need for a flamboyant spell when all we need is a little light on the situation." She tugged open the door, stepping into the room. Let her mother be the one to waste power on dramatic little touches, she'd keep her energy for more important things.

Shelves had crumbled, spilling scrolls, books, bottles and more over the dust covered floor. Broken bottles had leaked their contents over bails of cloth, glass crunched under foot along with shards of pottery and there, in the far corner of the storage area were the now sickly brown stains where two human lives had ended.

"Ah yes, I remember that maid and her lover tried hiding down here." Guinelia smiled, closing in on the stain. "Ah yes, and there, the page boy that was hiding. He did so well in keeping quiet until I skinned the maid. Pity really, looking back perhaps I was a little over zealous in killing everyone. We could do with a few servants. Perhaps one survived the carnage."

A survivor was doubtful. She'd counted the deaths, tallying them up in the back of her mind. More than the remaining servants had died, guards and guests had perished along side of them. She couldn't be certain that one had been missed but it was unlikely. Her mother had proven to be an efficient killer. Still, there would always be new bodies, new men and women to take the place of those who had died. "I sent word to the village along with one of Kaleb's familiars to gather new servants. I believe ten shall be enough for now. We only need a few sets of hands at first. Enough to make this place more livable." Dried blood, traces of body parts, it wasn't that she minded the mess but the smell in parts of her home had become more than a little unbearable. "Perhaps some lavender, or incense burning in the corners of a few of the rooms will improve matters."

"Suffering from a weak stomach, my dear?" Guinelia sneered, kicking over a basket that had somehow survived almost intact. "Something you will have to overcome. Lord Kaleb's taste in entertainment requires that you be made of far sterner stuff."

Better to ignore the biting comments. If they were the only weapons her mother now laid claim to then she had nothing to worry about. "He said there should be at least one scroll or book in the castle. He can sense it."

"But can't locate it fully or he wouldn't have sent you searching for it." Her mother replied quietly, sweeping one hand over the nearest shelf. "Dust, dirt, shreds of the past. We need more than the small pieces of information he has given us in order to better serve him."

Dangerous, she skated on thin ice speaking out against Kaleb. Still it was her life, her soul to loose. "We have enough to go on, or he would have given us more. He believes we will be able to sense the power in the fragments, the strands of energy."

The low snort spoke volumes.

It had to be here, some shred, a sign. Regardless of her mother's attitude she was determined to prove Guinelia wrong. Kaleb, her lord, her Master, had left her with a gift, a blessing and she was not about to risk his displeasure by failing.

Why would it, whatever it was, be hidden down here? Why not in the strong room, or in the lock boxes elsewhere?

Unless her family hadn't known what they were guardians too? It didn't quite fit with what she knew. She hadn't been prepared to take over as protector of this great secret for when her father died. Still, her father hadn't been a foolish man, he'd been well read, knew the lore of the land better than most did even if he had only scratched the surface of some of the legends. If he had suspected her duplicity, her ongoing contact with her mother he would have kept the matter a well hidden secret. He didn't travel that often, not since Riana's mother had passed away so it was unlikely he had been the one that had brought it, whatever it might be, into the castle. So who?

"The bitch's mother!"

"What?" Guinelia turned for a moment, eyes narrowed. "What did you say?"

"Riana's mother, she's the only one that could have brought in something of this nature into the castle without my father knowing." Where were the things she had brought with her? Those supplies, the few chests that Arinnana had taken great care to make sure had been put away after the Fae creature had died. "If father had known about them he wouldn't have kept it down here. They'd... it would be in a lock box, or the strong room. Not down here."

Fae. Creatures, not humans, not like her or her mother. They should never have been permitted to cross breed or wed decent humans. Another race created by those cross mating relationships. Little mistakes like her half blood sister. A mistake she would be delighted to rectify.

Before Kaleb she preferred to pay others to do such work for her, like the hired hands she had paid off to be rid of Riana. Pity that had backfired. Yet now, now the thought of slowly killing her sister, stripping the skin from her body inch by inch, appealed to her more than she had ever thought. It was her own fault, she'd brought this about by taking her prince, her mate. Using her foul Fae magic on her beloved. Like mother, like daughter.

Rhodan would be hers. No matter the cost.

No, there would be time to think of such delights later, for now there were other things she needed to focus on, like finding those boxes.

Screaming. All he could hear, even now, were the screams of the dying. Sounds he had never thought a human body could give life to. How many had been slaughtered? He couldn't be sure but his skin still crawled from the sounds he had heard. The dead, the dying, those tortured time and again before being granted the bliss of release. He could have been among their number. He still would be if those women discovered him.

Stupid. He shouldn't have even still been in the castle when the nightmare had begun. His own fault. He'd let a pretty skirt distract him from the fury Arinnana had triggered in him. He could still see her, the one that had caught his attention. A bold bright eyed wench, a serving girl, one that knew the comings and goings of both of Valer's daughters. So maybe he'd had more on his mind than just a quick moment of pleasure. She could have been a good source of information. Perhaps even the key to gaining his revenge on the elder daughter. Not now though. Not now. She was dead, like the rest of them now. Dead at the hands of those foul women.

The door. He could remember the door exploding inwards, shards of wood searing into his skin. Some of them still remained there, buried in his body, festering no doubt. He'd need to tend the small wounds when he had the chance, but not here. Because of those foul women he hadn't dared to pull them free. Just trying to might let them know where he was hiding. He couldn't risk it. Not after what he had seen.

Soldiers, men, women, children. They'd all died. It hadn't mattered if they had been loyal to Arinnana or not. The women had just wanted blood. Gods. He could feel the blood on his skin, caked there. The young kitchen hand, the look in her eyes when...

No. Don't think about it. Don't go there. Shut it out. He had to shut it out. Too many screams. The cries for mercy. Blood painting their faces, her face, the floor, it had never ended.

So much from just one body. He'd tried not to look but he'd been unable to draw his gaze away. Now he paid for that lack of strength, his mind all too willing to replay the long, drawn out death he had watched with stunned, sickening fascination.

Stop it. Don't think about it. He couldn't let the images strike him again, the memories. This time he might not be able to keep silent.

His teeth dug into the back of his hand, pain focusing him past the stark memories. If he made a sound they could find him. But only if they entered the kitchens again and no one had, not in nearly a day. Did they not need to eat?

He peered out from behind the sacks of flour, swallowing hard at the stench.

No one could eat what remained here. Not with the way it had all been coated by...

Focus. Breathe. He'd get out of this in one piece. He was Bevery, Squire, noble born. He'd trained along with the warriors his father had hired. Hunted. He'd seen blood before. Gutted animals. If he just thought of them as nothing more than beasts instead of people he'd be able to keep the contents of his stomach long enough to escape.

How though?

If he slipped out he could be caught then...

No. There had to be a way. Hadn't the maid tried to tell him. Yes. The same way out the young kitchen maid had tried for. A passage way, into the loading dock from the sea. Down through the caves. Most knew about it, and now, with everyone dead, they wouldn't be watching it. Would they?

He couldn't just stay there, hidden amongst the blood soaked sacks of flour and salt. Sooner or later he'd have to move so why not now, before their hunger finally got the better of them, or they hired new servants to clean up the mess. They'd bring others in eventually to take care of them. It was the nature of such people. The last thing they'd want to do would be pick up after themselves.

What would it take to get people to come back into the castle now that their beloved Lord was dead?

Threats? Spells? Both?

What if they didn't bring in humans, but some form of demon?

Gods no.

Slowly he crept out, searching for any signs of life, for the dark spawned pair with their craving for destruction. He'd never have guessed Arinnana could be capable of such acts. The blood had dripped from her face, coating her fingers, plastering her gown to a form that had looked lush. Once he'd almost thought her attractive, he'd been angry when she had turned him down during the ball. Now he could only feel relief that he had avoided her touch.

There, the door, cracked open. He just had to crawl a little further.

Sticky. His hand caught in something tacky on the stone floor. Honey?

His stomach rolled, threatening to betray him. His right hand resting in pooled and drying blood, but that wasn't what had him fighting not to vomit.

There, at the end of the pool, her honey blond hair fanning out across the stone, lay the decapitated head of the very same maid he'd planned on bedding. Her sightless eyes staring directly at him…

Chapter Five

"Up you get Rhodan dearie. You have such a busy day ahead of you and it's far too nice a day to play slug-a-bed." Simon's cheerful voice pulled him slowly from the warm, comforting realms of sleep he had sunk into sometime after he had stumbled into his room.

How much had he had to drink?

There'd been at least one keg, he could remember that much. And there had been a bottle of his father's best wine. The store laid down for him from the day he had been born ready for his marriage. Well it had seemed like a good thing to do, toasting his new found wife with the very brew his father had set aside for the occasion. What better use could there have been for the wine?

Had he drunk it all? There was a vague memory of glass shattering across the stone floor. Orent's disapproval grumbling at the back of his mind and Riana... hadn't there been something with Riana when he'd stumbled back to his room?

Too early to be awake. He didn't know what time it could be but it was way too early now. Light seared into the room, spears of pain that stabbed behind his eyes as the drapes where flung open in an all too dramatic gesture.

"Are you going to lie in bed all day, or get up and do something about this?" Simon tugged at the covers. "Up we get, I've got a bath prepared for you and you most certainly need one. Did you and that brute fall into the keg?"

Brute? "Cluiun?"

"Who else did you think I meant?" Simon plopped down on the edge of the bed, tugging out the familiar lace trimmed hankie from a lilac silk tunic. "My dear boy you've got mead stains all over your shirt. You look like you took a bath in the brew instead of drinking it, and your hair? I do declare it's sticking up all over the place. No wonder Riana refused to share the bed with you last night."

Riana? "Where is she?" He peered around the room, searching for a sign of his missing wife.

"Who dear boy, there are so many 'she's' in the castle."

"My wife of course." Why did he have to be so damn difficult? Simon knew full well who he was talking about. Punishment, that had to be it, he was being disciplined for daring to go off on a drinking binge. Not that he didn't deserve it, but it would have been so much easier to deal with if Simon had waited until the worst of the headache had eased.

"Oh, sleeping in my room. We thought it would be the best place for her and of course no one will think badly of the dear lady being there. She's perfectly safe there. Fast asleep when I left, all curled up on my bed." He dabbed at his upper lip delicately. "Quite the darling you've picked up there. Not quite what I had expected you to choose as a wife but you have my approval."

What did he need Simon's approval for? He'd married her because... why had he married her again. Other than the fact she was possibly the most beautiful woman he had ever seen. There had been a reason.

Love? That was it, he loved her. Didn't he? Yes, of course he did, but why did he. Gods he hated hangovers and the random thoughts that followed the headache. Damn it, what had she thought when he'd staggered into the room?

"Was she alright?" He almost groaned the words as he rolled half out of bed. His head pounded, throat felt raw and his stomach. No he didn't even want to think just how his stomach was playing up.

"Upset of course, well I can understand that now I've seen the state you're in but she calmed down soon enough, we shared a few warm drinks, exchanged some secrets, girl talk you understand."

"Do you have to do that?" He leaned against the edge of the bed, fighting to stay upright or at least on his feet. He had a full set of drums playing in the back of his head and a nest of snakes in his stomach. Mead and wine didn't mix. Why hadn't he remembered that last night? If he'd just stuck to the one drink, and maybe stopped before they'd reached the half way point on the first keg he wouldn't feel so sick this morning. "Girl talk, you're no more a girl than I am."

Girl talk indeed, what secrets had they shared? Not that Riana knew too much about him but Simon? There wasn't an event in Rhodan's life that his foppish friend didn't have information on. Gods above and below, if he'd told Riana about even a fraction of his dalliances prior to marriage then he'd spend the rest of his life explaining that he'd changed.

He had changed, hadn't he? No more skirt chasing or spending nights drowning himself in...

The throbbing behind his eyes put an end to that self deception. Okay, so maybe he hadn't changed as much as he thought he had. But he could try and change. He hadn't tried to bed any of the castle wenches since he'd brought Riana home. Not that he'd been home long enough for that to really be any test of the situation.

"True enough, but you have to admit I look better in this shade of lilac than most of the women in court do." He smiled, smoothing one hand over the soft material, barely glancing at Rhodan as he spoke. "I paid far too much for this of course, but one does what they need to in order to keep up appearances. Don't you think it suits me?"

It wasn't worth the fight, not while his head threatened to explode with each small movement towards the small door into the dressing chamber he was fortunate enough to have the use of. "The bath?"

"Is ready, I added some chamomile and lavender to the water." He smiled, waving towards the open door. Small curls of steam edged around the wood, carrying with them the very scents Simon had mentioned.

"Lavender? Do you want me smelling like a court doxie?" Lavender indeed, men didn't use scent, what was Simon thinking of? He'd never live it down if someone discovered him smelling like that. "Are you trying to completely ruin my reputation?" If he even had a reputation left to ruin.

"Anything would be better than how you smell right now." Simon wrinkled his nose in sheer disgust. "I've seen men stumble out of a three week binge smelling better than you do now. As for your reputation I think that you managed to ruin on your own long before last night."

"But lavender? It's just wrong for a man to be using scents like that. What's wrong with decent soap?" He grumbled, tugging off the shirt as he walked into the smaller room. "It would have got the job done just as well."

"I thought a little lavender might ease that headache of yours. It's always worked wonders for me. Besides, don't you want to see your wife smelling a little better than you do right now?" Simon leaned against the door frame wafting the handkerchief towards the large wooden tub.

He sank into the heated water, settling back against the wooden sides before looking back towards Simon. Riana, she would have had to have been very angry in order to storm off and seek out Simon the way she had. Just what had he done to her when he'd come back. No matter how he tried he couldn't remember anything about returning to the room. She would have been here though, where else could she have been? "Damnit, how angry was she? Did she say what happened before she stormed out of the room?"

"She told me enough that I would either apologize fully, with flowers and perhaps poetry as well. You might want to consider getting down on your knees to beg forgiveness or else not bother and be very careful how you sleep over the next few days. Yes the two kneed approach, one knee just won't do it, not this time." Simon tucked the cloth back into his sleeve before he continued. "She has quite the temper on her that one. You should hear what she has to say about that swine, Jeriah. Really, I always knew women were vicious but she could take on a new role as head torturer should your father ever need one. She has this wonderful idea about skinning a man in one very sensitive spot... well never, mind. It's not something you'd be that interested in."

He'd avoided half of the question. Could his Riana be that vicious? Well it made sense after everything she had been through in the past few days alone. "I've seen some of that temper, her spirit it's one of the things that attracted me to her." He brushed his hands back through his now damp hair, a wry smile tugging at the corners of his lips. "You should have seen her at the ball, the one her father held, such a bright spark, a living flame almost. She didn't back down to me, not one inch." It still amazed him how that simple ball had changed everything in his life. He'd entered a single man carefree and without a thought of settling down. Now he had a wife with children to follow soon no doubt and then one day the crown. No more trips off to the other side of Olain with Orent just because he wanted to escape the pressures of court not unless he wanted to take Riana with him.

Children. Great Dragon, he couldn't imagine himself as a father. He didn't even need to discuss it to know he'd make a terrible father. With luck that would be something he could avoid for a few years yet. Weren't there herbs, or charms that would prevent a woman from catching? Something he would have to look into and talk to Riana about it. She'd agree, obviously. Well why wouldn't she? They were far too young to be thinking of babies. All that mess. Both ends at once from what little he understood of such things.

Marriage fine. Family no. He just wasn't ready to settle down that much.

And what of the Cluiun. Now he had wed Riana what would their ally do? In the few short days he'd spent around the man he'd come to feel a grudging respect towards him, but beyond that there was a sense of friendship. Something he'd come across very rarely in his life. Few saw beyond the title and what spending time with the heir to the throne might gain them later in life. Cluiun didn't care about that, if anything he tended to ignore the rank that separated them completely.

"Well now considering how spirited she is didn't you think, before you went off to drain the cellar dry, that you might just upset your new wife by doing that? No, instead you ignored what she would be left doing and went to drink yourself silly with that brute of a pirate. Men, you're all the same a bunch of selfish brutes, only thinking of your own pleasure." Simon took a long breath before continuing his tirade. "Just what did you expect her to do last night? It's not as though she knew anyone else here, but you went and left her alone, all night. If I were your wife you'd be sleeping on the floor for a month."

"It was just a few drinks," so it hadn't been the brightest of ideas. "And who appointed you as the royal keeper?" Would drowning himself in the bath tub ease the searing pain in his head? Talking to Simon certainly wasn't improving his mood. "My head is killing me. I thought you said this scent stuff would help?"

"It will, just relax and give it a little time." Simon didn't hide his amusement as he moved further into the room, adding a little more lavender to the tub. "You did, a few years ago, after I pulled your sweet ass out of trouble over that merchant's daughter."...

Her fingers curled against the fabric, confusion gaining life at the back of her mind. Satin sheets, soft pillows and a bed far softer than she remembered curling up on, where was she? No, she hadn't fallen asleep on a bed, but a couch in the middle of talking to Simon. So how had she ended up back in Rhodan's room? Odd, she didn't recall him having satin sheets, good linen, plain but high quality.

Simon. Of course, she was still in his room and this must have been his bed. So where had he slept. Surely not with her? Oh gods if he had shared a bed, even though nothing had happened between them, and he mentioned it then the court rumors would start up again. She wasn't ready to face that. Not now, not ever.

Panic set in, forcing her to sit bolt upright on the bed, fingers gripping on the edge of the overstuffed mattress. She was still dressed, though the ties of her dress had been loosened a little and her court soft slippers sat at the edge of the bed. Of Simon there was no sign beyond the blanket and large pink pillow on the couch. He must have slept there over night after carrying her to the bed, but what about Rhodan. Had he even noticed she hadn't gone back to their room?

She doubted it, not in the state he'd been in. He'd been unable to stand without leaning against the wall, or the foot of the bed. Drunk hadn't even begun to describe it. She'd never seen a man as deep in his cups as Rhodan had been. Not even when her father had sunk into a depression after the death of her mother.

How she'd found her way to Simon's room had been more good luck than knowledge. The same page that had been sent to their room to summon Rhodan to the throne room had been in the corridors and had led her right to the door. If it had been anyone else in the well lit hallways she'd have been unwilling to ask how to find Simon, but she had a feeling the boy still felt bad for what had happened earlier in the day. She'd been right. With stumbling words and blushes he'd led the fuming Riana through the castle to Simon's rooms.

Poor boy, had he wondered what had sent her fleeing from Rhodan's room? No, not his room, their room. She'd let him chase her out of the room they shared.

Her teeth caught on the inside of her lip, chewing. That wasn't fair either, he hadn't chased her out, not physically. The smell, her anger, and the reluctance to deal with a drunk had pushed her through the door.

'He's awake, by the way and suffering for every drop of mead he had past the first cup' Orent purred at the back of her mind, the dragon's smug tone soothing some of Riana's annoyance. *'I don't think he's felt that bad in months. He over did it even by his standards.'*

"He didn't have to go and drink himself silly," it felt strange, talking to thin air but still knowing that Orent could hear her. "He doesn't do it too often, does he?"

'No, he didn't and no, it's not something he does that often compared to others in the court. However he thought it was a good idea at the time. Or at least that is what he will tell you. It's a very normal excuse you human's use. Perhaps if a few more of you thought things through these strange ideas would not be so amusing to you.' The sniff of disgust made it sound as if Orent was physically in the room with her. 'Humans they can be so annoying at times. And I had such high hopes for Cluiun.'

"Cluiun, why are you so interested in him? What about Rhodan? He's the one who came back in such a state last night. I've no idea where Cluiun slept and frankly don't care as I didn't have to face him." Not that she didn't hold Cluiun at least partially responsible for the drinking binge. It had been his idea, but she'd seen all too clearly how easy it had been to persuade her husband to join in on the celebration.

'I expected no less from Rhodan. He has a taste for his cups on occasions and it's a habit I am sure you will attempt to help break him of. Somehow you don't strike me as a woman who will put up with a mead soaked man on a regular basis. Not that he is the get drunk every night type as I said, he doesn't do it too often, but once or twice a month is normal for him. ' Orent paused for a moment before continuing. 'However, you did marry a man who has a well known reputation for following an inappropriate lifestyle.'

She'd rushed into the marriage that she couldn't deny, and now she couldn't help but wonder if it had been the wisest of actions. Love, it felt great at the time, she still loved him but now reality was settling in with an all too uncomfortable speed. Had she made a mistake?

He was handsome, a rogue at best, headstrong, gave little thought to anyone but himself if even a fraction of the rumors where to be believed but he'd come after her when Arinnana had had her abducted. Not just for a quick turn between the sheets either, if that had been all he had wanted then he wouldn't have risked marrying her and never before Lady Orent in such a manner.

'Oh he loves you, have no doubt on that.'

"I don't doubt his love, Lady. I just wonder if we should not have waited a little, found out if we could live together." What was she saying that she'd be content to live life without him? The thought left her feeling sick to her stomach. "I mean, what if we just don't work."

'I don't think that is really an option for both of you. Like it or not you were meant to wed. Why else do you think you fell for the type of man you'd normally throw a bucket of swill over?'

"I wouldn't do that to Rhodan."

'Oh, so why did you come close to grabbing a tray of drinks at the party *and throwing it over his head?'*

"Because he was being arrogant." She protested, recalling the moment all too clearly.

'Which annoys you.'

"Well yes, and he seemed to think he I should swoon over him." She should have thumped him instead of just slapping him. She knew how to punch, it just wasn't something she did that often. "He got so bold when I didn't fall into his arms. As if he wanted to push me into doing that, testing to see if it were all some sort of act."

'Which he tends to do with most women. Until you they all fell into his arms after a small show of resistance.'

"Well, he must have done something that night to appear different." This wasn't making sense at all. How could she have fallen in love with the type of man that normally made her skin crawl? But no matter how hard she tried to remember the night of the party she couldn't recall one moment where Rhodan had acted in any way other than the annoying, arrogant, every woman wants me, man that he continued to be.

'No, Riana. He did nothing different, he acted the same way he always does.'

"Then why, I mean how could I have, how could we…? It just doesn't sound reasonable. Nor make any sense to me." Riana tried to reconcile what she knew about Rhodan with the love she felt for him. Even now, with as angry as she felt towards him, she could remember how sweet his kiss had felt. How her body had molded eagerly against his, the soft tremors through her skin at each gentle caress. Bewitched. She'd heard the accusation before, about her mother and how she had changed her father from a rogue a hundred times worse than Rhodan had been into the loving man she had grown up with.

Had Rhodan found some way of enthralling her with a spell?

No, she'd have felt it. Or Orent would have warned against it. She couldn't see the dragon permitting such a deception. It didn't fit with what little she knew about the noble race.

'No, you can rest easy there. I would have never allowed him to force a woman into marriage. Such actions are reprehensible amongst dragon kind. But you're presuming love is both reasonable and follows some law of common sense. Silly girl. You know better. If that were true you would have been far more likely to fall in love with Cluiun than you did Rhodan. After all, even though he took part in your kidnapping he didn't ill treat you.'

Silly girl? Had the dragon really just called her that?

'What did you think I'd just called you then? You are still very young to me. Both of you are. When you've at least reached dragon teen years then I won't

look on you as children, but you've got a good four hundred years to go before you reach that.'

"So you're saying I had no choice in falling in love with Rhodan. It was just meant to be and I need to accept it and find a way to live with his faults?" Some other power controlled their destiny? She wanted to be angry, to scream against the twisted act of fortune that had put her in that position.

Energy crackled along her skin, lifting her hair upwards, the barest hint of the power she had nearly lost control of the day Rhodan and Cluiun had found her. Anger fueled it, rage bubbled within her core seeking a way to strike out at what ever had pushed her into this marriage."

'Peace, child.'

She'd been tricked. How could she not be angry about being tricked? Power surged from a low trickle into a raging force that rushed through the room, lifting up the couch into the air. Rattling the rare glass windows unleashing a power that sought out a target. No. She couldn't give into it. Wouldn't. She was better than this. Stronger.

'Calm, breathe, focus your way through this. Do not let your anger rule you. Do not become the very monsters some would have your kind be labeled as.' Orent whispered, wrapping her in a soft warmth from her heart outwards. *'There is so much to learn.'*

Monster, she wasn't a monster. Her fingers curled into tight fists on her lap, the couch lowering to the stone floor, her jaw clenched until it ached in protest. Slowly it eased, the crackling fading into a low prickling sensation, slipping back under the weak control she had struggled to put in place. "I'm sorry. I'm just upset about this. I don't want to be in a marriage through trickery."

'Yet you love him, you can't think about him, even now as angry as you are, without feeling some measure of peace. Could it truly be trickery when you feel this at peace with him? Accept it Riana. You wouldn't want to change who you are married to now. But that doesn't mean you won't try and persuade him to change a few of his less than savory ways. You won't be the first wife that has had to do that, and you won't be the last. Just as I am certain there will be a few things about your nature that will rub Rhodan up the wrong way and he'll either learn to live with them or he'll try and change them. That's the odd thing about you humans. You fall in love then instantly try to change something about the one you love.'

"I smell like I just rolled in a bottle of perfume," he grumbled pulling on a fresh set of pants. At least he had enough clean clothes around the place. So he didn't dress the same way Simon did but he seldom stinted himself on new clothing either.

"But you don't have your headache anymore, do you?" Simon tossed over a clean linen shirt. "As for the smell you must admit it is an improvement over how you smelled earlier. Besides, the scent suits you. Riana might enjoy it as well." He strode across the room, pushing open two windows. "Though you need to air this room out. It still smells of drunken prince and I don't think you want your good lady coming back in to this."

"I still can't get over the fact she spent the night in your room instead of coming back here." He kicked at the dirty clothes he'd peeled from his body earlier. Not even the scent from the tub masked the sickening smell rising from pile of clothing.

"Dearie I wouldn't have shared the room with you if you'd offered me exclusive use of that darling tailor down in Breckan Lane." He sniffed. "And you might want to consider having those burned. I doubt they can be salvaged not without the laundry woman passing out from the stench. They reek dear boy, absolutely reek. Yes burning them is for the best, unless you do have an enemy you want to punish. If so forcing them to wear those would be an ideal method. You'll need a locked box to store them in or they'll continue to coat your rooms in this foul stench."

They did smell bad, even to him and he had bigger concerns with what Riana now thought about him. Even though Simon's idea had merit. "Easily done, now what about my wife?"

"What about her?"

"Do I have to paint you a picture? She's upset, angry enough to sleep elsewhere only the day after we married, so what do I do to make it up to her?" He wasn't used to apologizing, not to men or women. It had been a luxury of station that he'd taken advantage of on more than one occasion. "How do I calm her down?"

"Saying sorry would be a start." Simon plopped down on the edge of Rhodan's bed only to wrinkle his nose. "Gods above and below, this entire bed will need to be stripped dear boy, stripped I say. Silk, satin, get something more appealing to your dear wife. Linen simply won't do. Perhaps sprinkled with a little lilac... no I suppose sandal wood might work better to preserve the remains of your masculine sensibilities."

"She didn't seem to mind the linen on our first night." He frowned ignoring the comment about scent as he ran a brush through his hair. If he tried to look a little more presentable for when Riana returned then it might ease a little of her bad mood. Well he could only hope.

"You're trying to apologize and make it appear you are not half the oaf you portrayed yourself as last night. You wandered in here, cup in hand and expected her to perform her wifely duties. Though I believe you said... now how did she phrase it?" Simon paused, one well manicured finger tapping against his cheek slowly.

"I don't think I want to know." Rhodan mumbled. Gods, had he been that bad?

"Oh but you must, it was an absolutely classic line."

"No! Thank you but no."

"Are you sure, you might want to use it again another day."

"Very sure," he came close to hissing the words.

"Well if..." A harsh knock rattled the closed door. "Well that doesn't sound like your dear lady now, does it. Unless she's doubled in size over night."

Grumbling under his breath, half expecting another summons from his father, Rhodan pulled open the door. Instead of a page wearing court colors a man easily six inches taller than Rhodan stood on the other side. Dressed in finely cut leathers with a well crafted short sword on his hip the new comer looked more like a Prince than Rhodan did right now.

"Your Highness? My apologies, I was not expecting you to look quite so... weary." The man made no attempt to hide the disdain in his words.

"A long night." His gaze narrowed, focusing on the small crest the man's sleeveless leather vest bore. A gryphon curled about a flame. Jeriah's personal emblem. Damn the man for his arrogance. His family had a crest, but his cousin had to push that one step further.

"Ah, yes. Well Lord Jeriah bid me seek you out and deliver a message." He made no move to enter the room, instead choosing to lean against the doorframe. He didn't need to enter, not to intimidate most he'd meet in life.

"And you are?" He should have known him but for the moment the name escaped him.

"Haon, son of Duke Racs." Sensual lips curled into a mocking sneer.

The name set off a few warning bells, though for the life of him he couldn't quite remember why. "And the message?"

"Lord Jeriah wishes to be done with the fight between you and has arranged for it to take place in the practice square at noon. He believes that should permit you enough time to prepare yourself and arrange for those witnesses you desire attend." Haon looked slowly over Rhodan, that same insolent smile twitching at the corners of his lips. "Though I am sure if you wished to publicly apologize he would be willing to come to some other arrangement. It would be a pity if your father was to loose his only son don't you think?"

His teeth clenched at the implied weakness. Noon? That soon? Jeriah was up to something, but that shouldn't have surprised him. "Tell your Master I will be there."

"Ah, quite brave of you Rhodan. Perhaps the rumors of your cowardice are exaggerations."

"What are you talking about?" He struggled to keep his voice calm.

"Everyone knows you prefer to lift skirts instead of a sword. If I weren't recovering from a small injury myself I would have been quite happy to take Lord Jeriah's place in the fight. He would never permit it however. Still, perhaps if he is gracious enough to allow you to live then I will take the time to give you a few… lessons in using your sword instead of your shaft." Haon waved his right hand, an all too clean linen dressing covered from the back of his knuckles upwards towards his elbow. "Once this has healed over of course. I wouldn't want to deprive you of a complete lesson."

And they called him arrogant?

"Then when I have finished with Jeriah I shall look forward to the lesson indeed." He barely kept the fury from his words.

"Of course, you'll need something to keep you amused whilst your new wife finds real men to keep her occupied." Haon lifted himself up from the side of the door, his good hand smoothing back through well tended shoulder length black hair that had been left in loose, flowing curls. The exact sort of style many women found to be attractive, though he'd never understood it himself. "She's quite the court beauty, who'd have thought it though, that a woman like that would hitch her cart to a fool of a prince. She doesn't appear to be the title hunting kind so one can only presume she hasn't been around a lot of men and was easily fooled by a few smooth lines."

"Get out." His hands clenched into tight fists, muscles growing taut across his shoulders. Every ounce of Rhodan now bristled with the sudden need to drive his fist into the all too smug face in front of him. "Get out of my sight now."

"Of course your Highness. I'm sure we'll have plenty of time to become better acquainted after the fight." He stepped backwards, offering a mockingly brief bow. "That is, of course, if you should survive the encounter with Lord Jeriah."

Rhodan waited only long enough for the arrogant man to step back before he slammed the door closed, rattling the wash pitcher and bowl on a nearby night stand.

"Don't let him get to you, Haon has taken time to perfect his rather irritating ways" Simon spoke quietly, with none of his usual flamboyant attitude. That alone worried Rhodan. "He's killed two men so far in spats over women, though he feigns injury and illness on a regular basis. For some reason the less level headed women of the court flock to him when he does that. Each one determined that they will be the one most suitable to nurse him back to health."

"And?" He settled on one of the few chairs in the room.

"He's dangerous, just not in the way he would like to think he is." Simon nodded towards the door. "He's a leech, professional trouble maker, provokes fights normally with men he assumes are weaker but has been known to target stronger men in the past. He has zero respect for women, doesn't believe they exist for any reason beyond what they can provide him with. A colder man I have never met, and that my dear Rhodan is saying something."

"Weaknesses?"

"Several."

"Details, Simon."

"You're in a terrible snarky mood today, did you know that?"

"Simon," he growled.

"Alright dear boy…he's got one that works well for the likes of you and I, but hasn't tripped him up too badly with women as yet. He can't keep his lies straight." Simon remained calm as he spoke. "He repeats injuries and illnesses, though so far only one woman has taken any real notice of that and she was only visiting court for a very short time, the Princess Shadoweaver…" Rhodan only vaguely recognized the name so could do little more than nod. "I'm sure you'll find time to collect the details of the encounter later but it was quite entertaining. Needless to say he wasn't impressed by her lack of interest in him. If she had stayed much longer then there might have been a chance of tripping him up in a more public way."

"But most fall for it?" Riana, she wouldn't be at risk from a man like that would she? Even if his wife wouldn't be at risk it was obvious a lot of the other women in the court were.

"Yes, most do. It's sad to say that some can be quite blind when the right window dressing is wafted in front of their face." Simon glanced towards the door. "He's managed to persuade three women that he is in love with them and only them and has slowly been relieving them of their money, property and their limited virtue. They claim, of course, that they cannot live without him or whatever it is about him that has addicted them. However sooner or later he will slip up fully in public or anger the wrong person. Until then he will need watching."

"Then I will be very sure to pay close attention to what he might be up to."

"If you have time to. The man is a leech yes, but he isn't your primary concern."

"Oh?"

"Your wife dear boy, your wife. Or have you forgotten that you have some serious groveling to do. I do suggest the down on both knees kissing her feet approach. I hear it works almost every time."

Chapter Six

Bevery edged past the door, crawling into the darkness that beckoned. He still hadn't heard anyone else, no other living soul in the castle beyond the two demon women and the man they served. If he was indeed a man. Not that Bevery believed in Gods, or Goddesses, at best the other had to be one of the Fae races.

Cursed beings. He'd never trusted them. Most thought them to be such peaceful races, creatures of healing, elemental beings. Some looked human like Riana's mother, others were odd spirits, wisps of air that wrapped themselves about any unwary soul. Could it be that some Fae were more like the demons spoken of in ancient lore? It would have made sense, filled in those gaps in what he was comfortable believing in. Dark, cold hearted beings, he'd have been happy if every single one of their kind vanished from the face of Erien.

Riana was different though. What little he had seen of her over the years, those brief visits for trade reasons, or to keep the lines of communication open. She'd been purified by her human father. Those visits were long gone now, just as Riana now was. Perhaps she'd been lucky in vanishing before the madness had claimed the castle.

Rhodan. The rumors had spoken of him being behind the disappearance of the youngest daughter of Valer. Could it be? A prince of the realm stooping to kidnapping women? No, even when he'd heard Valer had ordered Rhodan's arrest it hadn't made any sense. Less so with the way Arinnana felt about the man.

Arinnana, she could have been behind it. Nothing would have now surprised him about that woman, not after what he had seen, after what he had heard. Gods he could still hear the screams.

No, he wouldn't start down that path again. Not right now. Not in the darkness like this. Too dark. He would have near sold his soul for a torch or lamp. Anything that would have helped ease some of the fears that lurked within the deep shadows. He could have searched for a flint, something to light a basic torch but the fear of being caught outweighed his fear of what might lurk in the shadows.

How far would he have to go?

He'd never been this way, he just knew about it. Most did. Why the exit had not been sealed off, or checked he couldn't be sure. An assumption, perhaps, that everyone was dead so there would be no one left to try and use it as an escape.

Or would there be something waiting for him at the end of the passage? A foul and lingering death? A cage dangling in the center of the hall, nothing more than a source of entertainment, each shred of pain dragged out from his body until even the ability to scream had been destroyed?

A thousand deaths with no release.

No. Stop thinking about it. Keep going, finding the way through the dim light. That's all he had to do. Keep on moving down the well worn steps. They'd always been here, if the rumors were to be believed. A way in and out, just there to bring in stores. From everything he had been told the entrance was easy to defend from invasion just by a simple set of chains and a large block of stone. Not that he knew how to work it.

Gods. What if that stone block had been put in place? He'd be trapped in the darkness forever. Or worse, he might have to climb back out, into the kitchen and face those hell born bitches along with everything they might do to him. Would he have the courage to take his own life instead of falling into their clutches?

"Let it be open, please. I'll give anything you want. Anything." A plea to who? He didn't know, didn't care. Just as long as someone heard him. He could hear the ocean, waves crashing against the cliff face beyond, offering just enough hope to push him further onwards through the darkness. "I can't stay down here, I can't face them. Just let it be open." His hands moved over the carved stone wall, seeking the safe way down. Some parts were smooth, worn down over the years by a thousand sets of hands. Had one set belonged to the blond haired maid?

Her bodiless head, those eyes, the pool of blood. He could still remember the feel of it under his fingers. His stomach rolled, heaving violently until he could no longer control it. With a groan he sank to his knees on a wide step, his hands pressing over his stomach, retching until nothing remained in his disobedient body leaving him shaking, skin covered in a cold sweat as the harsh acidic taste coated the back of his throat. Slowly he wiped off his mouth, gulping in clean air. Still the taste remained there, burning with each swallow. Almost enough to set him back on his knees.

Move, he had to keep himself on the move. If he just stayed there he'd be caught for sure. Sweat fell into his eyes, catching on his lashes, his legs shook, skin cold and clammy but it would only be worse if he waited for his body to recover.

"Open, it has to be open."

How long had he been walking now? Long enough. He had to be close to the exit by now. He couldn't imagine it would be too much further from the last step. Not with the way he could hear, almost feel the ocean's roar echoing through the cavern.

He half stumbled, expecting to hit another step only to find himself on level ground once more. Thin shards of light filtering in from somewhere ahead. The door, but if it had been open there'd be more than just a little light. More than a few shafts. Just a crack around the doorway, the stone. Would it be enough to slip through?

Desperation roared into life, his fingers searching along the stone for the edge, the way out. Panic setting his limbs to shaking far more than a mere moment of vomiting could ever do. There, the gap, but not enough. Gods not enough, just a hand width of space. What had he done to deserve this, to have the way to freedom so close and so far out of reach?

He had to be wrong. He'd just not searched long enough. There would be a way out, there had to be. He couldn't be trapped here for all eternity, he just couldn't.

With a low, despair filled cry, Squire Bevery sank to the floor.

"We should have found something by now," Guinelia muttered, shifting aside a half ripped sack. Small bags of spices tumbled out across the floor, ignored by the two women as they continued their search. Rich scents mingled with the scent of corpses starting to bloat. "We've been down here a good portion of the day. If her chests where here we'd have fallen over the damn things."

Arinnana glanced up at the scowling older woman. The past few days had taken their toil on Guinelia. Once she had thought her mother to be a beautiful woman, now the lines were deeper, the harsh glint in her eyes was no longer hidden. Even the long elegant nails she had once envied now looked more like claws. And the smell, it almost left her gagging. Had the woman so much as even bathed? It wouldn't be too much longer before the bodies, or what remained of them, rotted past the point of ignoring the scent. The thought of her mother's stench and that of the dead mingling was almost too much to stand. If she had to force the older woman bound and gagged into a bath she would. "Stop wasting your breath complaining and get on with it."

"Don't order me around, daughter. You haven't earned that privilege."

She had, but arguing about it would be pointless. Only when her Lord gifted her with enough power to match and then better her mother without a shadow of a doubt would it be the time to face her down. "Once we find it we can get out of here. I don't know about you but I need to bathe. Something you could do with attending to yourself, Mother. Your dress, it looks like it's the same one you were wearing the night you entered the castle. And I don't think you've washed your hair in over a week."

"As if that matters now. It's not as though I have anyone I need to impress." Guinelia growled, grasping the edge of a barrel to pull it clear from the boxes behind. Wood splintered, cracking with the harsh shove that sent the barrel to the stone floor. "Perhaps if your father still lived, if Kaleb hadn't demanded his death as a sign of your loyalty I might have had something to strive for."

Regret or anger? Either way it would be a weapon she could use to undermine her mother's position with Kaleb even further. Every weapon, each small piece of information would help. Guinelia had rapidly become a liability and one she needed to be rid of as soon as possible. One wrong move from her mother, a bad word, or lack of devotion should her anger become too much to contain and she could cost Arinnana everything.

So the death of her father had been required. So what? Any ability the woman had left to feel some level of empathy or sorrow had vanished with Kaleb's first brutal taking. Her thighs clenched at the memory, the sweet pain, the darkness of his eyes. If he had been mortal he would have been enough to turn her attention fully from Rhodan, but she was no fool. In order to continue on she needed a human mate and who better than the man she had craved for more years than she could truly number?

"Found it!" Guinelia's cry pulled the younger woman's attention fully to the area her mother had been searching. "I know that chest anywhere, she brought it with her the day she entered the castle. Never let anyone else near it, even though I tried before leaving the castle again. I tried a dozen times after he ordered me out to get to the chest. Each time I slipped in I tried finding it."

"I thought my father had you thrown out of the castle with orders never to return. On pain of death if caught. The guards were given full descriptions of you, with reminders once a month." Arinnana tried to push past in order to get a good look at the chest. The guards, they'd come to expect the monthly briefings but it had taken many years before she'd understood the fear in their eyes at even a passing mention of Guinelia.

Not something she'd ever question again.

"He tried to keep me out but I had a few spells at my beck and call even then. It didn't take too much to use a deception spell. Everyone, including your father, assumed I was just one of the maids." Guinelia tugged the chest out into plain view, the heavy lock clanging against the wood. "I tried for close to a week to get to her or her room, but she had wards all over the place. Then someone tipped her off. They realized I was there and your father had me whipped from the castle walls."

"Why didn't I know about that?" She couldn't recall any incident that even remotely matched that story. Nor had she been too young to remember the day Einea, Lady Quilieinea of the Silver Forest, had arrived at Valer Castle. Tall, elegant, the Fae woman had moved with a grace most women would have killed to possess and in the moment she had stepped into the castle grounds all other women had ceased to exist in the eyes of her father.

Bewitched? She'd thought so for a while, but now spending so much time in close quarters with her mother it was easy to tell which woman had been using magic to ensnare her father.

"You're probably too young to recall."

"No, I remember that day very clearly, and a few days later when you were decreed not only banished but outlaw and to be killed should you be found within the castle grounds." Whipped from the castle walls, it didn't fit with the father she had known. No matter how angry her father had been he'd never raised his hand in anger to a woman. Another one of her mothers exaggerations no doubt. She reached out for the chest, growling a warning under her breath as her mother tried to keep her away. Oh no, she wasn't going to let her mother get in the way. Not this time. "Don't get in my way, mother. I won't permit it. He set this task to me and I allowed you to help find it to raise you up in his eyes. Not to steal the work from me."

The older woman turned without warning, her wild eyes lacking reason. She struck out, lashing towards her daughters face. A loud crack echoed through the room, sending Arinnana stumbling backwards from the chest. "So my whelp thinks she can take my place in the heart of our lord does she? I gave myself to him before you even knew he would step into your life. Gave myself over to summon the power needed to destroy your rival and you have the nerve to think yourself more important?"

A snarl tore from Arinnana's lips, her fingers clenching in a claw like manner, fury simmering beneath her skin until she could feel the dark energy, blood born magic, answer her untamed summons. "Never strike me again."

"Or you'll what? Go crying to Kaleb? Don't you think he'll find such a fight between mother and daughter amusing?" Guinelia advanced on her daughter, clearing the short distance between them. "You should take the time to learn a little more about the one we both serve. He'd like nothing more than to see the two of us fight it out."

Of that she had no doubt. "Touch me again and it will be the last thing you'll ever do." She pushed up to her feet, fire sparking into life about her fingernails. Dark skies, the rush. Nothing could have prepared her for this. She felt it, roaring in her veins, a drug more addictive than any she had known before. How easy it would have been to sink into that delight, give it full life, permission to seek out a target. "His touch, his mark has gifted me with a few small weapons of my own. Perhaps he foresaw this between us, I don't know, but lay one hand on me again and I'll take great delight in using every ounce of power he has blessed me with to strip the skin from your flesh."

"No, you won't. Oh my dear daughter, do you really think I am going to be afraid of the whelp I brought into this world?" Guinelia didn't hesitate. With a low snarl she reached out, grasping her daughter about the throat, nails digging into Arinnana's neck. "I have been doing this far longer than you can ever understand. No matter how much power you think you lay claim to I will always be far stronger."

Had she underestimated her mother? Arinnana grasped the fingers that now squeezed into her throat, small needles of pain pricked into her throat, just enough to warn. No, she hadn't underestimated, even this close she couldn't sense any build up of power, nor see it within eyes that had been claimed by madness. It wouldn't matter what Arinnana said, or did to warn her mother about the power she had been gifted with the older woman wouldn't accept it. No more than she had graciously been able to step aside when that Fae woman had taken Guinelia's place at Valer's side.

Foolish. Bluffing one who could now feel power in others. A death sentence in the making. She'd thrown away every ounce of caution. Her father's death had been too much. Nothing else made sense. All those years fixating on the man, only to witness him die on the whim of a God would have driven the strongest of souls insane.

"So be it."

Those three words didn't even appear to register with Guinelia.

With a growl Arinnana struck, fire dancing along her fingers, sparking out from her nails towards the older woman's face. Claws of flame scored out, biting deep into Guinelia's cheek, smoke and the bitter sweet smell of burning flesh filling the air in that moment. But the grip about her throat didn't ease.

"Stupid brat!"

"Release me or the next strike will remove your face!" She could do it, she had the power, so why did she hesitate?

"No, you'd have done it already if that were the case. Oh you may have some power Arinnana but you still lack the heart to use it against anyone who stands in your way. There's still a shred of innocence within you. A thread he can corrupt to his whims. He might find that attractive but to me it just shows how weak you still are." Guinelia snarled, closing her grip a little more, threatening to cut off the air Arinnana's body could not live without.

She scratched at the iron grip about her throat. Struggling to find a way free. Anyone else would have, should have, screamed at the pain her magic fueled attack must have caused. Yet there her mother stood, blood slowly dripping from her cheek, deep burned scores marring a face that had once been beautiful.

"It's time you learned just which of us has the power in this relationship darling daughter. You can strike at me, stab me, burn me and I won't feel it. Not any more. That, dear one, was the price I paid to focus on my revenge." Her grip tightened further, cutting off her daughter's air fully for a long count of five then dropped the gasping woman to the floor. "You've no idea what I have given up over the years. The sacrifices I have made in order to get my husband back. Now that's gone. I've nothing left to loose because of your desire to serve Kaleb in my place."

It hadn't been her idea. She'd not wanted to be pushed into service with the dark god who now waited for them in the hall. "You ignorant bitch. You pushed me to offer myself to our Lord." She scrambled up from the floor, keeping a healthy distance between them. "You told me it would give me Rhodan. Told me it was the best thing for me. That I should pay any price I had to in order to submit to him, to convince him that I was willing to be his for the taking."

"I never meant for you to..."

"To what? To do anything I had to the very way you had advised me to? Did you really think he would not push things to the limits? What better test than to have me kill my own father?" Had she wanted to kill the old man? There had been a moment when the idea had left her feeling ill even when Kaleb had ordered her to act, but that had passed. "If I hadn't killed father it would have been my skin hanging on the wall instead and we both know it. Our Lord does not suffer disobedience lightly."

'Enough!' His voice reached into their minds, silencing both women. 'I rule here, my desires, my law, my passion. It is on my whim that you both live and should you cease to prove of use to me your lives will end and another will take your places. Cease this bickering and continue on with your task. You have a candle mark to appear in my chambers with your task complete or one of you will die.'

Arinnana bit into her bottom lip before she summoned up the strength to reply. "As you will my Lord. It shall be done." Angering him further would have been a futile exercise. No matter how much power she gathered she would never be able to match Kaleb.

'And you my dear pet Guinelia, do you need a lesson in just how dangerous it is for you to delay assigned tasks in order to feed your petty needs for revenge? Do I need to have your daughter dispatch you as a sign of her devotion for me?'

"No my Lord, your will shall be done." For the first time since they had begun their slow decent into the bowels of the castle Arinnana witnessed fear marking a path across her mother's face. "My most humble apologies Lord Kaleb.

I did not mean to put my foolish desires above yours."

Did she believe the apology her mother offered? Of course not and she doubted Kaleb did either. Appearances, sometimes they held far more weight than reality ever would.

'Believe me my slave you have not yet learned what a humble apology is, but that can be corrected.'

Interesting. She'd been expecting him to blandly accept the offered words.

"My Lord, perhaps that will not be necessary. My Mother has located a chest that may well hold what you seek." Confusion ruled Guinelia's gaze at her words, but then how could she know that it was no sense of daughterly devotion that had pushed Arinnana to speak. When the time came for her mother to grovel, to plead for her life, it would be at her whim and hers alone.

'Bring the chest to me, my pets. Now. I grow weary of this waiting.'...

"I'm going to die... either down here or back up there," Bevery sobbed into the darkness, his arms wrapped tight about his knees as he rocked back and forth. Cold seeped into his bones, delighting in the fear that fed his imagination. "I don't want to die, please. I don't want to die."

No way out. He'd spent hours stumbling along the edge of the slab, seeking with his fingers for some way to pull it open. Nothing, after all that searching he'd found nothing. Just dust, rocks and darkness. A waste of time, energy, there might have been another way out elsewhere. A chance to slip out the main doors. Something. Anything would have been better than sitting in the darkness.

The front gates? He'd have died before reaching the courtyard.

"Don't want to die." He could still smell the vomit on his own breath.

"Who says you have to?" Soft, seductive, the voice whispered from the all consuming darkness.

"Who's there?" Not the women, they couldn't have found him. "Don't kill me," he whimpered. No where to run, only the darkness to hide in. She'd found him, others could as well. Stupid, he should have stayed in his sheltered spot upstairs, waited, fought his way clear when the time came.

A nice lie to cling to.

"I don't plan on killing you." It moved, little more than a shadow at first, stepping into one of the thin shafts of light that found a way into the cave. "In fact I want to help you Squire Bevery." Tall, elegant with ebony hair that brushed over her naked hips. The last thing he'd expected to see step out of the darkness had been a naked woman. Let alone one offering to help him. Yet there she was.

A flicker of hope in the cold despair that had engulfed him.

"Who are you?"

"Someone who can get you out of here." She cleared the distance between them, hips swaying with each silent step. Lush, that word suited her well. Full lips, a sensual teasing smile, her very walk would have attracted attention from any man and most women. Almost too beautiful.

He'd known women like this before. Dangerous didn't even begin to describe them. Always hunting for the next meal ticket. Well she'd come to the wrong man now. He had nothing to offer her. "Why should I believe you?"

"What other choice do you have? That's unless you want to spend the rest of your life down here? Did you have plans to meet Guinelia or Arinnana? I'm sure they'd be most pleased to know you wish to spend some time around them. I could always let them know you're down here."

"No, not that."

"Are you sure, it wouldn't take me but a moment. They'd be delighted to meet you again. Though didn't you have a slight run in with Arinnana at the ball?" She smiled, tapping one tapered nail against a full bottom lip. "It might be interesting to put the two of you together again. Lovers reunited as it were."

"We were never lovers."

"True, she wants Rhodan. All you'd ever be to her is a second rate substitute."

How did this woman, whoever she was, know about the events at the ball? Unless she'd been there? Another survivor? If so why was she lingering down here naked as the day she was born? "You said you could help me get out of here?"

"Yes, I can. If you're interested." She reached out, tracing one delicate finger across his chest.

Under other circumstances he would have been interested in more than a way out of the cave. Even with the fear, the uncertainty of what would happen, he could feel a familiar tightening about his loins. "I want to get out of here, alive."

"And if there is a price to pay?"

"I'll pay it." He didn't even hesitate.

"Are you sure?" She leaned closer, each word sending a cold breath across his lips. Cold? How could it be cold? Unless.

"Gods, you're not human!" Fear clutched his heart, sending him stumbling back.

"I never claimed to be," she shrugged. "But that doesn't change the fact I can get you out of here."

"How?" Whatever it was, it held the answer to his freedom. He'd deal with the consequences later.

"I can open the slab, move it for you."

"That's impossible…"

"For a human yes, not for me." She didn't move. "Now do you want out of here or not?"

"Yes."

"And if I said the price was your soul?"

"I'd pay it." After all what would it matter? He didn't believe in souls. They were nothing more than a creation of the priests as a way to enslave you to their beliefs.

"No hesitation or regret?"

"None."

"Interesting, most at least want a moment to think about it."

Why would he need the time? He couldn't miss something he didn't have to begin with. "If that is all you want in exchange for getting me out of here then it's yours."

"Well now, I believe we have a deal."

"Good, then open the damn slab." He growled, nodding towards the hefty weight that blocked him from freedom. "It's time I was out of here."

"First the payment." She took a step closer. "After all if I wait until after I open the way you might not want to pay."

"How is that done? Did you want me to sign something?" A contract no doubt. Signed with a dramatic flourish, perhaps with blood red ink. Not that it would be worth the paper it was written on.

"No. Do you think I can claim a soul that way?" A mocking smile twitched at the corners of those all too full lips. "No, I need a kiss from you in order to claim your soul."

A kiss from a creature that looked human but wasn't, that didn't sound so bad. Would her lips feel as cold as her breath had? She looked comely enough and he couldn't imagine that there would be a problem in kissing her. "Then do it and get it over with."

"Eager aren't you? Well then let's enjoy this sealing of the pact." She reached out, fingers tangling in his tunic as she pulled him close. "I confess I do relish these little moments where deals are sealed." Before he had the chance to speak again her lips locked against his.

Not a kiss, a taking. He couldn't move, breathe, barely could think. Ice seared at his lips, stealing his thoughts, turning him cold in a heart beat. Everything ceased beyond the kiss. Her tongue forced its way into his mouth, seeking, stroking, claiming every ounce of him that she could touch. Pain followed the cold. Shards of ice that cut the inside of his mouth, blood mingling with the taste of fear.

Never ending. She'd keep sealed against his lips for eternity. A false offer of freedom in order to claim a kiss. That's all she had wanted. To drink in the fear, pain and blood of his kiss.

"Done." She pulled back, licking the small trail of bright blood from her lips. "Such a delicious kiss. Perhaps you'd like to try another? No? Ah well, I can live in hope."

No more kisses. After that one he couldn't imagine ever wanting to kiss another living being again. Cold. He'd never been so cold in all his life. His limbs felt frozen. Shaking he forced his hand to his lips. Blocks of ice. What had she done to him?

"Now I can open the door." She didn't even look back at him but instead walked to the closed block, brushing her fingers over the stone. For a moment nothing happened, then it crumbled. Into dust. The block simply ceased to exist. Nothing but dust. "You're free to leave Bevery. Unless you'd like to stay for a new kiss or perhaps a little more? We could take a little time to get to know each other."

Even with as frozen as his limbs felt that offer spurred him into life. With a cry of terror he darted out into the still bright day...

Chapter Seven

A few more hours and it would be over. Rhodan would be dead at his feet. He would become the heir and Riana would be his. She might not like the idea too much at first but there were enough sources of potions and drafts around. Finding the right one wouldn't cost too much. Once she drank such a potion then her resistance would falter, they'd spend their first night together as husband and wife, then all arguments would cease.

Dealing with Arinnana would be another matter, but not an impossible one. He'd have to kill the woman, or find a suitable mate to replace the dead prince. Which one he hadn't decided as yet, but to simply brush her off would be a mistake. Dead men ignored the potential threat a woman might pose. He'd seen that error committed too many times.

A man would challenge you to a duel, he'd fight with warning. A woman, no they ran by different rules. No warnings needed. The attacks would come from no where.

"Well the prince did seem a little shocked at the short notice but he claims he will be there." Haon closed the door behind him.

"And Riana?"

"The girl? I saw no sign of her. Perhaps they have had a lovers tiff." The large man smirked, settling down on one of the spare chairs swinging one leg over a delicately carved arm. "Which should make it a little easier for you once the boy is dead."

"Indeed. It might well be that all is not well in newly wed land." That wouldn't have surprised him. He at least had tried to be discrete in his wenching, not something he could say about his cousin. Rhodan had never, apparently, learned what it took to be subtle about such matters, though now that would play in Jeriah's favor.

"Either way by the end of the day he'll be dead. It'll be over and you'll be taking his place." Haon shrugged, resting his feet on the edge of a low table. "You really need to get a few extra lamps in here. It's a little dull for my tastes. I prefer to see the faces of the women I entertain."

Entertain, that was one way of describing his recreational habits.

"It suits me." That was the problem with working with a man like Haon you ended up with unwanted opinions being offered. Still for now he was useful. "The men I instructed you to gather together?"

"They are ready."

"Their loyalty?"

"Without question. Many of them have been working either for myself or my family for years now." Haon yawned, making no attempt to hide his boredom. "Berin has been my second for five years now. Never baulked at anything I have had him do. You could say he takes great pride in being a part of the 'team'"

There were men and women like that. Followers. Those who lived through the fame or fortune of the ones they worked for. One thing bothered him though, the man had been well known for the second he had worked with until recently. What had been his name? "What ever happened to Onan? I thought he was your second?"

"I promoted him and now prefer to keep him for more important matters of a private nature." Haon's eyes narrowed for a moment, little more than a twitch of lines. Another might have missed the warning signs.

"Such as?" He didn't like the idea that his man would have private matters. Such things might affect plans he had running. Especially when he was reliant on a man like this.

"Family matters." Haon shrugged off the question. "Nothing that important. It won't interfere with your plans."

"That I would prefer to judge for myself." He needed Haon, for now at least. "You've no idea how far my interests reach."

Haon pushed one hand through his hair, making no attempt to hide the smugness in his smile. He knew something, that much was obvious. "Oh I think I have a fair idea now. We've been working together how long now. Four years, nearly five?"

"Something like that." What did he want?

"And in that time have I ever let you down? Either before I came to court or since?" He slid an elegant dagger free from a hip sheath.

"No." He couldn't argue that. Not once had Haon let him down or even come to it. The rules had changed. He wasn't looking to grab a little extra power in court; this was a matter of the throne.

"So perhaps it's time you learned to trust me."

"The day I make that mistake is the day I plan my own funeral."

"Ah now that's why I like working for you Jeriah. You've never been a fool." He started to clean underneath his nails with the tip of the dagger. "But you're walking on dangerous ground if you believe I'll just turn over information on my family's business to you. I'm working with you, for you, but I don't belong to you. Piss me off and I'll swap sides in a heartbeat. But you already know that about me, don't you." On anyone else the smile Haon flashed might have been seductive, but the glints in the man's eyes, slight tightening of lines, warning signs that Jeriah knew all too well.

"What's to stop me from killing you right here? I've more power at my command than even you might realize." Power, it always boiled down to power and the perception of it. A dangerous game to play with Haon, but it needed to be done. The lines had to be drawn.

"You need me." He looked up, that all too confident smile hadn't even faltered. Interesting. "You can't pull this off without me. Even with the magical edge you've got you still need good old fashioned man power. Oh you can summon your magical backer, wave some money around but at the end of the day unless you have the man power to back it all up you'll fail."

Jeriah bit back a growl. Like it or not Haon was right. He couldn't do this without help, without the constant back up that he provided. Others would already be looking at the throne. At just how they could take his place, become the heir once Rhodan had been taken care of. He couldn't risk that.

Once he had the throne, Riana and that bitch Arinnana taken care of, he could look at other ways of controlling the land. For now the smiling man in the corner of Jeriah's room was right. He needed the back up Haon could provide. The information he stumbled across and until that changed he would continue to need the man.

"I'm right and you know it."

"I know." Jeriah kept a civil tone, albeit barely.

"So keeping that in mind there's something I want from you."

Here it was the price. There was always a price sooner or later. Not that he hadn't been paid more money than most men his age would ever see in a lifetime. "And that would be?"

"A woman." The dagger flipped in his hand, ice claiming his tone.

"You have any woman you turn your attention to, so why would you need my help there?" Now he was curious. Haon had them flocking to him, no matter what little lies he spun.

"Not a woman, a specific woman."

Who?" He leaned forward, watching the play of emotions over Haon's face. Anger, need, desire. They flashed one after the other over a face Jeriah still thought to be too perfect.

"Shadoweaver." He all but hissed the name. "I want the so called Princess Shadoweaver in chains at my feet."

"Ah, the woman that turned you down." Pride, of course. With all the women he had access to the only reason he would need help with getting one would be because she'd dared to turn him down. He remembered the woman only too well. Not that tall, long red hair, almost living flame, and her eyes. Normal human's didn't have silver eyes. Attractive, as long as you didn't mind women with scars. She'd more than her fair share if the rumors were to be believed. A warrior, so she claimed. Unusual for a woman of noble blood.

The dance between the two had been quite public. Enough that Haon had been hard pressed to maintain his position after she'd left. No blows, but it had been a close call and not from Shadoweaver.

"She did more than that and I want her to learn how foolish that was." Haon growled. "She over stepped the lines, the boundaries, tried to make me appear stupid in front of the court. I won't allow a woman to do that and not go unpunished."

"Ah, well there might be a small problem with that, but I'll see what I can do." More than a small problem she was blood royal from some small country on the other side of Erien. Not exactly a person whose presence he could command at the court, even after he claimed the throne. Still it was better to at least let Haon think there was a chance. "I'll send out a request to deal with her on a matter of trade. I'm sure she'll do what is best for her land." He tossed out the answer without looking directly at the man.

"Good, because once I get my hands on that woman I'll teach her a lesson she'll never forget."

Cluiun groaned, dipping his hands into the bowl of water, washing off his face, blinking as he tried to think straight. How much had he had to drink? More than enough, that was certain. Still he'd drunk more in his time and certainly had felt far worse than he did now. A bite to eat, something to drink and he'd be fine. Just as long as he had a herb brew and not hair of the dog.

Long night, and it would be a longer day because of it.

Rhodan. Damn that boy had drunk too much. He wouldn't have wanted to be the one facing Riana last night. Not with the temper he'd seen in the woman.

A part of him envied Rhodan his good fortune, but no matter how attractive Riana was, or how a small part of him wondered what it would have been like to spend the rest of his life waking up next to her, she wasn't the one for him. When and if he found a woman it would be one that could match him passion for passion. Who didn't flinch at his scarred face and who understood that his love of the sea would never change. Not many women could live with that.

None that he had met at least.

If one existed he might go his entire life without meeting them. Perhaps that would be for the best. Women wanted men to settle down, buy pretties and father a dozen children. Not his way.

A thought for another time, another place, he had work to do. With Jeriah arould the newly weds would need his help. Jeriah, the man made his skin crawl. He'd met very few human beings that needed to be put out of their misery but he qualified. He'd seen the way Jeriah had looked at Riana. That sheer lust. A greed that had no end. If Rhodan had claim to something Jeriah wanted it.

The face that looked back at him from the mirror looked worn, eyes red rimmed. Too much mead in a very short time. He'd feel better after some fresh air.

He slipped out of the room, wiping the last of the water from his eyes. By now Rhodan would be awake and no doubt coming up with a dozen excuses for Riana. Or he'd be busy apologizing. He'd give the couple a little extra time before he went off in search of them.

It had been less than a week and he already missed the ocean. Stone walls had their place, for a short amount of time at least, but wooden floors, the smell of salt, sails billowing out as the wind filled them. There was nothing like it on Erien. He owed no loyalty to anyone but his mistress the ocean. It didn't matter that his ship was gone. He could replace it and had no doubt Rhodan would help there. But the nights on the ocean he missed and would need to return to soon.

"He wants us to strike when?"

The voice came from a door left half open. By instinct Cluiun flattened into the shadows, straining to hear. He didn't know who it was that had spoken, or what they were talking about, but the hair raising on the back of his neck told him far more than solid proof ever could.

"Not until Rhodan is dealt with."

"Dealt with?" Just two voices, no more. At least that he could hear as yet. He'd heard enough. The longer he stayed there the more likely he was to be discovered, but the next words kept him frozen against the wall.

"The duel is at noon. By two he'll be dead and Jeriah named heir." A cold chuckle followed the words. "Can you imagine the look on his face when our Jeriah slides his sword home?"

The fight, that soon, with Rhodan recovering from drinking the night before. Sounded almost like Jeriah had found out about their trip to the cellar and was acting on it. Foolish. He should have realized that a piece of slime like that man would take advantage of any situation he could. Noon would barely give Rhodan chance to sober up fully.

"You sure Jeriah can take him? Not that I don't want to be there when the boy dies, I'd just rather not be there if everything goes wrong."

"Yes, one way or another Rhodan won't be walking off that battle square."

"And the boss is okay with this?"

"I guess, or he wouldn't be helping Jeriah out. Don't know what it is between them but I'm not dumb enough to go and ask him either."

"Yah, I know what you mean. He's not the sort to take questions kindly. I guess that's why I'm confused about him helping out on this. Guess there must be something pretty big for him in this."

A sound, soft, but enough to make Cluiun turn, one hand reaching for the hilt of his sword. Pain shot through his face, lights dancing in front of his eyes as the blow sent him backwards, stumbling against the wall. Steel pulled from leather as he fought to clear his sight.

Not fast enough.

A flash of metal before the steel hilt slammed down against the back of his neck, sending him into the darkness...

'You can't hide in Simon's room for the rest of the day, Riana.' Orent spoke quietly. *'He is sorry about what he did. Very sorry. He does love you. I've found that to be a very rare emotion.'*

"I don't doubt that he loves me, just not sure what to do now." She could still remember how drunk he had been. What if he did that on a regular basis? She didn't know if she could cope with that.

'Hm, you're stronger than that.'

"Am I?" She sometimes wondered. "I don't feel it right about now." Curling into a ball around a very large pillow and buried under the softest of quilts sounded like the ideal plan at the moment. "All I want to do is hide. Not something a strong person does."

'You must be after what you've survived. And you're willing to face the world of court life. Knowing how many battles take place hidden behind silken words and fancy gowns. Perhaps you are better prepared for this life than you believed?'

"Anything is possible." She missed living on the edge of the ocean. The sounds had lulled her to sleep most nights, but here sounds of a different sort filled the air both day and night. It even smelled odd. Not salt but smoke, the kitchens worked day and night to feed noble born and servant alike. Not the ocean but boots on stone, calls from the guards, distant noises from the main courtyard and the houses beyond the castle. Her father's home had always been busy as well, but not to this level. So much smaller, she'd known nearly everyone there by name. Now she lived in an alien world.

'Don't underestimate yourself.' The Dragon chided. *'I have no doubt you will not only learn to cope with life here, but surprise everyone around you. And I wouldn't go thinking that your life will be nothing more than balls, court gatherings and avoiding the snide remarks of jealous men and women. There is far more than*

that in your future.'

"After the mad cap journey that brought me here I'm not sure if that's a good thing or bad." Riana half smiled. She could still feel the storm that had rocked her from one wall to the other in the Cluiun's ship, even the memory of it left her stomach clenching.

'What's this, are you trying to tell me you wouldn't want to repeat your trip? The adventure; excitement? Then meeting the man of your dreams? Why Riana I thought you enjoyed every step of that trip?' She could almost see the wry, knowing smile on the dragon's face.

"Oh yes, I loved being kidnapped, sold off to a pirate, ship wrecked, told I would never see my family again then presented to my future father in law wearing little more than a few strips of gossamer" Would she ever live that down? No one had spoken of it but she had almost seen the accusations in the eyes of the men and women of court. Nothing but a whore who'd caught the prince by spreading her legs at the right time. It didn't matter that he'd been her first, or that they'd waited until after their vows had been exchanged, no one who had seen or heard of how she had arrived would ever believe that. "And don't forget blasting a village apart with a power I have no way of controlling yet."

'I doubt anyone is going to call you a whore.'

"Not to my face."

'And do you really care what they think?' Orent probed gently.

"No, but I don't want who I am being used against Rhodan either. All it takes is one sign of weakness and they will be all over him. Deals will be made. Promises broken. Rumors will grow out of control and then he will end up fighting duels to protect my blemished honor. That cannot help the situation."

'There are other ways.'

"Oh?"

'You have the gifts of your race, more so than most know. A few carefully placed demonstrations would be enough to silence all but the most aggressive of court snipes.'

"You're saying I should kill one or two of them?" She couldn't believe what Orent seemed to be suggesting. "I can't do that."

'Court politics can be quite messy, Riana. Sometimes people have serious accidents in the most innocent of circumstances. I am not suggesting you kill anyone unless you have to and by the time such a situation arises you will be well able to judge that for yourself. I am saying that you shouldn't hide your gifts. A few public lessons would work just as well as a dead body or three.'

"I'm sorry, I misunderstood." Relief mixed with shame.

'You're young and will jump to assumptions on more than a rare occasion. Now, there is the matter of Rhodan.'

"Is he even awake?" He could have slept for hours with the amount he had drunk. She's seen that more than once amongst the guards. One had consumed so deeply one night that he had slept for nearly a day and a night. She didn't think Rhodan had been quite that bad, but it would be a close call.

'He's awake and Simon has been talking to him.'

"Oh gods, so he knows I spent the night here?" She couldn't be sure how he would react to her disappearing act.

'Yes, but I wouldn't worry. Out of all the people you could have gone to last night Simon was the safest. No one will even hint at you doing anything with him.' Something lay behind the amused tone. 'Simon will protect your reputation and honor with the same devotion he has shown Rhodan. If for no other reason that you sought him out last night. You expected nothing from him, didn't judge him for the way he acts.'

"I'm not like that." He could have died, with so much alcohol in his system it would have been normal for Rhodan to throw up, and alone he could have choked.

'No, you aren't but many human beings are. Some hide it better than others, some do not bother to hide it at all. Perhaps not being fully human yourself, hearing the soft rumors about your mother, helped you not be quite so judgmental about others?'

"Aren't you being a little… well judgmental yourself right now?" She felt odd asking the question, especially with as helpful as Orent had been.

'But of course I am, I am a dragon after all. Who's going to tell me off about that and risk ending up as a light snack?'

His head pounded, threatening to explode as he tried to peer into the darkness. His mouth felt odd, had he drunk something that had disagreed with him? It took him only a moment to realize he wasn't going to see anything not until he found a way to pull the blindfold from his eyes or the knot in his mouth had come from a cloth gag. And that wouldn't happen unless he broke free from whatever it was that had been used to restrain him.

Stupid. He'd been caught through stupidity. A dozen should of, could of's sprang to life in the back of his mind. Not that it mattered now. Hindsight was always perfect, or a decent version of perfect but it wasn't going to do him any good. He was still bound, gagged and blindfolded. Now what?

The low throb dulled into a manageable level, enough to let him think clearly. To recall every word he had overheard. The duel, Rhodan was in trouble, real trouble. If he couldn't get free and warn him his friend could end up dead. Worse still Riana might become Jeriah's.

He twisted, trying to figure out just where he was. Stone floor beneath him. Well that didn't help much in a castle built of stone. Cold, no smell of burning wood or oil lamps. Not even the scent of a candle. Yet there was something in the air. An almost cloying taste. Mothballs? Had he been put into a store room? A closet? It could have been either from the smell. He wriggled, edging along the floor, trying to find shelves, a chair, anything he could use to undo the bonds.

Larger area than he had thought with the smell.

Stone scraped his hands, the bond cutting deep into his wrists. Tight enough that he had no doubt they intended to leave him here for some time. But why not kill him outright? Unless they needed him alive for some reason?

To keep Riana in line, or Orent?

Rhodan. He had to warn Rhodan. With every ounce of energy he possessed Cluiun focused his thoughts into one mental scream for help. Hoping that somehow the great lady would hear him.

'Orent!'

"Where's Riana?" Rhodan demanded, pulling on his sword belt, buckling it into place. "I need to know she'll be safe during the fight." The last thing he needed right now was to head off into that duel, not with the way his head still felt, but what other choice did he have. Felt strange pulling on the sword again, so soon after marrying. "Damn Jeriah, he must have known about the little party last night."

"Of course he does dear boy. Half the castle heard you carousing down there, and the rest have been long since told by now." Simon lounged on a wide windowsill. "Not that it matters now. You'll be able to face Jeriah just as well as you would have done if you had been fully sober."

"What's that supposed to mean?" He frowned, shoving the end of the belt in through a loop.

"My dear Rhodan, if you think Jeriah doesn't have some pesky plan up his sleeve, one that he no doubt thinks is wonderfully clever. You know what he's like. He's always going for the twisted and devious plans." Simon looked about the room. "I had to be very careful in keeping him out of your room whilst you were away. He tried a dozen times perhaps more."

That did not surprise him. "And Riana?" A safe place, or protector would be needed during the fight.

"Should be on her way back by now if I know Orent."

"I can hope. The longer I have to wait to apologize to her, the harder it's going to be." He knew enough about women to understand that. No, that wasn't exactly fair either. He doubted it would be harder for her to accept the apology, the time just made it more difficult for him to form the right words. If there even were such things in the first place. He'd screwed up. There was little point in pretending otherwise. He would rather faced an angry dragon than his wife.

The door opened slowly, a glimmer of silver hair catching the light as his wife slipped into the room. For a moment she didn't speak, but the uncertainty in her eyes was all too clear.

"I'm sorry."

Riana didn't move, didn't speak at first.

"I should have thought about what wandering off would do to you."

"Wandering off, is that what you call it?" Her voice was low, soft, bordering on dangerous. "Funny, I would have thought it came closer to falling head first into a vat of mead."

"I know I shouldn't have..."

"Have you any idea just how I felt when you walked in like that. What I went through this morning not knowing if you were alive or dead."

"Aren't you over exaggerating the situation just a little?" He caught the warning look from Simon a moment too late.

"Oh you!" She whirled, grabbing one of the pillows, flinging it across the room with a deadly accuracy. "You've no idea how awful I felt this morning. All you cared about was going out having a few drinks then stumbling back to your room for a quick fumble. Did you even care how I felt?" Tears shone in her eyes, fury building to the point of explosion.

For a moment it jolted into life. A spark of energy threatening to be unleashed in the room. Then it died. Flickering out. Her hands clenching then releasing at her sides. "I'm sorry. I shouldn't have exploded like that. Came too close to loosing it."

"What have you got to be sorry about?" Rhodan paused for only a moment before asking. "I'm the one who walked in drunk, not you."

"I should have stayed with you through the night, in case you needed help. I've known men who've choked to death from over drinking. That left me angry. At you, me, the entire world. Nearly lost control of it. I can't risk it."

"Love, I wouldn't have stayed with me if I had been given the choice. I stank. I realized that this morning when I finally woke up." He cleared the distance between them, pulling her into his arms. She looked so pale, shaken when she had entered the room, almost waiflike despite her womanly figure. How she could be innocent and so mature at the same time would be a mystery he doubted he would ever come to understand. "I'm sorry. I let myself become so angry at Jeriah and how my father handled yesterday, at my own assumptions that I needed to let off steam. I think Cluiun understood that."

"I have to learn to control this, control the power and everything that goes with it. Can't do it if I'm going to run at the first hurdle. I should have stayed if for no other reason than to make sure you didn't choke to death."

He'd been expecting anger, frustration, perhaps accusations but not a woman apologizing to him for not being willing to sit in a room that had stunk of a drunken man. "Riana, has something upset you? Apart from me that is? I just, this feels odd. It's not like you did anything wrong and I never saw you as the type that would act this way."

A momentary flash of anger danced across her deep eyes. "Are you accusing me of being weak? I'm not weak like that. I just feel I should have tried harder. We're married, a partnership. Yes I was angry about last night. Because of that I nearly lost control, lashed out at you the same way I did in the village. My anger could have done Jeriah's work for him."

"Hells no, Riana I'm just worried about you. You didn't do anything wrong. So why are you apologizing?" Didn't she know how bad that made him feel, as if he had struck out at her and caused her to believe that him stumbling in drunk was her fault not his own choice. Even so he could see her point of view, though it was a struggle. No one had forced the mead into his hand and despite his carefree appearance at times he did believe in owning up to his own mistakes. Hells, some of them he'd outright flaunted in his father's face. "I'm sorry, I'm over reacting here. I know you must have your reasons for saying that. I guess the news about the duel has me on edge."

"Duel?" She frowned, eyes narrowing on his face. Energy crackled into life about her fingers, soothing away as her breathing calmed once more. She had so much to learn about the powers she that had been triggered to life in her and he had no way of helping her out. "He's brought it forward? To when?"

"Noon, today."

"What?" Her hands clenched at her sides, jaw tightening. "That bastard. When did you find out?"

"A hour ago, maybe a little more." He could see it, the struggle in her eyes for control. "He sent a messenger with the information." There would be time to tell her about Haon later.

"Wonderful, so as little notice as possible." Riana growled, turning away from Rhodan. "Damn coward." Tension played across her shoulders, anger bubbling under the surface of his new wife that could destroy anyone who stood in her way.

"No, not cowardice. Politics. He can claim he didn't know about the drinking, that he was being considerate towards your new marriage by getting the fight over and done with as quickly as possible. His fears that Rhodan would take off without warning again as our lovely boy has a habit of doing." Simon almost drawled the words out. "It's all the dance of the court my sweet lady."

Court politics. If it were not for that he could have just slit Jeriah's throat and be done with the matter. "And father wonders why I avoid the court."

"Something you have to learn to deal with." Simon tucked the ever present handkerchief away before rising. "Just as you, Riana will have to adapt to the rumors. No matter what you do there will be some snide little voices around the court seeking to paint you as a whore, doxie, floozy, gold seeker, perhaps a few that will claim you enchanted our dear prince with some nice little spell. Which, if you did I do hope you will teach me, there is a darling of a new corporal of the watch I would be delighted to awaken next to one morn... no oh well then we shall just have to accept those nasty rumors."

"They mention even one in my hearing and I'll..." He'd protect Riana, no matter what. She didn't deserve the sort of trouble the court could dish out.

"You'll leave it to me, Rhodan. I cannot have it seen that I need you to protect me from every danger out there. I'm not helpless, Orent reminded me of that fact. Besides she and I have a few plans in mind to help there." The anger had fled from her gaze, a sense of calm and purpose replacing it.

"Oh? How?" What had the two women discussed? Despite her size he still considered Orent to be a woman.

"We can discuss that later. Right now we need to get you ready for the duel." Riana turned back to look at him fully. "Where's Cluiun, you'll need him there as your second."

The mental cry nearly brought Rhodan to his knees.

'Cluiun. He needs help. Find him, find him now!'

Chapter Eight

Kaleb leaned back in the throne, watching as the two women returned to the hall. Between them they carried the chest that had been discovered down in the bowels of the castle.

Amusing the way the two women made no attempt to hide their hatred of each other, and Guinelia, did she really think that he could not see the anger she felt towards him? Had she forgotten that she knelt not to a mortal, but to a God?

She'd learn soon enough, such lessons could be quite entertaining. Mortals would never understand how the centuries could drag or what it took for a being like him to find a source of amusement. How could they, the wait of ages was unfathomable to them. They would never face it. Never know what it was like to know that you were going to live until the end of time.

Unless every single one of his worshippers died. What was the likelihood of that? Human's fought, battled, but with his pets scattered across the face of Erien it would take more than a few small fights to wipe out his supply of devoted lives. Such an undertaking would take years, centuries perhaps. Only then could he be truly killed and even should that happen there was but a slim chance another would have the skill to dispatch him.

He knew what would be needed, but how many of his kin did? And no mortal would have the skill to do so. The risk limited to being slim, almost nonexistent. So why did even that tiny chance bother him? He tired of the endless years, but feared death. Perhaps he was not that different from the two mortal women in front of him?

Did not they fear dying? Yes, he'd seen it, enough that they would try anything in order to cling to life through the harshest of treatments and foulest circumstances? No, they were not alike. Nothing but a foolish thought, even Gods were susceptible to them from time to time.

"We found it, my Lord. Though we haven't opened it." Arinnana avoided meeting his gaze. "I don't know if it contains the relics you hoped to find." He could hear it, the hope that if they were wrong that he would spare them his wrath. That chance did exist, he'd send them back to their search if needed, that came before his desire to see them squirm in purest agony.

"We will see soon enough and if it does not you will return to searching after a small lesson in the cost of failure." Did he have reason to punish them? Not right now, but what did it matter, they weren't in any position to argue and it would strengthen his hold over both women. "Set it down."

As one they stumbled forward, hefting the small but heavy chest with them over the blood stained stone floor. Within a few days he would have the hall cleared of the debris, for now it suited his mood. Just one extra element that kept the women believing he would do what he wanted, when he wanted and however he wished it.

With a cruel smile he turned his attention back to the chest. It had the look of the Fae about it, elegant carvings, the wood dark and heavy. Taken from Silver Woods no doubt. Only a few places on Erien provided such dark wood and as such it had become prized.   Old, older than the woman it had belonged to. Passed down from mother to daughter as was so often the way amongst those of the Silver Woods. Well it would not be passed on to Riana, that journey through time ended today.

It called to him.

"Step back," he growled, rising to his feet.

"My Lord?" Arinnana looked up, startled. "Did you not wish us to open it for you?"

"That is something I am quite capable of doing myself, pet." More than that, he didn't want any stray crumbs of power being gathered up by the two women. Better to keep them hungry for the gifts he could bestow.

"My Lord, I never meant that you wouldn't be." Arinnana backed away quickly, dropping to her belly against the cold stone.

"Of course not, I have no doubt you remember your lesson all too well." From the way she clung to the floor the memories of her time trying to meld to the floor were all to clear in her mind. The brief rags that were the only things left from dress she had once worn. And his mark, did she feel it still burning into her skin, the dragging touch of one talon as he scored the brand into her flesh?

"Yes my Lord, I know I live but to serve you."

Until she found the means to escape, to replace him or even overthrow him. Silly little girl. She looked so pleasing laying on the stone, her hair falling over her shoulders. Did her body find the cold floor seeping the warmth from her flesh? "Of course you do little pet, of course you do." Mortals, they were so very easy to read. Arinnana was one thing, her mother another. He could feel the anger vibrating from her, the desire to claw, rend, lash out at him regardless of the power he held over both women. Had he misjudged her love... no not love, her possessive desire for Valer? "And you, Guinelia do you still fight against my control?"

"Yes, My Lord."

Her honesty nearly caught him off guard. "Interesting, most would lie about it. Hope that I would not notice."

"I may be mad, but I am no fool my Lord." Guinelia hissed, her hands clenched tight, nails digging into her palms. "You know, why deny it? Why risk angering you further?"

Unexpected. "Well little Arinnana it would appear your mother has learned long before you have. How long will it be before you accept you can hide nothing from me pet? That I have watched human kind long enough to know how your kind think? Youth, it doesn't matter what race you always think that your elders know little to nothing, that we are blind, deaf and dumb. In time you'll learn."

With a soft whimper she edged back on the stone, hair tangling along her body, knees scraping against the edges of the slabs. "My Lord, I swear I mean but to follow you. I am sworn to you, now and always."

"For now, always is longer than you could ever imagine." He could feel it, the smile curling at the corner of his lips. It would have been so easy to grasp her by the hair or throat and toss her against the wall, shake her like a rag doll until the skin parted from her body. No, not this time, not yet. He still had need of her. Without another word he turned his attention back to chest. It was always better to keep them off balance.

His talon's caught under the edge of the lid. Lock or no lock it wouldn't stop him from being able to open it. With a sharp wrench the lid tore from the chest, hinges wrecked, parted all too easily. It had never been made to withstand the strength of his kind. By the time it hit the wall on the other side of the room he had already turned his attention to the contents of the chest.

Clothing, velvet pouches, paper packages. What else would she have kept in here? There had to be something apart from her personal items. Jewelry. What use did he have for that? They didn't resonate with the ancient power he sought. Pendants were tossed to the floor along with dried herbs, neither important to him. She had to have been the one that brought the source of power into the castle and it was close, close enough to cause his skin to tingle. It had to be in the chest.

No. Not in the chest. Part of the chest. Impressive.

With a snarl he turned, stalking across the room towards the lid he had sent across the room. It hadn't broken. It should have shattered when it hit the stone but it remained in one piece. Only the hinges had broken, not the wood itself.

"Right in plain sight, cunning bitch, very cunning."

"My Lord? Are you saying the chest is the item?" Arinnana looked up from the floor, but made no attempt to move just yet.

"Yes, the chest. Clever indeed. Hidden in plain view. Who would think a chest held a key, was a relic older than human's could understand?" His fingers turned numb as he gripped the wood, ward spells repelling his touch. Pain, what a delight, he could feel pain when none had been blessed with the power to cause that in a thousand years. "Very clever indeed. Guinelia come here I need you to hold this for me."

The older woman moved quickly, taking the heavy lid from his grasp. "What must I do?"

"Hold it in place and then only turn it when I tell you to." He shook out his hands. "Rune wards, nothing else would affect my kind." This was it, it had to be. Nothing else made sense. Why expend rune wards on a chest if the chest itself were not a valuable item. He glanced at the older woman. A slight strain from holding the wood but no sign of it causing her problems. Not warded against mortal kind then. Good. "The question is what other secrets this little chest contains."

"She kept others well away from the chest my Lord, even my husband."

There it was, that claim on ownership over a man now dead. A man that had cast her aside decades ago now. Foolish little mortal, there were hundreds of men that would have thrown themselves at her feet before she gave himself into the madness that now held her tighter than any lover. Did she believe he would rise from the grave welcoming her within his embrace once more? "Yes, she did, which means she knew what it was. Pity she's dead I could have pried some information from her. Your work I believe?"

"Yes, my work. She had my husband."

How long had she waited before striking? "Remind me how you did that." He purred the question, his gaze never leaving the wood.

"Three years of stalking, my Lord. I thought I had her at one point just after she came here, but the bitch was on to me and warned my husband. They kept me from here for four long years after that, but I found a way back." Pride flowed through each word. Few had the patience she must have used to wait so long. Then again one should never underestimate the possibilities a fanatic might display. "Hard, it was hard work. I waited, watched, set myself up as a herbs woman in the village. So many months crawling for work amongst those dregs. I wanted to kill them all but it would have done no good. I knew that."

Obsessive. Good. He'd been right about the fanatical gleam. That would prove useful later. Runes carved not into the wood but under the surface of it. Nothing raised, a simple touch wouldn't have resulted in the work being felt unless the runes struck out against the one holding the wood. Just as they had done with him. "And?"

There was more to the story. So much more.

"The guards, one of the guards came to me over time, courting me. It was amusing, he'd been one of the very men that had marched me out of the castle. I remember him lashing out at me, telling me to leave, that my foul kind was no longer welcome. A few years later he was trying to lift my skirts, declaring that he could not live without the pleasure I offered him. I suppose the herbs I added to his ale didn't hurt. He rather liked the flavor." Laughter followed her words, cold, owned by madness. Her mind had long since been lost. "Oh he never knew, never understood what I wanted from him until it was too late."

"Which was?" He knew, but hearing it from the woman gave him a greater insight into her mind. Strange, he should have been able to decipher the meaning behind the hidden runes, so why couldn't he? There had to be a way to read a least some of it. He wouldn't be foiled by that damn Fae creature.

"To carry a spell born illness into the castle. He worked so very well at that. Even commented on how wonderful my last batch of ale was. How I should go into the business and leave herb lore to one side. Never even knew that he had it until three days later. By then it was too late. Every woman in the castle was infected."

"You did that? You sent the illness?" Arinnana snarled from her place on the floor.

Ah there it was, the realization at just how little the daughter meant to the mother. A pawn, convenient and disposable. An interesting lesson, though he had other more important matters to attend to. But the damage was at last done, and the daughter's hatred of her mother would grow beyond all boundaries.

Runes, there had to be a way of reading them.

"Yes, who else did you think was behind it?" Guinelia turned a cold smile on her daughter.

There had to be a way. She couldn't have known enough magic to prevent a God from reading them.

"You could have killed me."

There, a small flaw in the protection. Or was it? Just the hint of one. Enough to trap the unwary?

"And your point would be?"

Yes, a hook to lure in the unwary. He was stronger than that.

"I'm your daughter!"

There, just hidden beneath the trap, a tiny thread of energy. He wouldn't be able to unravel the secret instantly but he would find out how in time. Just a little research, a few deaths offered.

"Replaceable."

"What!"

"You're replaceable. I made one child I could easily make another."

Ah, there it was, the fight, reality setting in.

"All I am to you is something replaceable?" Arinnana had had enough, her mothers words pushing her beyond the fear that had kept her pressed against the stones. "I'll kill you. You bitch, you lousy bitch. I've supported you, believed you, pleaded with father to take you back after she was dead and you still treat me as if I am nothing more than a pawn for you? A convenient excuse to enter the castle?"

"My dear daughter, what else did you think you were to me? Silly little girl. Don't tell me you actually believed all those lies about me loving you?"

The complexities of human relationships...

Sand ground against his feet, salt water heavy on his lashes, his breath burning in his lungs and still he ran. How long he had been running since the slab had dissolved he couldn't be certain, nor did he care. As long as he kept away from the castle and those within it.

The woman, what had she been? Not human, that much he knew. Then what?

No time for that. He had to move, get away, be free, stay free. The village would have resources he could use. He still had his money pouch, not that it would be much good if the village was under martial law. Without anyone to buy a horse from he would be forced to steal.

Him, a noble born, reduced to petty theft. He'd never live it down. Unless he told them how much of a hero he had been in the castle. Fighting to defend Valer. Yes, that was it. He'd been injured trying to defend the older man. That would explain the scrapes, cuts, he'd lost his sword and been reduced to fighting hand to hand. Against a dozen foul denizens of the demon plane. He'd struggled with every breath to save Valer only to see the older man ripped away from his side, torn apart by the very creatures that had then tried to take Bevery's life.

Would they believe it?

Well why wouldn't they? No one else would be around to say otherwise. He'd have to work on the telling of the tale, test it out on a few farmers, or bar wenches before reaching the capitol. If he played this right he'd come out as a full hero. The King might even knight him, or grant him some land for bringing word of the danger out here. If he made it that far.

If...

Wind picked up, lashing waves against the shore in angry fingers that reached out towards his feet. Cold, he was still cold from the kiss of that creature. Now the wind, salt and water seeped into his bones. He'd never be warm again.

Demons. Could the woman have been a demon? There'd been a legend, something he had heard in whispers as a child. Souls, didn't they steal souls? No, not steal, barter for them, trade them. For what he couldn't be sure. Too tired to remember, to worn out to care. Just a legend after all, nothing that would actually be true, they didn't exist.

Nor did the nightmares he'd lived through at the castle. Nothing more than a bard's twisted imagination, so why had he lived through it. If that had been real and not some hallucination brought on by bad mead, then demons could be as well. But that would mean he really had a soul and now it was gone.

Could a human live without a soul?

Well obviously they could, he was still alive, wasn't he?

For how long? A day, a few weeks? How long could he live without it? And was there a cure, a way of getting it back? A year and a day. He remembered something about a year and a day being important. Just like the hand fasting laws. Bond for a year and a day. He couldn't remember what it had to do with demon legends. Why couldn't he recall it now? And how could he trade something he didn't even know existed and had thought to be nothing more than a legend. The misguided belief of priests who had nothing better to do than gather converts for their gods.

Gods, demons, foul magic. What else existed on Erien that he had ignored, or tried to brush aside as myth? He didn't have time to think about it now. Not when he needed to get away, get that horse and tell King Justin about his heroic efforts to save the Lord of Valer Castle.

A good stiff drink, mulled wine to chase the cold away.

Lights beckoned in the distance, a hint of hope. The village, it had to be.

Not that far to go. He could make it. Just had to keep on moving, running. His legs burned, he'd never been in so much pain before. Pampered, he'd heard the remarks before, spoiled noble born, wealthy brat, wouldn't know a hard days work if it hit him upside the back of the head. Well maybe they'd been right after all. If he'd spent time working out a little in the practice square he might not have hurt so much. A few laps each day, some training would help.

Gods his legs hurt.

A horse, he'd have given his sou...

He'd already given that, to get out. Sold it to a demon. Jumped from a raging inferno into a small fire. Either way he was still damned.

What had he done...

"Enough!" The growled word sent her hurrying back from mother. Every instinct until that word had focused on tearing the smile from the woman's face. Destroying her utterly. But not now, not in front of Kaleb. It wasn't the right time. No it went beyond that. Inconvenient. That's how their God would view it, and that would be far more dangerous.

"Yes my Lord." She mumbled the words, cold sweat coating her forehead.

Becoming a minor annoyance would be too much, a dangerous step she wasn't prepared to take. Not just yet.

"As you will my Lord." Guinelia spoke all too calmly. "I was merely answering my daughter's questions. It seems a pity I raised one who has turned out to be so foolish. I had hoped she would show more intelligence than this."

Foolish. If she were foolish for holding on to a childhood hope of a loving mother than so be it, but it was over now. Ended by the cold words that had cut deeper than any blade could ever do. It didn't even matter that she had been planning on killing her mother as soon as possible, she'd half convinced herself that that would be a mercy killing. Never in her days had she expected the hateful words she had heard this day.

"You have more important matters to attend to my pet, if you wish to keep your prince alive."

"My Lord?" That focused her attention instantly.

"Jeriah wants the throne."

"I know my Lord, he believes you will gift it to him should he follow through with your wishes." She frowned, smoothing her hands down over her now bare thighs. She needed to bathe, change her clothes, do something to counter the turmoil of emotions she had been left with.

"Ah, you think he will not try and kill your Rhodan in this duel? When he wants the throne that much?" Kaleb's lips twisted into a mocking smile. "It seems you are truly naïve at just what human's will do in order to gain their heart's desire."

No, not her Rhodan. He couldn't die. She needed him. Jeriah knew that. "He wouldn't betray me that way."

"He would and will if he has but a chance to." Kaleb's cruel smile never faltered. "Even now he plans to do just that in the duel. If he had plans to keep to your rules don't you think he'd have let you know the time of the duel?"

"No, that was to be to the blood." Cold panic gripped her heart. If Rhodan died it would all be for nothing. Betrayed and by one who should have been helping her, just as her mother now felt. "I'll kill him." Three words, but they might as well have been the snarl of an animal.

"No, you'll warn him, punish him, but you will not kill him." Kaleb's gaze offered no chance for argument or mercy. She knew what would happen if she disobeyed and the idea of a repeat performance left her feeling cold to the core. "I have plans for him. So despite his petty attempts at manipulation I need him to remain alive for a few months yet."

Punishment, she could come up with some form a punishment, but only if she managed to stop him in time. He'd scream for this. "My Lord, by your leave…"

"You wish to prevent his plots." He glanced away from her, running one long talon across the wooden lid her mother still held. "To save your prince."

"Yes my Lord, please. I beg you to grant me permission to do so." She needed him to live, more with each passing moment. If he died would she follow her mother into the realms of madness, no longer caring if she lived or died, not feeling pain, sorrow, or anything beyond the need for revenge? "Let me save him, please. That we might create the new line for you, a line dedicated to your honor."

Such an easy thing to say.

"Go, save your prince. Perhaps you will still have the time, perhaps not." Kaleb didn't even look at her, not that she stayed around to see if he would. The moment the words had been granted life she turned, running from the room, bare feet slapping against the stone.

He had to still be alive; she needed to have him in her life. The very thought of him dying, of her never seeing him again turned her stomach. Her mother must have been loving the situation. Here she was, the woman that had killed Guinelia's focus, her reason for living, and now about to face the risk of loosing the very man she loved in return.

Fate had played a very cruel twist.

She fled without looking back, running through the corridors to the room she still claimed as her own. Even with Kaleb claiming the castle she still had her sanctuary in the well placed room. She had everything she needed to call him. The mirror. It had been hers before Kaleb but his arrival had given her the ability to use it at whim instead of spending hours preparing to summon the image of the one she needed to speak to. He'd answer or die. Regardless of what Kaleb said he would answer her or die where he stood.

Arinnana slid onto the velvet padded bench in front of the mirror, waving her hand towards the glass surface, muttering the spell under her breath. For a moment nothing happened, the slowly the surface shimmered, ripping as if the glass had been replaced by water.

"Jeriah!" Where was he? He had to be there. When would he be fighting against Rhodan? If he had already gone to the fight then she was too late. Rage replaced the fear, anger burning in every part of her body. She could see it, how she would grasp him, tearing his life from him one slow strip at a time. He'd scream, oh how he'd scream and she'd enjoy every dark sound. "Jeriah, answer me you fool. Answer me now!"

"What is it?" Jeriah's face appeared in the mirror. "I have business to attend to shortly."

"The duel," she hissed.

"Yes, the duel. An hour and I will be facing Rhodan."

"And when did you plan on letting me know you were going to kill him?"

One nail cracked under the pressure as her fingers dug into the wood.

"I didn't think I'd need to. How else am I to become heir?" He shrugged, a moment of confusion clear in his eyes. "I've never hid my ultimate goal from you."

"You fool! Did I not make it clear that Rhodan was not to die? That I needed him? He is to be my mate, my husband. He cannot be that if you kill him." Fool, the fool didn't think things through past his own desires. "And are you daring to suggest I would understand your willingness to break the rules?"

"There are other mates." He shrugged, downplaying the matter. It wouldn't work, she could see the gleam in his eyes, that lust for power. "You could find one far better suited for your desires."

"So you thought to go against my wishes?" How much power would it take for her to be able to reach through the mirror and grasp the man by the neck? She could do it, she knew that, but it would leave her weak and vulnerable for a time after she was done with him. "I need him alive!"

"And I need him dead or vanished for good. If he lives or appears to remain alive I cannot replace him as heir nor claim his bride as my own. Both of which I have plans to do." He peered through the shimmering surface, as if seeking sign of something or someone else before continuing. "So give me one good reason why I should listen to the whims of a mere woman when they stand between myself and the throne?"

Kaleb, he had been searching for the dark lord before speaking. Of course, he didn't fear her, but appeared to fear Kaleb. "I see, and you think me helpless to enforce my rulings?"

He leaned against the table the mirror apparently now sat on, lacing his fingers under his chin. "My dear lady, let's just say I have no reason to follow your rulings when they make no sense and would disrupt plans I have had in place for years now. Rhodan has to die. I would prefer he did so sooner rather than later. It makes for a cleaner situation."

She snapped, summoning the power that had built with her growing anger. With a hiss she gave life to the spell, reaching out through the mirror and past it into Jeriah's room. Shards of ice pierced her arm, but it didn't matter, the pain only added to her drive. Before he had the chance to react her fingers had closed about his throat, nails biting into his flesh. "Listen to me little man and listen well."

"Release me." He growled, his own hands moving to the one about his throat.

"Keep still or I'll rip your throat out before you have a chance to do anything else." Her fingers tightened a little more. "Do you think me stupid? Or without claws? An unarmed spectator? I'm no helpless girl, Jeriah. I have power at my disposal, the ability to rend your life from your flesh. I made it clear,

Rhodan is to live."

"Release me now!" His hands wrapped around her wrist, yanking at her grip. "You're a woman! You don't have the strength to... "

She choked off his words, nails piercing the skin. "I have more strength than you could ever imagine. It would take very little to pull you through this mirror and have you chained and cowering at my feet. Where would all your dreams of claiming the throne go then?" Men, they could be such idiots. Just because she had a female body it didn't mean she lacked power, or strength. So hers came from magical sources, but she could still use it and with deadly force.

He clawed at her grip, eyes widening. She could see it, the fear as he finally realized that he had underestimated her. "I... understand." He struggled to speak, impaired by her grip.

She smiled, watching him for a moment longer, the small trickles of blood that now marked a path over his skin, the pale fearful look, his wide eyes. It all fed into her desire to strike out a little more. Just to hear him whimper, plead for his life. How far could she push it before Kaleb stepped in?

Just a little more. Enough to see the fear grow beyond reason.

She released her grip, shaking her hand. Relief claiming his gaze only to shatter with the strike she landed across his left cheek. Even through the mirror she heard it, a crack that sated her needs, fear entering his widening eyes. Had he not been sat down he might well have stumbled and that only added to her delight.

"Cross me again Jeriah and the only crown you will be wearing will be one made of your own entrails." She drew her hand back through the mirror, ignoring the ice crystals coating her skin. "I will not be disobeyed in this or any other matter with you."

"Yes Lady, I understand." He kept the shaking from his voice but the fear remained in his eyes. She could see it just from the way he watched the mirror, ready to move if she went to grab him again. "Rhodan will not be killed. I cannot promise he will finish the fight unscathed, but you have my word he will not die from my hand."

Clever, very clever. "By your hand or the hand of any you command."

His eyes hardened. Good she'd guessed correctly. Better to be safe than sorry. Isn't that what her nurse had taught her? Funny, she never thought such a saying would apply to a situation like this. "Agreed. Not by my hand or any hand I command."

"Good, when is the duel?" He'd mentioned something about an hour, but she needed to be sure in order to cast the watch spells. He didn't have the contacts within the castle to prevent her from being able to observe the fight. Something she was certain he realized. She'd be watching and he'd be well aware of it. "And where will it be taking place?"

"An hour and in the practice square. Justin wanted me to wait until I suggested it would be better for the newly-weds if the matter were dealt with quickly. He seemed to like the idea that his son would be busy after the event getting his new wife with child." That small, tell tale smirk gained a brief life across his lips then vanished as he met her gaze. "Well that's the impression he left me with." Dangerous ground and he knew it. He rubbed at his neck, edging back a little from the mirror. "I will need time to pull the men back from the edge of the square. They are set up ready to strike. I'll have to do something to stop it. One of Rhodan's people overheard the plans between a few of my men. He'll have to be disposed of now. Pity, I had hoped to use him as leverage or pay him to join my people. Now I daren't take the risk." Small lines tightened about his lips, anger barely kept under control. She'd ruined all his plans and hated her for it. Not that she cared.

"Do so, and know I will be watching." Such a hatred she understood. She saw it every time she looked in the mirror. "Do not fail me this time, Jeriah. You're replaceable."

"Yes Lady, by your leave?"

"Go!" She waved her hand at the mirror, dismissing the image.

So close, she had cut it almost too close to save Rhodan's life. One day he would be grateful for that. Just as he would come to realize he loved her.

Pain, her hand, wrist, entire arm hurt from the ice that now melted slowly on her skin. She'd never thought it would hurt that much, but it had been worth it. Rhodan would remain safe...

Chapter Nine

His hands had turned numb, much longer and he'd risk loosing them entirely without the aid of a decent healer but still he tried to slip one free from the biting bonds. He'd twisted so much that the gag had rubbed at the corners of his mouth but it was slowly loosening. Between the cuts forming at the corners of his mouth and the lack of blood flowing into his fingers he hurt but for Cluiun the pain didn't matter as much as failing to warn Rhodan. He couldn't even be sure if Orent had heard his plea for help.

How long did he have left until the fight?

Not that long, less than an hour? Or had it already taken place?

No, if it had already been done they would have come to kill or release him. Jeriah wasn't the sort to just leave a possible danger sitting in a closet, even if he was bound and gagged. Not his style.

He couldn't let Rhodan die by the hands of that piece of slime or those working for him. It wasn't right. Lacked honor. Oh, he knew some would never understand how a man like him, an outlaw, could ever presume to speak of honor but he held it close to his heart. No matter what path he walked in life he'd never give up that personal code that had kept him going through the years.

Joran had often chided him for it, but at the same time he'd made no secret that he envied Cluiun's strength.

What good would it do him now though?

Footsteps? Hurried footfalls that seemed to be coming closer? Who? It could easily have been the same men that had bound him, but he had to take that chance. With a growl he turned, edging until his feet touched a wall. There, that should work. With every ounce of strength he possessed Cluiun began to growl through the gag and kick at the wall, hoping someone would hear him.

Voices, they sounded familiar but it could have just been his hopes. Damnit how did he end up like this? Because he hadn't been listening out. Sloppy, that sort of mistake could have cost him his life and it might well cost Rhodan his if he didn't get out of here.

"Can you hear that?" Riana? He stopped for a moment then growled louder, his throat becoming raw, calves screaming as he kicked the wall. "Sounds like there is someone in there."

Yes, Riana. Thank the Dragons. Orent must have heard his call, why the dragon hadn't replied he had no idea. Nor did it matter right now.

"Hold on, will get the door open. Someone locked it." Rhodan, she hadn't come alone. And the boy was alive. He wasn't too late. Wood rattled in the frame, a loud thumb repeated as Rhodan tried to batter the door in. "I can't get it open!"

"Let me."

"Riana?"

"I can do this, trust me. I can sense where he is."

Do what? Her magic?

"Okay, I do trust you Riana. Remember that."

As did he, but her control on her magic was weak at best from what he had seen first hand. He shuffled back from the direction of the door, holding his breath.

Wood shattered with a violent crash, shards scattering across the room but though he felt them brush against his skin not one pierced his body. Luck or magic, either way he was very grateful.

"Cluiun?" Rhodan's voice, with the door gone there was no mistaking it now. "Who in the darkest shades did this to you?" The gag was pulled from his mouth, the blindfold following quickly after.

"Men, plotting." His mouth hurt, making it difficult to speak. "Plotting against you. Duel set up. Jeriah." One painful word at a time, but it was enough.

"Slow down, and wait a minute. Riana his hands are near blue." Rhodan pulled at the bonds, then dragged a dagger free from his sheath cutting through the rope. "I don't think there is permanent damage but I need you to take a look at them."

She replaced Rhodan at Cluiun's side, reaching for his still numb hands rubbing them quickly. Gods that hurt, blood rushed into his fingers, sensation returning in a painful wave, but he welcomed it. Pain meant his hands would be undamaged or so he hoped.

"I don't think there is any damage. I wish I could be certain but I only learned the basics of healing. Enough to help out." Riana continued to rub his hands, helping him sit up as Rhodan cut through the bonds on Cluiun's ankles. "If he'd been left much longer though it would have been another story."

"Thanks," he pulled his hands reluctantly from her grasp. Not that he didn't enjoy her touch, he did, but there were other matters to attend to. Gods his fingers hurt, but despite Riana's claim of lack of knowledge her words were welcomed. "Jeriah plans to kill you at the duel."

"That much I had expected, but you make it sound as though he has help?" Rhodan helped the pirate to his feet.

"He does, men answering to him. Even should Jeriah loose the fight you aren't to be allowed to leave the square alive." He rubbed at the corners of his mouth. Annoying but the cuts would heal quickly enough. Ointment would help. Eating and drinking would be uncomfortable for a few days. "I overheard them talking, next thing I know I'm waking up in here."

"What has he got planned, how many men?" Rhodan pressed.

"Not sure, just know Jeriah is behind it, his name was mentioned, and there were several men involved. I didn't recognize the voices." Not enough information, he knew that.

"An ambush?"

"Over zealous protector, that's what he could put it down to, or a hired hit from a husband you annoyed years ago. I don't know how the ambush would take place but he would have thought it through, planned it so he didn't look guilty." Cluiun rubbed at his wrists. "How did you find me?"

"Orent, she gave a warning."

"So why didn't she reply? I wasn't sure she'd heard the call for help."

'Because someone set a ward inside the door. I could hear you when you focused enough to call for help, but couldn't reply. No matter how much I tried. A rare ward indeed and I do not know where it came from but whoever provided it might have access to more.'

"And when the door was destroyed the ward was as well?" He frowned, glancing back at the small storage room now covered in shred of wood. He'd been lucky not to be struck by the flying debris. Riana had... "How could Riana protect me with the ward in place?"

'That I am not sure of, but I have my suspicions. If I am right Riana's marriage to Rhodan just tripled in importance. I will need to look into this, but first we need to end the problem with Jeriah, though I fear we may already be too late.'

Damn that woman. If it hadn't been for Arinnana he would have been able to complete his plans. Rhodan would have been dead before the end of the day and he, the dutiful and grieving but righteous next of kin would have been proclaimed heir. What little chance there would have been at Riana being named in his place would have been dealt with via the captive Cluiun.

Now he fled for cover, riding at full pace away from the castle with but a handful of men. Arinnana would pay for this, once he got his hands on her she would pay. She'd beg for death before he would grant it to her.

Bitch. He could have been expressing his regret to Justin by now, preparing for his place as the new heir. Reduced to fleeing into the country like a common criminal was disgusting, he was the King, or would be. One day.

A minor set back.

He leaned back against the velvet and padded seats within the dark wood coach, his body jolted with each pothole and rut in the roads. Some had been smoothed out, but once you were out of the city itself the road became little more than packed earth. Still he hadn't hesitated at the idea of using the coach.

What nobleman would ever ride on horseback for such a long trip? It made no sense. Soldiers, thieves, even farmers and swords for hire would do so, but a man of his rank? Never. He had better things he could be doing with his time. If he wished he could stop and find a woman for company for the rest of the trip. Not an option he would have had on horseback.

Not that he wanted such company right now, not with the problems women had caused him in the last day alone. He'd be more likely to slit a woman's throat than enjoy the softer side of such company.

No one could blame him for being this angry. He'd lost everything.

Perhaps lost was the wrong word. His plans had been put on hold.

So much had been left behind, he hadn't even dared to leave traps, that would have only made him appear even more guilty and right now he was clinging to the fact he might be able to remain protected on his family estates. He could claim he had been called back there for business reasons, yes that would work. That he knew nothing of the accusations, if he had then wouldn't his room have been stripped? Or he could have staged a coup. Justin would fall for it, if for no other reason than to protect the memory of his dead sister, Jeriah's mother.

Yes, he had to cling to that hope or he'd be facing an order for his execution.

Women. The bane of life.

Two days hard riding should see him at the estates. It would have been faster if he had access to a dragon the way Rhodan did. Another thing he hated his cousin for. He should have been the one honored with the bond, not a man who ignored his responsibilities on a regular basis.

There would be a way back into favor. No serious member of court could ever look at Rhodan and see a potential King. They'd want him back, to help him find a way to over come this. The last thing they would want would be Rhodan on the throne.

Overlooked in favor of a womanizing fool. Stupid. The entire land would suffer if Rhodan survived to claim the throne. He had no knowledge of what it took to be King and Jeriah doubted the man knew his way around the financial records that were a daily part of life for Justin.

They'd pay, they'd all pay.

Haon had stayed behind, he'd keep him informed and no one would assume he had had anything to do with a plot to kill Rhodan if that plot was even believed, not with him remaining behind at court. Haon would become his eyes, his ears, perhaps even his voice when the time was right. Until then he'd play the fearful, misunderstood cousin. In Haon he had the chance of information, a helping hand, if only for the woman he had been promised.

"Speed up the horses," he called out through the coach. Rhodan would have ridden instead of sitting back in the coach this way, but that would have been well beneath his station. This way he could rest, reach home faster and had been able to grab a few small items to carry back to the home he hoped never to step foot in again.

"Are you trying to claim that your cousin tried to arrange for your assassination?" Justin made no attempt to hide his disbelief. Not that Rhodan blamed his father, he'd have struggled to believe the situation if someone had come to him about it.

"Father, it's not as simple as that."

"You're right about that. It makes no sense. He would have known he would be the first man suspected and as such never sworn in as my heir if you died. Worse you expect me to take the word of a well known pirate and personal friend. Half the court are going to think you staged this as a way of avoiding the duel." His father had aged since they'd entered the room. Visibly aged at least a dozen years.

His fault? No, not entirely. Jeriah was equally to blame.

Rhodan took a long slow breath before he spoke. "I know father, but it's true nevertheless. Jeriah would do anything to replace me as heir and we both know it."

'Stay calm snackling, your father has had a long day and you know how grumpy he gets.' Orent yawned at the back of his mind. *'I believe he's been too long without a bed partner. Perhaps you should help him find one. Not a wife you understand, but nothing wrong in helping him find a playmate or three. He'd look so much more at peace if he did that. Might loose a few of those worry lines around his eyes.'*

Rhodan struggled to keep a straight face at the Dragon's words. He couldn't imagine his father spending time with women at his stage in life. He'd grown too old for that, hadn't he?

'What's so strange about it, dragons do it all the time. We help match our Elders up with suitable companions if they start showing signs of becoming too grumpy. Too old indeed, he's in his prime as you well know, or should do. Maybe you should ask him for advice on keeping your wife happy. I'm sure he'd be able to fill you in on a lot of interesting details.'

He nearly choked, covering his mouth quickly to mask the sound. Ask his father? The man couldn't have had a woman in his life in years.

'And does that mean he's forgotten how to use his equipment? I don't think you humans work that way. You really should take a better look at the world around you, some of the biggest skirt chasers in court are twenty years older than

your father. It all makes sense you know, about his mood swings if he hasn't had a companion in a while. Well don't you humans say you can tell when someone hasn't been... now what's that odd term you use... laid in a while by how bad tempered the person gets.'

"And I am supposed to stand before the court and present Cluiun as my only evidence?" Justin rubbed his temples as he paced, distracting Rhodan from Orent's words. "Can you even be sure of what you heard?"

"I know what I heard, your Majesty." Cluiun did his best to keep his tone respectful. "And even if I am wrong then it had to be someone with power, perhaps trying to trap Jeriah. So would it not be worth checking with Jeriah, perhaps asking to check his quarters?"

Rhodan shot his friend a look, but calmed the moment that he saw the confident look in the older man's gaze. He knew something, or suspected it.

"Indeed father, it would protect Jeriah if he is innocent."

Justin drew to a halt, turning to look his son square in the eyes. "Perhaps that would be for the best, and I cannot see anyone in court objecting to you making sure your cousin's name had been cleared. However I would advise against letting it be known just who had provided the information that led to these actions. I cannot stress enough how dangerous it would be to you if anyone thought Cluiun was working with you in an attempt to discredit your cousin."

"Father I..."

"I know, it is not something you would do, but your cousin has gained a wealth of loyal followers. It wouldn't take much to start a rumor that could destroy what little support still remains here for you my son." Justin walked towards the two men, nodding once to the still silent Riana in the far corner of the room. "I have worried about you for many years. The death of your mother stole the focus of the joy in my life and I kept myself distant from you perhaps too much. Now it may be too late and you have to settle yourself, prepare for the years ahead when you will rule in my stead."

"That won't be for many years yet," Rhodan began to protest only to be silenced by a wave of his father's hand. At least Orent had chosen to be silent for a while. Hard enough to focus without her helpful hints about his fathers sex life.

"It might be tomorrow, it could be next week or twenty years from now. The point is you need to learn. The breaches must be closed between you and those of court." Justin laid a heavy hand on his shoulder, leaving Rhodan fighting the unease the words and the unshielded love in his fathers eyes brought to life. "For pushing you away all these years I am sorry. I never forgave myself for either your mother's death or failing Olain in not being bonded with a dragon, but the day Orent chose you was one of the happiest of my life. I felt as though the curse on our family had been lifted."

"What are you talking about?" He couldn't help but be confused at the sudden turn in his fathers' behavior. "Is something wrong, have you become ill?"

"I suppose it would look like that, after the way I have acted towards you." Justin shook his head, taking a seat nearby. He'd aged, in just the last few days he'd aged almost a decade. The lines were deeper about his eyes; they held a weariness within them that he had never noticed before.

"Hear your father out, love." Riana slipped her arm through his. He'd never even heard her move across the room. "I have the feeling he's trying to tell you something you should have known many years ago."

Even without Riana's words he would have done just that now.

"I'm sorry, Rhodan. I blamed you for so much, you were easy to use as an excuse. Like your mother you have a love of life, you hate duty, and you see things without the bonds of the rules of court life. I've envied you, hated you, pitied you and forgotten to love you. Now I fear it's too late." Justin rubbed one hand across his forehead. "If I had not done that then Jeriah would not have the hold on court that he now has. Your marriage would have been a cause for celebration not threats and duels. Now I have to find a way to make it right."

"And if it's too late," he tried and failed to keep the bitterness from his words. All those years he had run to his father, sought out help, advice to be sent elsewhere as a burden. No, he couldn't think about that right now. Not when there was still even a slim chance of healing the damage.

"I don't know, but I want to try, if you'll let me." Justin spoke quietly, meeting Rhodan's gaze. "We can start with this business with Jeriah. I believe you, I believe Cluiun. I've known for a long time what your cousin was capable of but I never did anything to try and prevent it. Now we have a reason to search his room and talk to him, or rather I do."

Regret, his father didn't even attempt to hide the pain behind his words.

"You?" Rhodan frowned, he wanted to talk to Jeriah, not leave it to his father. "I guess that makes sense. If I talked directly to him it would come across as bullying, trying to jostle for place again."

"Exactly, we can't allow that to happen."

"I understand," for the first time in years he did believe he understood his father, offering a low bow that nearly ended as Orent's liquid silver voice murmured in a way that only he could hear.

'Bah, I still think he needs to loosen up a bit and get laid.'

'He's gone.' Orent purred at the back of her mind. *'Fled before you found Cluiun, the report is being taken to Justin now. It should be safe for the three of you to go and check his room out now.'*

"What caused him to run?" Riana glanced about the room. The two men hadn't returned as yet from checking out the small room in which Cluiun had been held captive. Though the chance that anything had been left behind in the rubble of the door was slim, Cluiun had wanted to check through it to be sure.

'Threatened by another, that would be my guess. The only way we'll know for certain is checking through his room and capturing him for questioning. If we're lucky he won't have had time to strip down his room.'

"To capture him would mean being given permission to do so from the King." She fought not to knot her fingers into her skirts.

'And the odds of that happening are slim. Justin means well, he's made mistakes and knows about them, but he is still human and wary of doing something that would so obviously turn the remains of the court against him.'

Frustrating, she could blast down a door, destroy a small town, but couldn't understand the workings of the court. Or this court at least. Dodging squires in her father's castle, or dealing with trade agreements had been one thing but this… she'd never known a situation like it.

'It's the same thing, just taken to a higher level. As long as you don't let it overwhelm you then you'll be able to cope with anything the court throws at you. Don't let them fluster you. Try to think before speaking or acting and you'll have won half the battle.'

"Right, a country born noble, half Fae, magic out of control and I am supposed to be able to deal with the games they play."

'You're missing the obvious, they are games and all games have rules. All you need to do is learn the rules. If you let them get you upset then they will win, if you keep calm, think before making your move then you'll be fine.'

"A game?" In an odd way that made sense. She'd played games since childhood, her mother had loved them and as long as she looked at it that way it wouldn't become too overwhelming. "Yes, I can see how that would work. There are rules to this, at least from what I've seen so far. Power plays, structure. Like a warped form of chess."

'Exactly, and you watch people, I've seen that already about you. Now all you have to do is continue watching. Do not let them lull you into a false sense of security. Smile, let them think of you what they wish to, remember our discussion about this. Then when we need to we will have our little demonstration and if that doesn't work I can always eat one of two of them.'

"I thought killing one of them would be a bad idea." She rubbed the palm of her hand nervously over the dress one of the servants had found for her. If they were to stay at court she would have to seek out a dress maker. Not because of wanting to appear in fashion but to play the very game Orent spoke of. Dress, appearance, what people believed they saw were all a part of the game. Simon had taught her that much. They took him for a fool, a fop and never dared to look beneath the show he put on for them.

'For you, yes, for me no. Though I'll have to see if I can find several mint bushes afterwards. I swear more than a few of those creatures bathe in perfume.'

"So he ran, why doesn't that surprise me?" Cluiun rubbed his wrists without thinking about it. Even after a few hours he could still feel the rope circling his flesh, cutting off the flow of blood to his fingers. A healer had assured him there was no long term damage to his hands but that hadn't stopped the phantom tingling that remained in his fingers.

Riana had been relieved about the news, she doubted herself that one. Not unusual. She'd either settle into her new role or she wouldn't. There were no half way points on something like this.

"It's enough to give us leave to search his rooms." The prince glanced back at him as they waited for the guard to open up the door. He looked every inch a member of the blood royal now. Shaking off the drink of the night before, the words from his father and a new set of clothes had changed him. Pity, he preferred the rogue like youngster he'd met up with only a few days ago.

Marriage and his father had changed him, but that was life. People changed, adapted or they died.

"Good, though I would have thought your father would want someone else to do the searching." For appearances sake if nothing else, but he refrained from adding that. Each meeting with the King had him respecting the man less. He'd lost the courage to stand up for himself, for his family and that was something Cluiun could not accept. The excuse of the way court was run, the game played, was just that to him, an excuse.

Courts, he wasn't cut out for life here. Once matters were settled he would see about getting a new ship and head back out. He had a need, a drive to be back on the ocean that grew stronger with each passing day. A new ship, his old crew and he could shake off the smell of the castle within a day.

"He has his reasons. I won't say I agree with them however." Rhodan curled one arm about the waist of his silver haired wife. "Hopefully we will find something in here to change his edict concerning Jeriah from banishment into a death sentence."

"If so I might apply to a position as executioner, as a one off arrangement you understand." There were very few beings in this life he could honestly say he would enjoy killing, but Jeriah had jumped to the head of the list. "I'd work for free on that one, but it would only raise suspicion in court so I would reluctantly accept the fees that came with the job."

'Oh you are a bad bad man Cluiun. I knew there was a reason I liked you. However you will have to wait your turn, dear one. I believe I have first claim on him. I don't like it when people bring strange magic into the castle.'

"Well now, I'd never have put you down for the blood thirsty type." Cluiun could almost imagine the look on Jeriah's face should he be faced down by the large black dragon.

'I'm not, but ask pet over there, I do so enjoy a good snack from time to time and he might as well be of some use. Throwing him into the midden would be a complete waste.'

"Pet?" Cluiun glanced over to Rhodan as the guard finally found a key that would open the door.

"One of her names for me, along with snack, lunch and anything else she might find suitable at the time." Rhodan explained.

Somehow that didn't surprise him.

'Don't all higher beings have cute names for their pets?'

"Well, let's see what we can find." He nodded towards the now open door, following the others into the room. Opulent would have best described the furnishings. Lush tastes, rich beyond the norm in the castle, at least that he had seen so far. Expensive silk tapestries decorated the walls, furniture that had to have been made from rare woods, inlaid with gold, jewels and silver. More money had been spent to deck out the one room they now stood in than had been expended on the entire court room.

"He must have been hoarding money for years to be able to afford this." Riana moved further into the room. "Some of these items would have cost more than the taxes my father collected in a dozen years."

"Not sure where he got the money, but he certainly has a good source of income. That wall hanging alone must have cost a thousand gold." Cluiun looked over the tapestry, he'd traded more than a few of them in his time after acquiring them from their original owners.

"Where to start?" Riana moved through the room towards a large dressing table. "What are we looking for anyway?"

"Simple enough, we're looking for anything that might link into him having a desire to claim the throne." The young prince explained, uncovering a heavy chest from beneath a soft woolen blanket. "Not sure we'll find but we might as well get it over and done with."

There could be a dozen or more such chests in the room, along with bags, other furniture, scrolls had been carefully organized on a long shelf, though there were enough spaces to suggest that some had left the room along with Jeriah.

"How long had he been gone before it was discovered he'd left?" Riana spoke softly, trailing her fingers over the large dressing table finally lingering on a dark wooden box.

"Several hours at least." Rhodan explained. "He might have already left by the time we located Cluiun, he certainly didn't leave much after that."

"I'd like to know what spooked him." Cluiun found his gaze moving to focus on Riana. He couldn't be sure why, but a tension exuded from her as her hand hovered over the still closed box. "Riana?"

'I don't like the feel of this, Cluiun, it's like the marker on the door that stopped me talking to you.' Orent murmured. *'Jeriah's been collecting sources of power, greedy little human that he is. I need you to watch Riana closely. Rhodan will be too caught up in his love for her to do what might be needed.'*

Why did that sound ominous?

'I could dress it up a little for you, if that would make you more comfortable.'

"Something important is in here, I can ... feel it." A soft quiver entered her voice, her hand trembling as she tried to move it closer to the lid. "Something that won't let me open the box, but wants me to at the same time. I don't know why, but it's there, calling to me, taunting me."

Her hair transformed slowly into liquid silver fire, a fire that overtook her skin, threatening to dance through the air into the box. He didn't hesitate. Cluiun cleared the distance between them, his hands circling her waist, pulling her away from the box. Whatever was in the box he needed to keep her away from it until it could be proven safe. Together they hit the floor, rolling until his back touched the rugs, the slender silver haired woman resting on his chest, thighs straddling her hips.

"What the..." Rhodan began.

"The box, whatever was in the box triggered her powers. If she'd stayed there who knows what would have happen. I don't know about you but I've no desire to see your wife spread across the room in some magic fueled explosion."

Orent's amused voice filled the minds of all three within the room.

'No, you'd much rather have her spread over your lap, not that I'm faulting your taste in females dear Cluiun she is very attractive. But don't you think it would be better if you tried that little move with a woman who isn't married hmmm?'

"Well you have to admin she is very ravishable.' Cluiun grinned, sitting up as he lifted Riana from his lap. He couldn't help but enjoy the rapid spread of the blush that now claimed Riana's face. Perhaps he was a rogue after all, but if that meant he got to enjoy seeing a beautiful woman blush and turn into a tongue tied lass then he was quite content in being a rogue.

"True enough, one of the many reasons I married her." Rhodan smiled, pulling the stammering woman into his arms. "Open the box, Cluiun. She's a safe enough distance away from it so it shouldn't cause her to react. At least I'm hoping it won't."

He didn't think mentioning that magical reactions might not come with safe distance instructions was such a good idea. "Alright, but I'm betting what ever is in that box is something Jeriah is now cursing that he left behind."

"I don't take sucker bets."

"I can still feel it, the energy vibrating from inside the box. Calling to me, trying to push me away, trying to tear me in two different directions." Riana spoke quietly, leaning back in Rhodan's arms. So confident but shy, almost vulnerable at the same time. No wonder she brought out the protective part of his nature. "It's dangerous, but I don't think it will hurt you Cluiun."

"Good, I don't believe I have a magical bone in my body." He reached out slowly. No matter what he said, or the reassurances from Riana, he had no intention of rushing into this. He'd seen more than one friend turned into dust because they hadn't respected the work of a mage.

'Oh, I wouldn't be so sure of that. You've got several very interesting aspects to your body. One or two parts I could become quite attached to if I were human.' Orent whispered into the room.

"This isn't the time for..."

'For us, I know, but a girl can dream can't she?'

"Orent," he wanted to warn her off but how did you tell a dragon to stop?

'I love the way you say my name. Almost poetic.'

Growling under his breath Cluiun turned his full attention to the box, well aware that the dragon was enjoying her own brand of fun. Old wood, smooth, unmarked on the outside. It didn't quite fit in with the more decadent tastes Jeriah appeared to prefer for the rest of the room. Even without the magic Riana held he could feel something as he touched the box. A low vibration that played through his body. Power, energy, nerves, it didn't matter what he called it, it was still there and very real.

Light reflected from the crown nestled on deep velvet inside the box. Gems, finely cut, richer than he had seen in many a year decorated the golden form. A crown fit for a King. "Seems our Jeriah wasn't happy waiting to wear the crown of Olain, he went and had one made for himself."

"Great Dragons!" Rhodan stepped closer, keeping one arm about Riana. "That has to be old. He couldn't have just had that made up. Not with the work in the crown. Someone would have mentioned it."

'He's right, the crown is old, but I have no doubt that Jeriah thought it had been made for him. He wouldn't have looked past paying over the money needed

and moving on from there. But in paying for this he's brought a very old artifact back to the castle.'

"You know this? The crown I mean?" Rhodan reached out for the crown but pulled back, wary of touching it.

'Every dragon does. It's the first true crown of your family line, Rhodan. The crown my people had made to seal the bond between our kind.'

"It can't be, that was stolen, generations ago now."

'It is, I know the feel of it, or the stone in the center. We all do, every one of dragon kind. It vibrates within us.'

Cluiun turned the crown in his hands, light reflecting from the gem, a stone of a type he had never seen before. "What is this? I don't recognize the gem type."

'You won't have, they're rare. Seldom seen by human kind. It's carved soul gem. Normally they are left untouched but this one was prepared, carved by a skilled hand then set into the crown. The smaller gems along the rest of the crown, some are diamonds, emeralds, but a few have been made from the cast off parts of the gem. Just one part of a soul gem, carved the way these have been, could buy Olain.'

"But why did it, they, whatever... react to Riana?" Cluiun couldn't take his eyes off the crown.

"Don't know about Riana but my hands are tingling just from being in the same room as that thing." Rhodan shook his head, taking a half step closer.

'Riana, hold the crown.'

"But."

'Trust me, hold the crown. I need to know if I'm right about this.'

"Alright, I'll try." Riana agreed, slipping free from her husbands grasp. Slowly she reached out brushing one hand over the crown, not quite touching it. "It's like it's alive, calling me. Wanting me to wear it."

'Calm, focus then touch the largest gem.' Orent continued. *'Whatever you do, do not give in to the call to wear the crown. I don't think any of us would be ready to deal with what I think might happen.'*

Her eyes closed, brushing out over the gem.

Light blazed from the gem, blinding them, filling the room. It shouldn't have struck them but it did, pushing Cluiun back against the wall, his grip lost on the crown as it clattered to the floor. The same force repelling everyone in the room except Riana.

Through the brightness he somehow still saw her, standing there, reaching for the crown.

'Don't, don't touch it!'

"It wants me," she murmured. "Wants me to pick it up, wear it, claim it.

I can hear it calling me" She snatched her hand back. "Cluiun, Rhodan, stop me. You have to stop me. I can't... I can't..."

Something snapped within, a source of strength and will that had kept him alive through darker times. He didn't know where it came from, he'd never known, and right now he didn't care. With a growl he moved, before Rhodan could, before Orent could scream a warning. Diving forward, his arms wrapping around her body as he slammed her to the floor. "Cover the crown, cover it up now!"

"Wants me, I can't ignore it. Cluiun!" Light shone from her eyes, power, a warning he couldn't ignore.

'We can't let her touch it, she's not prepared.'

"Cluiun, don't you dare touch her!" Rhodan tried to move from the wall, but the light, whatever it was, still held him in place.

"Forgive me." He didn't want to strike her but what other choice did he have right now. He struck, hard and fast, one balled up fist connecting with her chin. That's all it took to knock the light from her eyes...

Chapter Ten

"No!" The word screamed into life, rage fueling his strike across the room, exploding against the far wall. Shards of stone erupted into the air, not that he cared. He was immune to such missiles. "That fool, human scum. He left the crown behind. Now they have it."

"My Lord?" Guinelia whimpered. Scrapes marred her flesh, small splinters of stone imbedded in her skin. She knew enough not to complain, that he was not pleased to see. Her disobedience would have given him reason to destroy her, use her body to soothe his anger. Tempting. She'd scream, delighting him with her pain, her suffering. Feeding him with each whimper. A focus that would calm him. For a moment he reached for the trembling woman. No. Later, there would be plenty of time for his explorations of her ability to scream once matters were settled.

"The crown, Jeriah left the crown behind when he fled." Foolish mortal, didn't he know what he had done. "The Fae girl touched it, the dragons know, she knows, if she unlocks the power in the crown then... No there are other ways. Fetch your daughter, I wish her presence at once."

"At once my Lord." She didn't hesitate, but pushed to her feet running from the room before he could change his mind. Had she seen his hand moving towards her for that heartbeat, known she had only just avoided becoming his latest play thing in a way even Guinelia was not prepared to face? Not that it mattered. She ran. She obeyed. The task would be completed.

The crown. Darkest night Jeriah's cowardice had come close to undoing them all.

All those centuries searching for a way to get the crown, the jewel and now Riana held it within her grasp. She didn't know the power it contained, the spells it could unleash. He couldn't leave it in their hands, but how to claim it? How to remove it from the castle?

The women he controlled held the answer. He couldn't enter the home of the Dragon throne without a strong summons. Sending either of the women would be a risk, Arinnana would be recognized by her sister, and he doubted Riana would believe she had been acting under the control of another. Guinelia was less predictable, harder to control, she feared very little in life beyond facing him in person which would not be possible from such a distance.

He needed the crown, the gem, the power it held the key to. Just a moment with it in his hand and his kin would tremble. No more dawn chorus. What bliss that would be. But for that he had to reclaim the crown.

Powerless, it was a sensation he didn't experience that often and it infuriated him. He was a god, all powerful, mortals bowed down to him, worshipped him, obeyed him knowing if they didn't they would suffer until their last breath. Yet he had no way of appearing in that castle and claiming what rightfully belonged to him.

Oh he could imagine the look on the faces of the mortals if he could just walk into the center of the great hall. The screams, terror, pleas for mercy. A pretty little scene. Impossible but seductive nevertheless.

The box, the gem, two parts of the same desire. More would be needed, but the gems the crown held were the largest part.

Did the dragons still know how to use the basic magic? No, if they did they would have used it many years ago. Before the crown had gone missing. He held onto that as a thread, a comfort against the situation he now faced.

Still he didn't know how to retrieve it.

A pawn, an innocent would work best, unless he could bind an imp to his will. They alone held the ability to slip in and out of any domain. No wards kept them out, only a mage box could hold them. Binding one to his whims would mean capturing a newly formed imp, one that had yet to learn what its life would entail. He needed someone from the village, one he could twist to his whims and force an imp to appear. There were some small runes he could use, that would help delay the actions of an imp, others that would pull it to appear.

Deity or not he had no true power over imps, demons or any of their kind. He could ask, suggest, add a few compelling spells that might encourage them to put in an appearance, but beyond that there was little he could do to force them to appear. Once he had control of the ancient magic that would also change. They'd obey him and worship him as would the rest of mortal kind.

Still, if he found one that was new there would be a chance to confuse it, persuade it to obey him. Long enough, at least, to regain the crown.

"My Lord, you summoned me?" Arinnana dropped to her knees at his feet, lowering her gaze. Wet hair soaked the thin gown she'd pulled on, interesting was she attempting to attract him. Nothing would surprise him about humans.

"Have a woman and her children brought to me. Or a man with children. It matters not, either way make sure the children are unharmed when they are brought here." Children, almost as annoying as bird song, but they had their uses.

"My Lord?" She glanced upwards, making no attempt to hide the confusion in her eyes. "What do you need children for?"

"You will learn soon enough, now fetch them. It is time you learned a little more about the magic of Erien." It would be an interesting lesson to teach his willing student, one he was sure she would take to with ease. "Guinelia, you will help me prepare the room, the markings will have to be precise. Make a mistake and I will repaint them with your blood."

A farm. Not large by any stretch of the imagination. Just enough room to make it viable. He doubted the place supported more than a small family plus a small income in trade on the side. But it was on the edge of the village and the perfect place to pick up a horse. Any further into the group of houses and he ran the risk of being discovered. Though with the confusion at the castle most of the men would be away. Or that was his hope. Bevery hadn't seen many men or women around since he'd crept into edge of the village, some would have fled for cover at the first sign of trouble. Others would be hiding out until the right moment, just as he had.

Three small white washed buildings lay in a semi circle, a fenced off area just within line of sight, vegetables growing in a small patch nearby. A picture of homely bliss. Right, until the smashing, tearing and killing. Everything looked lovely until that happened, then bam, blood everywhere. So much for peaceful living.

The people at the castle thought they had a good peaceful life. Nice source of income, good clothing, never going hungry. And they had been right, up to the moment it had been their blood coating the stones.

Blood. He could still taste it on the air. Thick, coppery, heady. Gods he didn't need this. Muscles clenched, his stomach rolling as it threatened to spill out the acid that remained.

He'd never be able to look at a rare steak in the same way again. Or hamburger. The kitchens had looked like someone had taken a whole cow, ground it up, then splattered the walls with the remains.

Maybe he'd become a vegetarian?

A good stiff drink. That would help. Maybe he'd be able to hunt out a bottle of cider or wine before heading out. Farms were good about stuff like that. Ale would work. Wasn't his favorite beverage but it would certainly take the edge of his nerves. He had every right to be suffering from nervous after what he'd been through. Any man would have the shakes, or be curled up in a tight ball, wondering where the next blow would come from. Not him, he'd pulled through. Well what else would be expected from a survivor, a hero of his caliber?

Even Riana would not be able to avoid looking his way now. If she were still alive that is. He had no way of knowing. Not that it mattered, if she were dead there would be other suitable women.

No, she lived, he lived and with Valer dead and Arinnana a traitor perhaps there were some other benefits to the situation. She'd need a husband, one willing to look after her, present her case to the King in order to gain the men needed to retake the castle. Of course she'd be grateful. Women normally were.

Wife, ownership of the castle, rank and fame in one simple move. He couldn't have planned it better himself.

Horses, where were they. None in the pasture, so if there were any left on the farm they'd be in the small stable. A place like this would have had a couple of horses, and maybe oxen for tilling the land. He couldn't be sure. If there weren't any here he'd have to move on to the next place. Each one he had to search would increase his chance of being caught by some of the people from the castle. That thought alone was enough to re-awaken the chill in his bones.

He'd feel better once he had that drink inside him. One quick one before he went to look for a horse.

Homely. He'd expected that. Nicely laid out. Fire burning in the hearth but low enough that he could assume no one was left home, and hadn't been around for an hour or so. Empty kettle over the main fire, cups knocked over on the large table. A broken pottery mug near one table leg. Salt scattered from a knocked over shaker left a pattern of small coarse white grains on the table. They'd left in a hurry whoever they were. Not that he blamed them. He'd have done the same.

Rich enough to have access to good salt. Interesting. He'd struck lucky with the farm then. Any horses left behind would be decent quality. Good. He didn't need to be left with a lame mount.

He could still taste the blood. Rich. Sickeningly so. Cloying at the back of his throat. Gods he'd never be free of it.

Where would they have kept the ale?

So maybe he wasn't doing the most sensible of things, he should have grabbed a horse and gotten out, but the trouble was up at the castle, no sign of them here and he needed something to take the edge off his nerves after everything he'd been through. No more demons or those vile women seeking to bathe in blood. A drink, a quick rummage through the house for anything worth stealing, maybe find a cloak and some cleaner clothes, then he'd be off.

It wouldn't take too long.

Kegs, they'd be in the cellar, if the place had one. Of course they would. Between roots and ale they'd need a cool place for storage. He just had to find the way down there.

Bevery swore, stumbling forward as his foot caught on a large metal ring. "Damn trap door." He should have kept a closer eye on where he was walking, instead he now sat on the floor rubbing his leg as he cursed his own stupidity.

"What are you doing in here?" A girl's voice, little more than a child when he glanced up, no a teenager would have been more accurate. Maybe. He'd given up judging the real age of females. Stringy blond hair, wide eyes, a kitchen knife held in her left hand. Yeah, just a kid, he could handle her without any problems.

"I'm just looking for a few things, nothing to worry about."

"This isn't your home." Her voice shook, bottom lip quivering. Great, a crier. Just what he needed.

"Does it matter?"

"You should leave, now." She took a half step forward, lowering the knife a little. At least the lip quiver had stopped. "This is my home, my father's place. He won't like you being here."

"And where is he?" His gaze narrowed, watching the girl as he stood up. From the way she held the knife he doubted she knew how to use it beyond butchering animals. She didn't move like one trained to fight. Not with the stumbling steps, glazed look in her eyes and the slowly shifting grip about the handle of the knife. In fact she moved more like one in shock. Good. Easier to handle.

"Up at the castle. He went up there a few days ago." Her gaze shifted towards the door for a moment. A heart beat of focus, then it was gone. The glaze returning to her pale eyes.

"Then I don't think he's coming back. I just came down from there lass. No one's alive. No one." He saw little point in hiding the facts to her. "I saw them die, heard some of the others, the only two left alive at the castle are two women. Arinnana and an older woman."

"No," a whisper of a word, the color draining from her face. "It can't be. He was fine. They all where. He can't be dead." Light trembling turned into a full body shake. Focus chased the glaze away. Fear. The need for his words to be a lie.

"Well he is, they all are up there. I heard them scream loud enough."

"You're lying. You want something here and you think if you lie I'll let you walk in and steal!" Her voice turned into a near scream.

"Calm down."

"He's alive! You're a liar and he's alive!"

"Stupid girl. Why do you think no one has come down from the castle in days? They're all dead, there's no one left to come down from there except me and those women. Believe me better you see me than the women from up there. You don't want to end up dealing with those creatures." He had to walk into a girl who didn't want to believe the truth when it was right in front of her, wonderful. Now he'd spend hours trying to explain things to her or she'd bring down the watch on him.

If they still existed.

There'd been no cries for help, no signs of relief entering the castle. Still they might have fought their way into the castle. Not something he planned on staying long enough to find out.

"Cruel, hateful lies. He's alive, tell me he's alive." Tears ran down her face, dripping from her chin onto the floor. Women, some could cry and still look attractive but the girl, she'd be red faced and blotchy in only a few moments. "Tell me he's still alive damn you!"

"Why lie to you?" Her shrieks had grown louder with each new breath. "Where's the watch?"

She didn't answer for a moment, blinking. "What?"

"The village watch. The peacekeepers. I assume there's one, or are they all up at the castle?" If there wasn't one then he'd be fine to just take what he needed and be gone. Being that close to the castle the village might not have needed one. Valer had always run a pretty peaceful land. Low crime, good trade areas, it would almost make sense that the watch if any, would have been at the castle. It would explain a few things. The lack of life in the village, and around the farm as a whole.

"No watch, not a real one. Few of the local farmers and business owners worked to fill the gap," she mumbled. "Where's my father?"

Good, one less problem to deal with. Now he could ignore the brat, leave her to snivel in the kitchen. He'd go without his drink, but at least he knew he wouldn't be followed.

"Where is he!"

"You're hysterical, go wash up or something. Keep yourself calm and just accept the fact you're never going to see him again." Farming wenches, mush for brains. One track mind. Best to be gone and rid of her. "The horses?"

She didn't answer him, her hands limp at her sides, blinking slowly.

"Where are the horses? I presume you do have some here?" He glared at her. They had to have horses here. "Snap out of it and answer me!"

Nothing, a blank stare, tears silently coating her cheeks, hitting the clean wooden floor in large splashes before soaking into the grain. "

"Answer me you silly little bitch." He growled, clearing the distance between them. He didn't have time for this. He'd have to slap her if she didn't give an answer. Any time now they might come down from the castle, looking for more victims and this girl was holding him up.

"You killed them," barely more than a whisper.

"What? Are you insane?"

"You came from the castle, you said so. Said you'd heard their screams, that no one else was alive, so it must be you that killed them." She mumbled, not meeting his gaze.

"Just answer th..." Pain lanced through his stomach, sharp, without mercy. A thrust that pushed him back towards the wall. He didn't understand, couldn't figure it out. He shouldn't be stumbling like this. "Wh...what?"

"You killed them," her voice remained low, calmer than it had been but moments before. "Now you'll die just like they did."

Her hands were empty. The knife, where had the kitchen knife gone? Blood bubbled along his lips, his own hands moving to grasp about the pain in his stomach, fumbling as he brushed over the handle of the knife. Stabbed? She'd attacked him? "What have you done to me?"

"What my Daddy always told me to do with thieves, kill them, strike once, just do it and think later. He'd like that, like what I just did. Don't you like it?" She smiled, almost innocent now despite the blood that she smeared from her hands onto her skirts. "He'll be pleased I remembered. I know he will be. He taught me everything I needed to know in life. Said I had to learn if I wanted to make it out of the farm one day. Don't think he ever understood that I liked the farm. Gone now, all gone, but I can build it back up. If I remember to do what he wanted me to then I can protect the farm, look after it, make him proud of me."

Mad. Gods she was insane.

Blood pulsed from between his fingers as he pressed them against his stomach. Bad strike, but he lived. Would still live. Just needed to stop the pain. The blood. A cloth. Needed a cloth.

"You're still standing up. Aren't you supposed to be on the floor by now, dead?" A small frown crinkled across her brow. "Maybe I didn't do it right after all? That's not good, he'd be upset with me for being sloppy. I can't have him upset with me."

What did it matter if her father would have been upset, he was dead, just like everyone else up at the castle. He'd make it though. No matter what he'd make it. With a low groan he stumbled back, reaching for the edge of the table, trying to keep on his feet. "Have to stop the bleeding." He didn't want to die, he didn't think she'd struck deep enough, not if he could stop the bleeding and find the right herbs, a healer, something. There had to be one still in the village.

Cloth tangled in his fingers, a moment taken to press it against the wound.

"I know, I know what to do. He taught me how to do so many things. Healing the animals, butchering, training some of the animals. I learned everything he could show me. Even taught me how to brew ale. Said some man would want that skill, maybe I'd catch the right husband that way." She chattered on. Didn't it matter to her that she'd stuck him with a knife, that he bled out slowly on her kitchen floor? "He even taught me how to clean up in the slaughter area so we didn't end with vermin coming in."

Clinging to what she knew, that had to be it. Her mind had rejected the news and now sought out a way to survive. Stupid. He should have kept his distance, grabbed a horse and got out. Now he'd be here a few days healing up. At least it didn't feel as bad as it could have been. Struck his side more than his stomach, maybe. He couldn't be sure, not without getting another set of eyes to check the wound.

Blood, he could see it, feel it. It soaked into the cloth. No he wasn't going to die. He'd survived the castle, the demon woman, he could survive this. Dizzy. The room swirled about him, forcing him to sit down hard by the table.

"I know what I did wrong." Her fingers curled into his hair, smoothing through sweat damp locks. "I forgot the basics."

Mad, quite insane. "Get away from me."

She gripped his hair, pulling back on his head. "He always told me, when butchering slit the throat first to bleed the animal out before gutting them." Steel flashed before his eyes, a moment of bold, bright pain. Blood spurted out over her face, covering it even as his vision faded, his mind desperately clinging to life even as he slipped fully into the darkness. "And this is just the same thing. Just like he told me, always easier if you bleed them out first."....

Candles flickered along the walls, two spluttering out fully splashing wax onto the stones, the soft pops and low hissing sounds from the remaining candles the only source of light and sound within the room. They'd obeyed. Not that there had even been a doubt. Preparing the room exactly how he required. Fortunate for the two women in many ways. He lacked both the time and patience to enjoy their correction fully had they failed him even by mistake.

They knew better than to fail on purpose.

Blood marked the floor with ancient symbols that even he had problems recalling the meanings. Chalk filled in the rest. Enough life force remained in the blood to draw a new and hungry imp if they were close enough and once he had the pawns from the village he could...

A tiny movement, little more than a few grains of chalk dust, caught his eye. Not alone. Interesting. He hadn't forced an imp into being, yet they were the only beings that could have entered the room in such a manner. There. It moved again, disturbing a small pile of chalk dust. Confused, new enough to be confused and uncertain.

"Where am I?" A male voice, shaking with each word. Still very human in nature. Emotions raw.

"Show yourself. You know you need to if I'm going to help you."
Interesting, it didn't even know what had happened. Normally they had at least a
vague idea. "Step into the center of the room. There's no need to be afraid. I can't
hurt you and I might be able to help you understand what's happened to you."
Kaleb refrained from laughing, shifting form slightly, enough to hide the features
that normally would frighten others around him. Better to lull the creature into a
false sense of security.

Footsteps, good, it retained its past memories. That would make the
creature easier to contain, control and bend to his whim. Until another of its kind
found it and helped. Imps, they may jostle with each other for power and position
but they were loathe to let others outside their kind gain the upper hand over
them. Odd like that.

Too late for this one though.

"Where am I? I don't know how I got here." A shadowy figure, little more
than the outline of a human male. Clothes. He still wore them. Or rather the faint
image of them. Good lines to them. Expensive by human standards.

"What do you recall last?"

"I don't know, just images." The image solidified, becoming more
human with each passing moment. "Darkness. I remember being pulled into the
darkness. Pain. Sharp then dull. I don't remember much else. I feel odd, like I'm
only half here."

Interesting, the shift couldn't have happened more than a few moments
ago. A chance in a million. Fate was on his side at last. "Your name?"

"Name, I have a name. I just... I'm a hero, I think. No, that's not a name.
Bev... Bevery, Squire Bevery." Each word added to his form and now a young
man, perhaps in his mid twenties, stood in the center of the markings. "My
name's Squire Bevery."

"Good." A squire. Matters improved by the moment. A man of rank
however limited. It would be easier for him to walk into the castle that way even
in human form. "What brought you here?"

A small frown creased the brow of the confused young man. "I... died,
didn't I? Is this the after life? Where are the lights, the warmth?" His bottom
lip trembled, much like a small child's would after being told no to a piece of
chocolate. "This can't be happening. I can't be dead. How could I be dead and still
be here talking to you?"

"To have an after life you must have a soul, and if I am not mistaken you
sold yours." Now he allowed the smile to gain life. "Such a pity really, most who
sell them have no idea what they are getting themselves into."

"The woman, demon, whatever she was. The one who got me out of
Valer's castle." Panic ruled the watery eyes in front of him. "Oh gods, what did I

do, what did I do to myself?" He dropped to his knees, arms wrapping about his stomach, rocking as he sat on his ass. "This can't be happening to me! I'm not supposed to be here. Not like this."

"Ah but this is where you are meant to be young one, and I'm afraid you're no longer a mortal." He drank in each whimper, letting it sate his needs. "When you sold your soul to her, the female demon, you gave up your humanity. Even if something hadn't happened earlier to kill you, you'd have died within a year and a day unless you'd found a way to regain your soul. A slim chance but possible, it's been done before by rare individuals. Most die. They become imps like you, the lowest form of demons." There was one other option, but there seemed little point in telling him the fate he had avoided. Not just yet at least.

"I'm an imp?" Bevery blinked, looking up from his tears. "I'm a demon thing? That's not right, it shouldn't have happened. I have work to do, I can go to the capitol and become a hero, get Riana to notice me, maybe marry me then her fathers lands... this... this is Valer's castle isn't it? Oh gods, you're the one those women were killing everyone for, for you, all that death, the pain, destruction. I can't stay here!"

"But you can and will, at least for a short time. I have some work for you and if you complete a few small tasks then maybe I will find it in my heart to either grant you your life back, or help you move on to the afterlife." Of course he couldn't do either, but it sounded good. Bevery didn't know the first thing about being an imp, or the legends of the demons or he would have left already. At the first understanding of what he had become he'd have vanished in a puff of smoke. Or whatever it was imps tended to do. "A little work, a few minor tasks and it will all be over."

"Why should I trust you, for all I know you were the one behind all of this. You killed everyone in here, so why would you want to give me my life back?" He rose, shaking his head as he backed away from the center of the room. "What are you?"

"Kaleb, you might have heard the name a few times before. A well educated young Squire like you is bound to wandered past a few of my temples from time to time." He might have even taken a look into a temple on a rare occasion then no doubt, hurried past before someone realized who he was.

"Yes, I know what you are." What little color he had in his face drained, human reactions, human emotions. In time they would fade, but for now they would play in his favor. "God, a dark, evil god."

"Ah, evil. An over used word. What is evil? How can you be sure that what you think is evil truly is that?" Fear, confusion, these were the tools at his command. He could blast apart entire cities but he found tearing into the beliefs held by a single mind attracted him even more than the prospect of a thousand deaths. "Why am I evil."

"You kill people." Too quick an answer.

"So does old age, is that evil also?"

"No, but that's different, it's just a fact of life. You're a god, a creature, something that can control its actions."

Kaleb slowly gestured around the room. "Do I look evil to you? And how do you know old age is just a fact of life and not some dark force slowly hunting down every man, woman and child on the face of Erien. What proof do you have?"

"I don't have any proof, it's just how life is." Bevery stuttered, edging back a little further. "I want to leave."

"Why now, when we were having such a wonderful conversation."

"I just want to leave."

"Ah, you wish to join the other imps, well I am sure they would enjoy tormenting you. You see right now you're helpless and a ripe target for their little games."

"Games?"

"Well they can tear you apart, then watch your new form heal only to redo it again. It is a game they enjoy with new imps." The emotions playing across Bevery's face fed him like the sweetest of wines. Fear. Denial. Pain. Confusion. They rose and blended in the mock eyes formed from a still fresh memory. "Imp's can do that to each other. And you'll be such a tempting target for them. So new, so uncertain of yourself."

"Oh gods." He sank down to the floor, giving up on his plans to escape. Tears fell, gathering on his cheeks. Dripping down from his chin fading into nothing as soon as they left his face. Interesting. He'd never been close enough to an imp before to see this side of them. "I can't do this. What am I to do?"

Good, he was ripe for the plucking. "You could listen to me, I have ways to help. Just a few small tasks and it will all be over for you." He held out his hand, waiting for the frightened form to move.

"Why should I trust you?"

"What other choice do you have, Bevery?"

Chapter Eleven

Her fingers still tingled. She'd not even had the chance to fully touch the crown but her whole body craved to grasp it once more. Every time she used her new found gifts they backfired in some way. Better that she had never discovered this part of her nature than face the turmoil they created.

She could have killed them all, just as she had destroyed the village the day Cluiun and Rhodan had found her. A danger to herself and everyone else around her, she knew that now. Perhaps it would have been better if she had never been found. If she had stayed with the other Fae in the village, let them teach her what she needed to do, how to control her gifts.

'Peace Riana, all will be well. You should have been taught how to use your innate gifts many years ago but the death of your mother put an end to that. It will become easier in time. The gems would have caused problems for even an experienced mage. Your mother would have been put in the same situation. Once we are able to heal the breach between the crown and Rhodan's family all will be well. Or at least the crown will be back where it belongs.'

"What can we do, about the crown I mean?" Rhodan pulled her into his arms, settling onto the edge of the bed. "We can't leave it lying around for someone else to claim, and in family hands it might call to Riana again."

"I could always take it off your hands," Cluiun grinned, rubbing one finger over the scars on his face. "For a small price of course. I'd cut the fee to the bare minimum out of friendship."

"You're incorrigible." She couldn't help but smile. "There has to be another way though. The crown belongs to Rhodan's family." A Soul gem, she'd only heard of those in passing, vague references to artifacts no one had seen before. Or at least no one she had known.

What magic did it hold?

More than she had the ability to control right now. Or knowledge. Both could change if she believed the hints Orent had given her. And why would the dragon ever lie? Some of them would. Younger ones with the need to tease the humans. Older ones with an intense dislike of her kind. But not Orent.

'There is a way.' Orent spoke slowly, her voice carrying that odd vibration behind it. Enough that she knew the Dragon spoke to all within the room. *'A way to reform the bond between the crown and Rhodan's family, but I am not sure your father will permit it, snack. He's grown very odd over the last few years.'*

"What would we need to do?" Riana asked, leaning back into her husband's welcoming grasp. Here, within his arms, she felt safe, ready to take on the rest of the world. A moment where she could almost close her eyes and shut out the events of the week. "Perhaps if we presented the problem to the King he would be willing to let us try... whatever it is that needs doing."

'The soul gem was formed many years ago, long before the castle was ever built by a race that vanished.'

"A vanished race, okay. Now I don't want to get into anything too deep right now. I'd like nothing better than to get a new ship and do a little vanishing act myself, so can we ignore the old races, mystical talk and just cut to the chase?" Cluiun yawned, hooking his fingers into his sword belt. "Jeriah stole it for a reason, the crown had a funny reaction with Riana I'm the first to admit that, so if there's a way to fix all this great, but can we leave the children's tales for later?"

"Cluiun, how can you talk like that? You've seen some amazing things during your trips across Erien and you're telling me you aren't interested in the background of the stone?" Riana stared at him in sheer disbelief.

"I never said I wasn't interested lass, I love nothing better than a good tale, but I doubt we have the time to sit around exchanging stories right now." He offered her a smile. "Besides such things always sound better curled up next to a half naked wench with a few glasses of mead in her belly. I can see her now, fire red hair eyes bright with life and well padded er..." He glanced towards Riana, having the good grace to change track slightly. "Pillows, goose down pillows."

'Ah Cluiun, I grow to like you more each day. I wonder if you would ever consider finding a way to change into Dragon form? You'd make an interesting mate.'

"Has anyone ever told you Orent, that you have an unhealthy interest in mates, bedding practices and human males?" Cluiun didn't hide the grin. Few had the courage to banter so openly with a dragon but then again she'd not met that many dragons, or pirates.

'I wouldn't call it unhealthy, a good sex life helps keep the rest of the body stable. Ever noticed men can't seem to think straight if they haven't indulged for a while. Now Cluiun, you have to admit the first thing you sailors do when you arrive in port is go looking for a friendly lass or three to pass the time with.'

A few weeks ago she could never have imagined hearing a dragon bantering with anyone. Or being in the same room as a pirate, it just wouldn't have fitted into the small corner of the world as she knew it. "We're getting off track, what about the crown?"

'Yes, the crown. A days ride from here, at the edge of the sea, there is a stone circle. Rhodan, remember it from your childhood?'

"Yes, the one with the odd markings?" Rhodan held her tight, his voice a warm caress against her ear. Here, sitting on the bed, she could almost believe they were alone, recapturing their first night together. The feel of his hands about her waist, how they'd cupped her body, explored her with a tenderness she had almost forgotten existed in the world. There would be such moments again, soon. When the matters of the crown and Jeriah were done with she would know his touch, his kiss, the sensations that would follow as she clung to him, giving into the desire he had awoken.

'You need to take the crown and Riana there. She has the power in her blood to re-bound it to your line. It will not be easy, there will be pain for you both, but it can and must be done.'

"Pain?" She felt Rhodan's grip tighten about her waist as she spoke. "How could it cause pain?"

'You will be healing the rift between the crown and the royal line. It will take time, pull you in two different directions at once. I would not blame you for refusing to do this but you are the first in many generations that could be asked to take this risk.'

"How much of a risk are you asking my wife to take, Orent?"

There was always risk, in every aspect of life. She had found that out the hard way. Could she do it, face this danger, the pain Orent spoke of?

'More than I have the right to ever ask of you.' Orent sighed, the flick of wings within the large courtyard heard even through the windows. *'Forgive me, both of you. We can find another way. The pain, the risk of the magic backfiring through Riana, of both of you being killed, it is too much. Yet the chance to bond the crown to you, place you back where by birth you should have been. If the bond returned then the damage done by your father would be wiped clean. Not one Dragon would refuse a call for help. Not one would state "But this is the family that destroyed one of our own" There will be another way.'*

"There is no other way you know of?" Riana kept the fear from her voice, thinking carefully as she spoke. "Or you would have spoken of it. And this healing, it's why you are the only dragon that deals with those of the Dragon throne now?"

'Yes, something that happened many years ago, before Rhodan was born.'

"What happened to pull the dragons back, the legends speak of a bond so tight between Dragon kind and my family that nothing could ever break it." Rhodan slid Riana from his lap, settling her next to him. "I never heard of the breach, nor what could have caused such. If I am to take the throne when my father dies I need to know what happened and why."

'You need only know that it happened, Rhodan and that the way to fix it lays in your grasp. In one thing Cluiun is right, this is not the time for children's tales, but if this works I swear to you by the oldest dragon I will answer your

questions on this and many other matters.'

"Why not before, it's not just a matter of time is it?" Riana pressed. There was something in the Dragon's tone. A stress she'd not heard before.

'You know I may not answer that now, Riana. You've felt the call of the crown. What it can offer if you but let yourself be pulled to it. You know better than any other here the dangers present should the healing not take place.' It took a moment before she realized Orent spoke only to her. *'Trust me, Riana of the silver hair, daughter of the woods, Fae born child, you must trust me in this.'*

For Orent to keep something from Rhodan meant trouble, a deep old trouble, or worse news that her husband might not be strong enough to hear. But what that could be she had no way of guessing. Fear built within her stomach, threatening to overwhelm her, the weight of ages pressed down on her shoulders, so much now rode on her ability to heal a breach she knew nothing about beyond the fact it existed.

'When the time is right you have my oath he will be told.'

"Well now, I suppose you'll be off adventuring again without me. I don't know why you think it's fine to take Riana and Cluiun but leave me behind." Simon sniffed, dabbing his cheeks with the corner of the aqua linen handkerchief. "It's almost like you don't believe I could manage on such a trek. You're not even going that far. I'm heartbroken, cut deep, look at me, I'm a wreck you have me in tears again you brute."

"Simon, I'll only be gone for a few days at most." He tried not to look at the sniffling courtier, by now there would be smudges of make-up from the new black lines Simon had taken to painting under his eyes. Fashion Simon would call it. Not that he would admit why he followed the call of whatever fashions took over the dress of the court. A part of the game. "Orent, Riana and Cluiun have to come with me but I need you here. Haon, I don't trust him. Jeriah is bound to have left him behind to keep an eye on the workings of court."

"Hmph," Simon blew at the strands of hair that brushed down over his eyes. "I suppose I can understand that. He is an interesting piece of slime. Not half as complicated as he thinks he is. Over inflated ego. Not that uncommon, but smart enough and lucky enough to be a mild problem from time to time."

"Indeed, so I need you to watch him, make sure he doesn't strike against my father or my holdings whilst I'm gone." He tried to keep the concern from showing across his face. Just a few days away, it could be too much, leaving the court and his father open to further rumors. More rumors, just what his father needed to deal with. "What's he been up to?"

"He's been busy since Jeriah left, has a new interest, the lady of the moment is one Katrina. Not a major player in the court and she dabbles in petty attempts at heart games of her own. More men have lifted her skirts than a whore working the docks." Simon threw out the snippets of information, tucking the swatch of bright colored silk into his sleeve. "She might have had a chance of becoming a player, if she had ever learned the first rule. Never be public with your indiscretions if you are female. A man can get away with it, a woman cannot."

All too true, a few women could get away with their small affairs, but where a man would be congratulated for his adventures a woman could be ruined by them. Katrina, the name sounded familiar. "Dark haired woman, owns a stretch of land about three days ride from here, never bothers spending time there?"

"That's the one. Employs a group of people to run it for her and has been looking for a husband for a few years now. Silly chit thinks she's going to be the one to snare Haon. I can't wait until she finds out how wrong she is. Do you know she had the nerve to criticize one of my outfits last month, and this is the woman who never wears the right style of shoe and insists on dying her hair that awful black color. Washes her out. You'd think she have the common sense to look in a mirror from time to time."

"Has anyone ever told you that you can be more bitchy than a dozen women in a cat fight?" He glanced over at Simon, tying up the travel sack. "Don't get me wrong, I rely on the advice I get from you. No one understands the court the way you do, but have you heard yourself lately?"

"My darling boy, everyone expects me to be this way. If I didn't continue my little tirades against poor dress taste, whose spending the night with so and so's husband or wife or parading around in my newest creation people would assume I had taken ill. I have an image to keep up and I can tell you that there are times it's hard work." He smiled, smoothing off his silk tunic, plucking a small stray hair from one section. "I have a duty to keep my adoring fans babbling every time I walk into a room."

One day he'd get a straight answer from the man. Not today though, that had become obvious. Simon was everything he appeared to be, a flirt, whose taste in lovers fell into the category that Rhodan would rather not know about and his choice of clothing produced a mix of colors that had left him feeling ill on more than one occasion. So what was he missing?

"Why is it you want to come on these trips with me? It's not as though they are ones you'd enjoy. I don't stop around markets trying to pick out new colors for my wardrobe." He hefted the bag up from the bed, shouldering it. "They're hard riding, no baths, often nothing more than a brush for a privy, yet you keep asking me to let you come along? Have you ever even stepped outside of the palace walls since you took up residence here nine... no ten years ago?"

Maybe that wasn't entirely fair, he knew Simon did wander through the market place and rumor held that he had a lover out in the richer quarters of the city, but that was nothing compared to the rides across Erien.

"Oh I take a wander beyond the city from time to time. Nothing too strenuous you understand. Just a brief ride." Simon's eyes narrowed slightly, a tension forming about his shoulder that was gone a moment later. "But you're right. Bushes for privies, how positively revolting. Not even paper. Next you'll be telling me I'd have to sleep on the floor by some petty little camp fire."

"Where else did you think we slept?" Rhodan tried not to chuckle at the look of disgust he had been faced with.

"Inn's of course, Inns. What do you think they were built for? Decoration? Have we located a part of your education that was completely missed. I'm very disappointed in you." Simon gave a long low snort, the end of his nose wrinkling. "I really must attend to correcting your tutors. There appears to be some rather uncomfortable gaps there. I had thought so much better of you." He stalked across the room, looking around for something he could pick on. His eyes lit up as he reached over and tugged at the sack Rhodan had packed. "Look at this, just look at this. You have wonderful cases, mahogany wood, first grade leather and you go off gallivanting with a second rate sack that a peasant might use."

"It does the job. I'm not out there trying to look good." At least he'd found something to play around with. Better the sack than asking why he and Riana were heading out. What did Orent want them to do out at the stones? That part he didn't know, but he trusted the dragon beyond anyone else on Erien. She might have her own agenda from time to time, but she had never steered him wrong.

"Ever think that is where you are going wrong?" Simon walked slowly around him. "You're a prince dear boy, a prince, the heir to the throne. Isn't it about time that you started looking like one?"

Cluiun smiled, resisting the urge to pat the swaying ass of the maid as she sashayed past him carrying a tray of drinks. One thing you could rely on in a court was the constant supply of alcohol dispensed by pretty young things seeking husbands with the right connections.

Or dangerous men to pass the time of day with until the *right* man came along.

He was neither, though if they weren't leaving so soon he might have been open to entertaining a few of the court ladies.

Damn headache wouldn't shift. Even with the powders he'd reluctantly taken just to stop Riana from worrying too much. He could still feel it, the lump on the back of his head. Just about the right size to match the pommel of a sword. Not that he knew for certain who'd been behind the blow. Oh he had an idea, they all did. Haon or one of his men. Most knew they worked for Jeriah. No secret. Just how far that service went was the question.

He didn't like unknown quantities.

On ship they could mean the difference between surviving the storm and being claimed by it. Here a dagger between the ribs would be more likely. He didn't want to risk either.

Hm, Haon appeared to be in his element tonight. Waited on by two maids, a blond nearly in his lap and a dark haired woman lingering near the table. Nursing a bandaged hand with obvious over care. Each move, each slight and badly hidden wince was exaggerated. The sort of flinches that Cluiun knew were faked. A well practiced act.

He'd make a slip at some point. By then most of the women wouldn't care just as long as he looked their way from time to time. They even seemed content enough to share him. All but one.

Black hair, pale skin, a dye job that was too obvious with her skin tone. He'd seen cheap whores do a better job, but then again their looks where the first thing they traded on. The second, well he was certain more than a few women here practiced the same trade. They'd notice the poor attempt to change color and would use it as a weapon when they needed it. Human nature. Strike out with whatever blade you had to hand.

Dark hair bristled every time another woman looked at Haon. Fingers clenching, nails threatening to pierce her palms. She'd staked a claim. One the others ignored. One she expected Haon to honor. Interesting.

With a mug of mead, untouched, in one hand Cluiun moved through the hall, leaning against a pillar close to a card game. Poor hands, but a diversion most would accept he'd be interested in.

"We have business to attend to." Her words could have been mistaken for shards of ice.

"Impatient Katrina? We'll have plenty of time soon enough." Haon curled his *injured* arm around the blond. "I don't want to appear rude to our guests here."

Fine lines tightened about her narrow lips. "Your guests. Not mine."

"You could always go and wait in your room until I am done." He gave Katrina little more than a brief glance.

"Or in your room."

"I catch you trying to enter my room without my permission and your life will take a twist in a manner not even your depraved soul can handle." If her voice had carried shards of ice, his had become the north wind. "Do I make myself clear, Katrina?"

If the woman had had any color remaining in her face it would have drained. "Completely."

"Good, I wouldn't want to have to remind you how I dislike being displeased."

Cluiun felt his grip tighten about the mug. If there was one thing he disliked more than anything else it was a bully. And Haon fit the bill.

"I wouldn't do that." Katrina's voice dropped into a shaky whisper.

"No, I don't think you would. But no harm in reminding you. Is there?" The coldness lifted, an all too smooth smile gracing his lips. "I wouldn't want you to think I had misled you about something this important."

"Of course. I didn't mean to make it seem otherwise my love."

"Your what?" His eyes narrowed, any warmth he had shown her vanished in a heartbeat. His grip on the blond tightened until she squealed in fright. "What did you call me?"

"A slip of the tongue, nothing more. My apologies. I was thinking about something else." The words tumbled from her lips, weight shifting from foot to foot. Fear. Nothing else would have made the woman apologize that quickly.

"A slip that will not happen again."

"No, of course not. Never again." Katrina chewed on her bottom lip, one hand moving to her loose hair, fingers tangling in dark locks. "I'm a little more tired than I had thought I would be. Perhaps it would be best if I retire for a short while?"

Cluiun tensed against a pillar, the pretense of watching the card game long since passed. Not that it mattered. Haon didn't care who saw. Arrogance like that tended to get a man killed sooner or later.

He wasn't here just for Jeriah's benefit, the man had his own agenda.

"No, I don't think so. I'd prefer your company." His grip on the blond eased, a mocking smile returning to his lips. "In fact I'd prefer your company right there, where you are, silent of course. Perhaps that will encourage you to think before speaking again."

Men like that gave the rest of the gender a bad name.

"You want to leave now. After Jeriah has fled? Just up and wander off on some jaunt?" Justin growled. Anger flaring brighter by the moment. "What has gotten into you. Jeriah has left the castle. You've proven he was ready to try and take the throne even if we can't announce this to court as yet and instead of solidifying your position you want to up and leave?"

"Father I..."

"No, I won't permit it." The older man was beyond reason. Riana hadn't known him that long but flashed within his eyes. Anger. No, sheer fury. "You will stay here, formalize your marriage for the court and deal with the outcome from Jeriah's betrayal."

"Will you please give me a moment to explain." Rhodan struggled to remain calm.

"There is nothing to explain. I know what you're like. Gods alone knows I've watched you over the years."

This was going well. Not. Like two children squaring off in a courtyard. Neither one prepared to give the other true time to think.

"And kept your distance, shut me out. Weren't those your words?"

"You insolent pup. How dare you!"

"I'll dare far more Sirrah. You've been the worst kind of father any in my position could have been cursed with."

Words flew like weapons, cutting deeper with each new strike.

"And you've been the dutiful son? I might have been better proclaiming Jeriah as my heir after all." Justin cleared the distance between them. "He at least knew where his duties lay instead of spending his time wenching, drinking and traveling across the face of Erien. You've done little more than flout your bond to the Lady Orent since she chose you."

Rhodan's fist clenched. He'd pushed too far. Any moment the first blow would be struck, the first real blow and the breach would never be healed. She couldn't remain silent.

"Your Majesty, please. If you will not listen to Rhodan I beg you heed my words."

"This doesn't concern you lady."

"But it does, your Majesty. Not just because Rhodan is my husband but because the crown, the stones in it, react to me."

"Crown? Stones?" He faltered, the anger easing for a moment. Reason reclaimed his eyes. "What is she talking about Rhodan?"

"The same information I was trying to tell you about and you wouldn't give me the chance to. We've found the crown. In Jeriah's room."

"The fake crown. I know. The guards told me. Part of the reason we can now prove what he was doing. But I don't see what this has to do with a trip away from the castle."

Why did men make it so difficult at times? Life would have been so much easier if he'd just have listened first and exploded later. "Not a fake crown, your

Majesty. The missing crown. Your family crown."

"I don't under…" He blinked. Twice. Silent but for a soft gulp for air. Beads of sweat glistened across his brow. Lips moved without sound. A swallow that turned into a sharp cough before he finally spoke again. "The crown of the ancestors?"

"The soul gem." She couldn't be sure he meant the same one, but the odds were in her favor.

"It's just a myth." The words should have been a protest, but lacked conviction. "That's what my father told me."

"I'm told some places still believe dragons to be myths." Riana tried to feel some measure of sympathy for the older man. Tried and failed. "It's real. I've seen it. Touched it. Lady Orent confirmed it to be real."

"The crown has been missing for generations." He half mumbled the words. At least his desire to argue with Rhodan had faded. "Jeriah had it? Good Gods. If he'd worn it, on the throne, then all hell would have broken loose. I'm not sure his blood line claim would have been strong enough. The entire castle could have been destroyed." He shook with each new word. Fear replacing the anger.

"Destroyed?" Rhodan moved back towards his wife. "Orent didn't mention that."

Orent hadn't mentioned a lot of things by the sound of it.

"Riana shouldn't have been able to touch it. Not this close to the throne. Neither should Jeriah and I doubt he left it laying in a box." The older man sat back down, rubbing his temples. "I only know the myths. The legends that my own father told me about. There's no written information about the crown. I don't think anyone thought the crown would re-appear."

"Well I was able to hold it. Just for a moment." Her fingers tingled at the memory, the soft tug of the artifact, of the soul gem, replayed over in the back of her mind. "Well touch would be closer to the truth but there was a danger to it. Orent made that clear. There's something wrong with the crown and that's why we need to go. Orent knows the way to heal the breach between the crown and your family line. Do you really think this is a chance we can let slip past?"

Riana took a slow breath. Each time she mentioned the ancient creation she felt it. The pull to find it. Seek it out. Place it on her brow. It wanted her. No, not just her. Anyone with the right blood.

'Now you begin to understand.'

Understand?

'It's not just who you are, or who you've wed. The blood that flows through your veins is as vital to the line of the Dragon Throne as that which pulses through Rhodan's body.'

"Heal the breach. Is that possible after all these years?"

"Orent thinks so." Rhodan pulled Riana close against his side. "I'm not about to start distrusting her word now. Not after so many years."

"I wouldn't ask you to, son." Justin's voice had lost its edge, almost as if a form of shock had settled in. But it was more than that. She could see it, in his eyes. Calculations working too rapidly at the back of his mind, shutting off other reactions until he spoke in a low, dull tone. "Where do you have to go?"

"The stone circle, the one you used to take me to." Tension seeped from her husband's body. A sideways look her way enough to confirm her belief. He didn't want to fight with his father. It had become a habit. A bad one.

Maybe in time they would be able to heal the breach between them, but it wouldn't be over night. And she knew enough to understand that it might never happen. At least there would be an uneasy truce. In public if nothing more they would show a united front.

'You can't choose your relatives, Riana. But you can make choices on how you live with them or not.'

"Makes sense. It's been a place of power, according to legend, since before our family built the castle." Justin nodded slightly, half lost in thought as he spoke. Uncertainty blended with reluctant acceptance across his silk creased face. "I don't like it, but I understand why it must be done and why it has to be done now."

Chapter Twelve

A harsh jolt rocked him against the back of the coach. Adding to his growing ill mood. If something existed that would have brought him out of the foul temper that now wrapped about his form, other than his cousin laying dead at his feet, he didn't know what it could be.

So close. So very close. Another few hours and Rhodan's life would have spilled across the stones. A few low gasps for that last needful breath of air and then death. A crown. A place in power and history.

He could have been in his rooms, waited on by servants and lackeys. Every whim catered to. Instead he was forced to flee like a common criminal. He'd never live this down. Unless. He could turn it. Make it seem as though he had left for the good of the Kingdom. To avoid the court being torn apart by the petty manipulations of a jealous heir. Enough would buy it. More than a few would run with the story and turn it into Rhodan framing Jeriah. All without him lifting a finger.

Ripped away from him.

Patience. A wonderful if inconvenient skill.

The coach jolted, wheels hitting pot holes or ruts. Either one. It didn't matter. The result was the same sending him half out of his seat in a flurry of curses.

"Watch where you're driving." He growled towards the window once he'd steadied himself.

"Sorry Milord. Fog. Came out of no where." The driver called back. "Taking it slower now. Can't see the road."

Fog? Unusual but not unheard of this close to the coast. Still it shouldn't have blocked the vision of the driver. Not that fast. The air had been clear but a few moments earlier. Frowning he moved to the window, half leaning out to get a better look. If this slowed them down too much they'd run the risk of being caught if Justin had sent the watch out after them. Not what he needed.

Wisps of clinging grey white dampness enfolded the coach. Chilling fingers seeking to drain the warmth from his body. Wonderful. How to add to an already bad mood in one easy move. Strange, it had been so clear one minute. Not unheard of though, for fog or weather to change with little or no warning.

The coach slowed, jolting ever few moments. A sharper bump forced him back to the floor of the coach. Bruises forming under fine velvet. Breath knocked from his body as the wheels threatened to crack under the force of the last jolt. Another little problem he would have to discuss with his cousin when the moment arose.

"Milord, we'll need to stop. I can't see my hand in front of my face." The driver's voice held more than a hint of fear. "If we continue we're going to loose a wheel or worse."

Worse. He didn't need to hear things like 'worse' right now. "Okay, find a place to stop. Shelter of some kind. A few trees will do." Not what he had had in mind for the night.

"Yes Milord." His voice sounded strained. With the thickness of the fog it didn't surprise him. At least the coach was still in one piece. Even if he were bruised he'd reward the driver. Better marked up then trapped in a damaged coach, or dead.

Oddly enough death was a state of life he wanted to avoid as long as possible.

Jagged fingers of fog drifted in through the open windows. Grasping at the wood only to move further in. Strange. Was fog supposed to act that way? Might have just been his imagination but it really did seem to move with a purpose.

He'd gone too long without eating. That made more sense. Fog wasn't a living thing.

So why did it reach for him?

He frowned, jaw clenching until his teeth ground down. Just fog. Nothing more than overactive imagination. But that didn't stop him from edging back against the chair when the fingers clawed out for him.

Not fast enough.

Cloth parted. Lines of blood marked his arm between the slices.

A joke. Had to be. A magical based prank.

Reality settled in, bringing with it pain. A low hiss slipped from his lips, one hand pressed against the cuts. Pranks didn't burn. Didn't bleed. Real. Gods, this was real.

"Milord! I can't see through the fog. There's something in this. Claws. Claws everywhere. I can't..!" The drivers words turned into screams. The coach lurched. Hitting left with a sharp jolt. Screams. Both from the driver and the horses.

No time to think about them. He had to save himself. Dispensable. It described the driver and horses well enough. Not something he would ever be. No matter how many other lives it cost.

Jeriah twisted, trying to avoid the next strike. Tried and failed. New lines. New pain. Clawed marks parting the flesh of his back. Not deep. At least he hoped. The door. Had to get out. But where? Into the fog? More vile fingers seeking to rend flesh from bone. No. Not that. Another way.

Two, three. No four sets of claws closed in on him. Trapping him in the corner of the coach. No where left to run. They lashed out, slower this time. Taunting. Then nothing. They just lingered there as the blood dripped from his back, his arm. Forming sticky, growing pools on the plush cushions. His blood.

Where had the riders gone? The men he'd been traveling with. Not enough noise out there to account for them. Where had they gone? If they were in range of the noise they would have come to help him. Unless they couldn't hear him. Or the coach driver. Far enough away that the screams couldn't be heard. Too far to get to his aid with any decent amount of speed.

"Did you really think you could slip away from my anger little Jeriah?"

"Arinnana." A hissed word. Anger he took no attempt to hide.

"You were expecting a pretty little dream goddess instead?" A face formed in the fog, smiling, seductive. "Or a dryad ready to lull you into a welcoming embrace?"

"I didn't kill him." Stupid. She'd been angry. More so than any woman he had met before. Maybe he had been foolish running but staying would have meant more danger than he had been prepared for.

"No, but you were going to. Then you ran. Left behind something my Lord wanted kept away from the Fae girl." Wisps of fog curled into human like form. Naked. Fog in the image of a naked woman. Interesting. Not a trick he'd seen before. Then again he'd never been attacked by a fog spell before tonight either. "You ran without ever thinking beyond saving your own worthless life."

Something left behind that Kaleb wanted? If he'd known that it would have been brought with him. A bargaining point. If one could ever presume to hold such a thing against a god. Of course, she could always be lying. With Arinnana one could never be entirely sure. "What are you claiming I left behind?"

"The crown. Silly little human. You went to all that trouble. Laid down plans, gathered resources, even found yourself a nice crown then you left it all behind. Not even bothering to grab the one thing you prized in your material possessions. Why do you think that is?"

The crown. He'd meant to grab it. Until that moment he'd been certain it had been shoved into his carry sack. Out of everything he owned in the small suite of rooms that crown had meant the most to him. "I thought..."

"You didn't think. That's the problem. You seldom do Jeriah."

"This is why you killed the driver, the horses? Over a crown?" Why did Kaleb need it? He was missing something here. It was a pretty little piece of jewelry, but a dozen crowns would have been the same. He could have had a new one made up just as he had this one.

Hadn't he?

No. He hadn't had it made. Found. He'd found it. Where? He couldn't remember. It had been there for a while. Sitting on one of his dressers in a box. A simple box. But where...

"No, those I killed because I wished to. Nothing more. Nothing less. Haven't you ever killed something just for the sheer pleasure of the moment?" She smoothed down the mockery of wisp like clothing that now formed over her body. "You should try it some time. Taste the fear that drips from them."

"Sick bitch."

"By whose standards? Yours?" A near playful smile tugged across her lips. "You've no idea how sick I can be little man. One day you might get the chance to find out. You might even enjoy it."

His stomach rolled. Even formed from fog he could almost see the look in her eyes. "I think not."

"Pity. Still you might change your mind later." She reached out towards him, tracing the line of his jaw with a cold damp finger. "The crown Jeriah. You didn't have it made, it found you. Then abandoned you when you proved to be of no use to it."

"Crowns don't make decisions like that. They're inanimate objects." Did she think him stupid? "I just forgot to pick it up."

"In your hurry to save your life?" That mocking smile had his fists clenching, ready to strike out. "Oh dear, you really don't understand what you've gotten yourself involved in. Do you?"

"I'm not going to fall for this."

"For what?"

"Your attempt to make me feel foolish." Could he hit a being made from fog? No, his fist would go right through her. But she'd managed to strike out at him. So there had to be a way to act. Blood dripped from his arm, slower now, but a steady loss of blood. He couldn't avoid any blows she tried to send his way. Had no way of defending himself. So why was he still alive? "You're not going to kill me, or you'd have done it already. Why are you here?"

Disappointment appeared for a moment. A pout. Then it was gone. "Why to remind you not to cross me again Jeriah. Why else. You're right. If I had planned on killing you I would have just done it."

"So why are you here?"

"A warning." She shrugged, her form dissipating slowly. "Nothing more. Don't cross me again."

"All this just to warn me. No. I don't think so. You're testing what you can do." Jeriah brushed one finger tip over the marks on his arms. "And the men who were with the coach. I didn't hear them scream so you cut me off from them. At least for a short time."

"A short time," that shrug again. "They'll be here soon enough. You'll need new horses, a new driver. And I wouldn't look too closely at the remains unless you have a very strong stomach. There's not a lot left of them."

Power. All about the show of power. Not just to him. This was too much just to be about him. What was he missing?

"I understand. And the crown. You want me to go back and get it?"

"No. We'll find another way to collect it. You'd just better hope we don't run out of uses for you Jeriah. If my Lord ever feels you can no longer fulfill a part of his plans then you die. Slowly. At my hands." She reached out, cupping Jeriah's cheek. Real. Cold, cruel fingers. Fog made. But real. Nails that he knew could cut. Had cut. They still burned. Scars. He could live with scars just as long as he remained alive.

All this just to prove a point.

Foolish. He knew that. She didn't. Good, he had a chance at leverage on her. Just not right now.

"Run away to your safe little home. Sit there in the hopes I can't follow you and flinch every time the shadows move. You'll never know for certain if the fog, rain, shadows or the wind are really harmless or another message. Another lesson for you to learn." Her touch faded, pulling back. Fog parting into soft shreds that vanished with a soft puff of wind.

Gone. Nothing left but the scratches and blood. He could believe that, just as long as he avoided looking at the mess that remained from his driver and the horses.

"Believe me, this is one lesson I'll learn very well indeed."

Dead. He was dead. How could that be? He felt alive. Well mostly. Just a few things didn't quite feel the way they were supposed to and he could remember the feel of the knife slicing across his throat. That brief moment of pain, then calm. A calm so deep he'd sunk into it.

No bright lights. No welcoming embrace. Just darkness after that.

An imp. Wonderful. Just what would that mean in the long term. Kaleb had spoken of other imps. Creatures like the one he'd sold his soul to. Is that what imps did with their days, steal souls?

Strange, for a dead man he felt oddly alive. He still breathed, or thought he did. Still felt the cold and riding for more than an hour left his ass feeling odd. Bruised. He preferred coaches but Kaleb had provided a horse. He wasn't about to argue with a God. Weird that, a few days ago he'd have laughed at the idea of either gods or demons. Now he had spoken to one, and was the other.

What did imps do with their lives? Afterlives. Whatever it was he'd become.

Go back to the castle. Find Justin. Play up what he'd been through at Valer's castle, be the big dramatic hero just as he'd planned. Only this time he wouldn't be playing it up quite as much. He'd died. Wonderful. But if he did this one little task for Kaleb then it would all be over. He'd get his life back. Be a hero. Get Riana and the castle and be the lord he was meant to be. Simple really.

A crown. Not even the crown Justin wore. Just some simple piece of costume jewelry the God wanted. A test? Would make sense. If he completed this task there might be one or two others, and rewards. Other rewards when he'd been given his life back.

First thing he was going to do was kill that damn girl in the farm. She'd still be there. Lingering in the area. People like that didn't wander off. Once he had the wench she'd die. Slowly. Insane or not he wasn't going to let her get away with killing him.

Gods that sounded odd.

Was he dead, or undead?

Not that it mattered either way.

A long ride, or would have been. The horse seemed to be moving faster than they

should. Another gift from Kaleb no doubt. A demon spawn mount? Did such things exist? Well now he knew about demons and gods he didn't doubt so quickly. A god could call on a demon horse, or whatever it was. What should have taken a full day's travel had been cleared in less than a few hours. Fields, houses, farms, they sped past in moments.

Weird. He hadn't noticed it at first. Now he had the horse seemed to move faster yet, but still the same steady rock. They were moving, at greater speed with each stride, yet the stride itself didn't change. He'd figure it out eventually. Maybe. Or find someone who could explain it to him.

His stomach rolled, watching the flashing landscape didn't agree with him. Needed to find a way to...

Slow down. They were slowing down. Could Kaleb read his mind?

No, not the God. He was doing this. The horse, demon or not, was obeying his whims. What else could he do? Imps, demons, they had power. So what other powers did he have access to?

What else could he do?

He frowned, focusing. Wanting the horse to stop. For a moment longer it continued, then shuddered to a stop. A complete stop. No snorts, whinnies, no noises of protest. Nothing at all. It just stopped, not even lowering its head with the need to gulp in air.

Well, maybe demon steeds didn't breathe real air. Or eat for that matter. What could they do? If they didn't need to eat, or breathe, or need rests from long trips maybe it didn't need to run on the ground either? Hey he didn't have to give it verbal commands so the laws of reality didn't apply.

Only one way to find out.

Clouds, low level clouds. Pretty in an odd sort of way. What would it be like to ride over the top of them?

Proud, ebony, a bold bright steed. Noble, demon or not, unreal or not it was the sort of horse he'd have given his right arm for in another life. Perhaps being dead had advantages. A good horse, money, fame. Could he die? No, Kaleb had made that pretty clear. The other imps could rip him apart and then watch him heal so they could do it all over again. So death was out of the question.

It moved. A shudder. Breaking into a brisk trot. Nothing strange about that right? Except they headed up into the air. Hooves moving through the air, barely touching across the clouds. They leveled out, racing along the tops of the first layer of clouds. He'd never even dreamed of such a thing.

Rhodan and his dragon. People like that had the chance to fly. Maybe a few of the Fae born kind, he couldn't be sure what type of powers they had. But people like him. No they didn't get to fly.

He wasn't just a person anymore. A demon. Imp. Creature of the damned. It didn't matter. He had power now, ability. No longer a second rate Squire getting by on the reputation of his father, or others. He was someone. Finally someone.

Strange how these human's took delight in the simplest of things. Guinelia sat rocking in a corner, clutching the remains of a wedding dress, cackling in delight each time she tore a little more from it. He'd never used the word cackling before now, but it suited the situation and the human involved. Her grip on what human's classed as sanity had crumbled since he'd claimed her as one of his servants. Not that it mattered. Insane but usable.

Arinnana was another matter. Sane, bright, eager to learn. She might become a small threat one day. But not just now. She had a long way to go in learning how to use the powers he had gifted her. The little show off scene with Jeriah had been but a part of that. A warning to her mother? It would fit with the little power play between the two women.

Expendable described them both. Their greed, powers, grasp on the world. Nothing about them put them in the do not destroy category. Pity really. He hadn't bound a non expendable servant to his will in over ten centuries.

Riana held promise. If he could tear her away from that damn dragon and the crown. Neither of which were very likely. Dragons protected vulnerable Fae and human kind. And this one, well he had no doubt Orent knew some of the potential that burned within the core of the Fae girl. Just touching the stones would have been enough. If he'd felt it then Orent would have also.

Oh he knew about the black dragon. How could he not. The oldest of Dragon kind to venture outside of their own realm. He'd not dealt with her directly and for that he was grateful. Head on against an elder black dragon in a time of strife might call the rest of her kind out. Even those who wanted little or nothing to do with humans. A risk he wasn't prepared to take this time.

There were a few things that even a God would be wary of, but elder dragons numbered among them.

"Daddy?" Soft, low, the voice pulled him out of his thoughts. A new voice. Not the two women that now served him. But another female. Younger this time. Blood covered didn't do her justice. Long dark hair, matted from now congealed blood. Spots of it that flaked from her face, arms and hands. Her peasant dress, a simple enough one half suited for working in the fields, had been splattered with it.

"You can enter, child."

"Where's my father?" No trace of fear in either her voice or words. She had to have seen the destruction in the castle. The remains of those that had been caught. Ah, yes. Denial. A form of insanity. What other type of human would enter the castle now, or remain behind.

He seemed to be collecting unstable human females.

"Your father? Now why would you come looking for him here?" For once he kept his voice low, almost soft, welcoming. She exuded a form of calm. An innocence wrapped around the heart of a killer. She'd flip in a second and they'd never see it coming.

"He came here, said he'd come home for supper. Never did. Where is he?" She took a step further in. "The bad man, the thief, he said everyone was dead. I don't like liars."

Delicious. She'd dispatched Bevery. Such a useful child. "Ah my dear, I'm afraid he wasn't lying. They are all dead as no doubt you saw when you walked in. But they've gone to a better place. No more pain. No hunger. Your father's quite happy there my dear."

"But he promised he'd be back. He doesn't break promises like that." Her bottom lip trembled, tears welling in soft blue eyes. "He's always come home before. Please, where is he? I need to see him, to tell him. He'd be so proud of me. I killed the thief you see. Did just what he'd told me to do."

A part of her knew, even accepted her father was dead, but the rest of her mind clung to the idea of life. Hope. Normally he would have taken great delight in crushing that hope. Not this time. She had potential. "Can't you see him?"

She frowned, squinting as she moved further into the hall, bare feet near silent against the stone. "No. Please Sir, I need my father."

"And you shall have him dear one." Just a touch, a slight push. That's all it took to seep into her mind. All she seemed to think about was that one man. Oh there were fleeting images of others. Younger, older, children, even Bevery, but her thoughts kept returning to the grey haired man. A little more. He just needed a little longer. There. A shift, little more than a fraction of the power at his beck and call. An illusion only the girl would see.

"Father?" Confusion lingered behind the lone word.

"Yes. Who else would it be?" Had he got the voice right? He prided himself on such matters.

"I thought someone else... that I'd been..." He pushed, just a little further into her already confused mind. A touch here, tweak there. "Father, where have you been? You never came home." Her fists balled, resting on her hips.

"But I am home my lass, we both are."...

Chapter Thirteen

A bag lay half open on the bed, little more than standard travel sacks as the young couple sorted through what they would need.

"Not like we'll be gone for very long, not with using Orent to travel there." Rhodan frowned as he tugged open one of the sacks. "Two days at most. Maybe less."

'A lot depends on what resistance if any, we meet on the way there. Once we're at the circle I doubt anyone can stop us.' The ancient dragon yawned halfway through her words. *'Should have got a little more sleep last night.'*

"Late night oh great beast? Too much gallivanting around with other's of your kin?" Rhodan glanced towards the window.

'Beast?'

"Would you prefer lizard?" Rhodan teased.

'Lizard!' She hissed, her nose pressing against the open. *'If we weren't bonded I'd fry you just for that comment.'*

"Has she ever done that? Fried someone I mean?" Cluiun winked at the Dragon, unable to avoid noticing the small trails of smoke curling upwards from her nostrils. He could think of more than a few members of court who would be all the better for meeting the business end of the dragon.

"Once before, well in my memory."

'He had it coming. Great brute of a man, kept trying to get in the way of things.' She snorted. *'But that doesn't mean you get to call me a lizard, or a beast. Maybe I should drop you on the head a few times during the trip.'*

"This trip, just what will we be doing once we get to this circle?" Cluiun leaned against the closed door his arms lazily crossed about his chest. "Don't get me wrong, I understand that the crown, for whatever reason has to be taken to the stones in order to heal whatever it is between you and the crown. I'm just not sure how you're going to do it."

'Riana will do it, she and she alone will repair the bond.'

"How?" Not that he didn't trust the great dragon but there were a few matters he needed to straighten out in the back of his mind.

'By invoking the magic of the circle.' Orent paused a moment longer before her voice rumbled at the back of their minds. *'She and Rhodan will enter the circle, with the words I will give her, and the channel of power the stones control the bond will be healed.'*

"So let me get this right, you only actually need Riana and Rhodan present for this?" He nodded towards the newly weds as they halted in their packing for a moment. "You don't need me there."

"Cluiun, you don't mean to stay behind do you? We need you there." Riana frowned, looking between the two men. "You've become our dearest friend, our alley."

"Yes, but as such perhaps it would be best if stayed behind. You'll need a set of eyes here, more than Simon can provide and I am well aware he has been your eyes and ears in other times Rhodan." Cluiun rubbed his thumb over the scars that marked his face. "Haon and the woman he seems to be controlling, Katrina, they might cause more problems than expected if we all left at the same time."

"I trust Simon."

"Not saying you shouldn't, Rhodan. Just think about this for a moment. What if he needs help, back up in some way? Or he's dealing with a high court matter when Haon makes his move?" Cluiun moved away from the door and sat down on the edge of the bed. "You don't need me with you at the circle, you will need me back here, trust me on this one."

"You saw something that made you uncomfortable?" Riana rested one hand on his shoulder. "When you were in the court?"

"Yes, more than uncomfortable, as though someone was running a blade down my back. He's dangerous. Perhaps more than Jeriah is aware of. If you don't have someone watching your back whilst you're away then you might come back to find you don't have a crown, a throne or a father waiting for you."

"Haon isn't that powerful." Rhodan protested.

"Maybe he wouldn't be if it weren't for the women that would do anything to gain a moment in his arms. If I didn't know better I'd say the man has a touch of the Fae blood in him. Or perhaps another strain. He has an ability to charm any woman, or close to, that he sets his sights on. More than that, from just what little I've seen, seducing them, claiming them, seems to make him stronger than ever."

'He's not Fae, I can sense them easily enough thanks to the bonds of blood. But there are others on Erien who might be able to persuade men and women to their sides in the manner he does. Something to look into when there is time to do so. And I agree, someone should remain behind to watch over things here.'

"Just what sort creatures could have that hold over others, that aren't Fae I mean?" Riana glanced curiously between the dragon and Cluiun.

'Shaman gifted for one, but very few of those who follow the shamanic paths will misuse those gifts. Those who do loose themselves are more likely to during a shape shift. No, this has the feel of something else, if there is anything there. Demon kind can persuade and there are soul drinkers.'

"Vampires you mean?" Cluiun felt the hair rise on the back of his neck. "Those are just legends."

'Hmm are you sure about that? There are some on Erien that would say dragons, gods and powers of the Fae are nothing more than legends.' Orent smirked, licking an incredibly long tongue over her lips. *'However you know very well that not everything in life that is named a myth, superstition or legend turns out to be that.'*

"Well now, I guess I'll be keeping a very close eye on Haon after all."

Vampires, crowns that demanded her attention, a marriage she hadn't planned on, powers she could barely control, what else would suddenly force it's way into her life? Riana glanced over towards Rhodan as her husband sorted through what he would need for the trip, reluctant to bring up her concerns.

It didn't silence them though.

What if she couldn't do it, if she couldn't heal the breach between the crown and Rhodan's line? No, she couldn't think that way, just letting the doubts gain a greater hold on her heart would only serve to make matters worse.

'You'll do just fine, Riana. Everything you need is already in the back of your mind.' Orent rumbled softly at the back of her mind. *'You're stronger now than you were even a few days ago. I see it, feel it, sense it about you. You just have to believe in yourself. I know it's more than you ever dreamed you would have to face in life but think about it. If you weren't strong enough, with everything that has happened, you'd already be dead.'*

That sounded simple enough, so why didn't she believe it?

'Doubts are a very human and fae aspect of life. Even dragons have them from time to time, but I wouldn't let pet in on that, he might well try to take advantage of the situation. You know what men are like, give them too much information and they find themselves unable to do anything but run with it.'

It took every ounce of self control he owned to keep a straight face in place and not give into the laughter that bubbled in the back of her throat.

'Another day, two at the most, and you'll be able to relax at least for a while. Just follow through on your instincts when we're at the stones. Listen to that inner voice, it won't let you down.'

Riana glanced towards the window then back towards the still busy Rhodan. Wonderful. She'd just got married, this was supposed to be the time of her life when she was enjoying her new husband's company, getting to know him, setting up their life together and instead they were going to have to spend the next day or so fixing some mystical bond between the crown and her husband's family. Not exactly her idea of a honeymoon.

'What, are you trying to tell me that the excitement of storms, magic, gods chasing you just pales next to a few days in bed curled next to a half naked human. I really don't understand your kind one little bit. Though if Rhodan ever got around to letting me peek in on you both I might be a little more sympathetic.' Orent smiled, her face pressing to the window for a moment. 'I suppose you could always talk to him about that for me?'

'Orent, why do you need to ask him? You could take a look into his mind at any time you wanted to.'

A soft chuckle bubbled at the back of her mind. 'Well now, if I did that I'd lose one of my chances to bug him.'

"Orent, you're a wicked wicked female, did anyone ever tell you that?"

Rhodan frowned, looking from his wife to the dragon. "Did I miss something here?"

"Oh nothing of importance love." She smiled, barely keeping her own need to laugh under control. "Nothing I would worry about, just girl talk."

"Between you and Simon every time I hear the phrase girl talk I end up wincing." He cleared the distance between them, circling her waist as he pulled her close, lips brushing over her own in a soft caress. "Just one of those things we'll have to talk about when we arrive home."

Talking. Oh they'd be doing a lot more than just talking.

"Well if you two ladies are quite finished with your little gossip session perhaps we could be on our way?" Only the smile that tugged at the corners of Rhodan's lips prevented his words from becoming hurtful.

"Everything ready?" Riana stood, smoothing down the tunic and pants she had borrowed from her husband. Just one ride on Orent had taught her that riding a dragon back in a dress wasn't the wisest of ideas. Too damn cold, even sandwiched between Cluiun and Rhodan she'd felt the chill.

"As we'll ever be." Rhodan shouldered the pack. "Orent, we'll meet you in the courtyard."

'I'm already there my sweet pet.'

Haon. The more he thought about the man the tighter his muscles knotted across his shoulders. Jeriah was one thing, slime like that he'd dealt with a dozen times over, but Haon and his tactics, using women, tossing them aside, or keeping them dancing on the end of his strings sat ill at ease with Cluiun. Strange in many ways, he'd been pulled up by Joran a dozen times over about letting his hero complex get the better of him any time he saw a woman being ill used. Foolish when one part of being a pirate might well include enslaving men and women alike.

Except he didn't lie about it. He didn't try and hide what he was doing or could do if the need called for it. Every foul deed he had committed was right there, out in the open and for the most part he didn't regret any of it.

Yet Haon lied, hid and seduced his way through the court. Small tugs on heart strings, like a spider setting a trap for any pretty little creature that dared to look his way. Worse still he knew exactly what he was doing, played on their insecurities, their fears, needs, desires. Feeding from them...

Vampire? Could Orent be right about that? The man was driven by another need, to feed from the very emotions he evoked in the women he stalked? It would also have explained why they near fell at his feet. All but one, the one fire touched red head with a spirit that had blazed a path through the court and left Haon fuming, plotting to gain his revenge should the chance ever arise.

Pity the woman had left the court and returned to her own land, she would have been the perfect bait to urge Haon's schemes out into the open.

Instead he needed another way. Another way to trick Haon.

A small frown tightened across his brow as he leaned against the wall, watching the gaggle of women around Haon. All but one of them smiled, a woman he'd seen before with badly dyed black hair that had been forced onto the outer edge of the group. Her dark eyes were red rimmed, barely covered by a thick layer of make up, anger lingered as a dull red coal in her gaze, a gaze that never left Haon despite her obvious lack of favor with him at the moment.

Perhaps there was an answer after all. Katrina.

The idea of using the woman, of stooping to that level, sat ill at ease with him, but when he was looking at a man like Haon and the trouble he could cause then Cluiun was about ready to take any option that came his way.

If nothing else it would end the hero to the rescue comments from Joran. If he ever got the chance to tell his old first mate what had happened.

She lingered on the edge of the group of women that surrounded the lazy eyed Haon. Ignored even by the other women, no one even glanced her way. Interesting. She hadn't been sent away, but it had been made very clear that she was no longer one of the chosen. Something had happened. The question was what, and how could he find out.

Simon. Out of all of the men and women in the castle he was the only one left that would be able to help him out here. He knew everyone within the castle. Each man and woman, their weaknesses, their interests, and how to use them. Not that Simon had used that information for anything except keeping Rhodan out of trouble as far as Cluiun could figure out, but he had little doubt the flamboyant courtier would bend over backwards in order to help him out now.

"Thought I'd find you here." Simon smiled as he settled down on a long couch, leaning back against the thick cushions.

"They've left?" He nodded once towards the windows looking out on the courtyard. He couldn't be certain but he thought he'd heard the sounds of the Lady Orent lifting into flight just before he'd taken up position in the large room.

"A short while ago. All in those drab traveling clothes. Not sure how Rhodan thinks he could ever look the part of the prince dressed like that." He tapped one thoughtful finger against the side of his face. "I'll have to go back to basics with him, though I'm sure more than a few in court will put it down to some odd attempt to impress his new bride."

Hard not to smile when Simon started his little games.

"Going to need a little information from you, Simon." He nodded towards Katrina, keeping his voice low.

"Ah, the lady of questionable needs and poor judgment." Simon glanced for less than a heartbeat at the lonely Katrina. "I think I see where you're going with this, but it's a dangerous game. You might well find yourself with an unwanted admirer tagging after you for the rest of your life."

"I've had worse things happen to me." He could deal with that, it might take a little work to ease the woman down without destroying her completely but it was worth the risk. Wasn't it?

"You don't know the beast in question. Once she has the scent of her prey she isn't one to let go. Ever. Just look at how she's hanging around Haon. She's been tossed aside, cut out, and she's still there." Simon didn't even look towards Katrina as he spoke, keeping his voice as low as Cluiun's.

Simon had a point. Even dock women would have left by now, but she still remained on the edge of the group, watching, hoping for a small sign of approval from Haon. What sort of hold did Haon have over the woman? And what could he do to shake that free.

Dark hair, dark eyes, slightly over weight. The court fashions of the moment sat ill on her form, only seeking to accentuate her slight roll of her stomach. More than slight. Pasty faced under the make-up. Had she been so pale a few days ago? Hard to tell right now, but perhaps something had happened to drain her a little more, steal some of her energy. Life force? That would fit with the idea he was a vampire.

Foolish. Even with Orent's words he had a hard time believing such creatures existed. Still, she was right, he might have said the same thing about dragons at one point, despite all the evidence that they really did exist before he had met Orent. Just one of those wonderful facts about human beings. It was always easier to dismiss the fantastical than believe in them without proof. A little like the gods when he thought about it.

"There might be a way." Simon offered. "It's a long shot but it might just work. A blatant play for her, in front of Haon. Cause a fight. Everyone knows she's his property right now. Even though she's out of favor. He'd have no choice but to get in your face, do the macho thing. He might even forget that he's supposed to have a damaged wrist."

Interesting. That would fit in with everything he had seen so far from Haon. As little as that had been. He seemed the possessive type. More than that. Property. That's what he viewed the woman as. And he wasn't about to let her go, not in public, not when it meant letting another man steal what he'd claimed as his own. Good.

"Could get messy. A fight in the middle of the castle."

"I suggest we make it as nasty as possible then. Tonight. During the evening dance. There's normally one. With Rhodan away the King is going to want to make everything seem as if nothing is going on." Simon turned to face him fully. "Which means, dear boy, we're going to really have to do something about your dress. I can't imagine the guards letting you into the grand ball room looking like this can you?"

Smiling would have given the game away, or at least hinted that something was going on, but it took more control that he had thought he laid claim to not to smile at Simon's words. "I do believe you're right Simon, but I think I'd rather play on my image of being the bad boy of the court. It might just play in my favor in this."

For a moment the pink and purple dressed fop didn't speak, his gaze moving over the older man before a true smile claimed his lips. "I do believe you might have a workable idea there dear boy. And I might just have something that would fit you well for this. Very well indeed. Just need you to agree to a few things."

A few things? The image of himself dressed in pink, purple and feathers sprang to mind. Gods and Goddesses of the chaos pits what had he walked into?

"Don't stress yourself on this, and trust me. Put yourself into my hands, I believe I can mold you, turn you into the darkest pirate to ever enter the court." Simon pushed to his feet, nodding towards the doors. "Follow me oh bold bad pirate, feared wolf of the high seas."

"No pink."

"Oh Cluiun, my dear sweet Cluiun. I wouldn't dream of such a thing." Simon linked one arm through Cluiun's, walking him towards the door. "No pink, my word on it. But maybe, just maybe a dash of purple."….

Chapter Fourteen

"Bitch." Jeriah scowled, staring at the wreckage of his coach. They'd all gone, the horses, his men, everything. Thanks to that bloody woman. What did she think she was doing, using her magic, trying to frighten him, scaring away his men and the horses. Miles from anywhere and possibly hunted and she'd left him standing in the damn middle of no where without any other choice but walking to his home.

Where was he anyway?

Nearest place he could find some shelter had to be on the other side of the stone circle. Nothing much managed to survive out here, thanks to the dragons and their damn legends. Circles of stone, dragon spawn, Justin, Arinnana, and now Rhodan and his pet bride had his crown. Could anything else go wrong today?

They shouldn't have even taken this route. Inland, the road was supposed to have led inland. Had Arinnana changed where they had been as well? He wouldn't put anything past that creature now. Not after what she'd pulled in the coach, that mist, the claws. How had she suddenly garnered such power.

By becoming Kaleb's pet. His toy. A glimmer of the dark gods favor had been granted to her and with it more power than she might ever have laid claim to otherwise. He'd underestimated the woman. Not a mistake he would make again.

If he had the chance to make any further mistakes.

Storm coming in. No shelter. A long walk to even find a decent place to wait it out. Just what he needed to deal with.

Growling he turned towards the distant outline of the stone circle. How long had it been since he had visited it. Ten years, perhaps more? Rhodan had even avoided the place, so had Justin. Odd when you thought about it. Everyone knew about the runes, the history of the place, the weird legends. You would have thought with all that mystery that at least some investigation would have taken place around the area. But no, people stayed clear. Bad feelings, odd dreams, rumors that spoke of shadows that walked out from the stones, lightening that danced from one to the other during the full moon.

Foolish rumors.

Should be at least enough shelter there that he could catch his breath. And he had enough in the way of cloaks, blankets, perhaps a little food so he could hold up there for a few hours. Bah, men like him were not supposed to have to walk this sort of distance. Ride yes, be transported in luxury coaches, but never walk. Another matter he would have to seek retribution for. But from who?

Arinnana, yes, he'd beat it from her before slitting her throat.

If he could find a way to strip her of the power that Kaleb had granted her. If not then he'd find a way. Foolish woman. She'd learn soon enough. They all would. Riana would be his bride. Justin would die. Rhodan would live long enough to know his wife had squirmed willingly beneath Jeriah's body, then the crown would be his. Even that annoying pirate would be dealt with.

And Orent? Who cared? Without her bonded human she'd be in grief, easy to handle. After all a dragon she might be but she was still a female. Prone to emotions, which made her potentially easy to distract when the time arose. Good. They'd pay for it, for each painful step across the land. Every blister, each curse, he'd make them scream for mercy before he granted it. If he ever did.

Growling he searched through the coach, tugging out a small shoulder sack, filling it with two cloaks, water and some travel food. He needed to get away from the coach. Just incase the bitch tried to come back after him. Right now there was nothing here that could help to protect him from the woman. At least at the stone circle, if only a fraction of the rumors were true, he'd be able to use them to seek shelter not just from the elements but Arinnana.

Great, now he was clinging onto some foolish folklore in order to keep safe. What sort of lunacy was he letting himself feed into?

The winds tugged at his clothing, cold fingers snagging against his skin, the court wear offering little in the way of protection or warmth. He'd be chilled to the bone before he even reached the stones. Perhaps he would be better off staying with the over turned carriage, build a fire and hope that someone would come along and help him, or that one of the horses would return.

Not that he had much hope of that happening.

Bandits. There could be bandits, pirates, robbers around here. Patrolling the road. He'd be helpless out here.

Fear gripped his stomach, his hands clutching the bag as he glanced around quickly trying to peer into the distance searching for some sign of problems. Nothing. Still he couldn't take the risk. He needed to find a way clear now. Get out of here, plan revenge, build a fire, re-settle his life on the right track.

Damn storms. Picking up again. He didn't need this, didn't deserve this. He had everything in place, life, a chance to reach his goals.

With a low snarl he turned, shifting the sack on his shoulders, a thick cloak now fastened about his body, and began the long walk towards the distant hill. The stones he could barely see through the rain that now fell in cold lances from the heavy clouds.

Barely a hundred steps into the storm and he was soaked, nearly to the skin. Cold, he'd be more than that by the time he reached the shelter he hoped existed in the distance. Another set of wrongs he would have to seek retribution for from Rhodan. It all back tracked to him, that ignorant boy. He'd been given everything any many could want, could dream of, only to disregard it and glad about on that damn dragon instead of becoming the heir the land needed.

The bag rubbed against his back, ice shards disguised as rain drops scoured his cheeks. Might as well have been needles hidden in the rain instead, would have hurt just as much. His cheeks would be raw soon enough. Bleeding if his luck continued this way. Soft skin, he wasn't meant to be doing things like this. He should have been wrapped up in thick clothing, nursing a cup of mulled wine or mead before a raging fire. Listening to the sounds of the court in the background. Maybe with a pretty lass close to his knee, fingers kneading into his shoulders, rubbing out the tension.

Now there was an image he could sink into.

Soon enough. He'd be back where he belonged within a short time, he just had to make it through the night at most. Perhaps little more than a few candle marks of walking, then he'd find a cottage, a farm, something to hide out in. Demand a horse to ride back to his lands, the family retreat, it would be over and done with before the new day cracked it's first finger of light on the land.

If this was what being a demon meant, imp, whatever, he couldn't imagine why many others hadn't found a way to become one. The faster he wanted to move across Olain the quicker the horse moved. Fire collected about the hooves of the stead, wind tugged through his hair, eyes wild as he leaned across the neck of the horse laughing in the sheer joy of the moment. Alive, he may have been dead in the eyes of most, but he felt more alive than he had ever done before. Even the feel of fear, the emotions that had choked his throat as he had stood before the beast in the castle had faded.

Power, life, energy, hope. He could re form his life, set new goals, new hopes, become the hero to the King. No one else would need to know about this.

What about the crown, whatever the thing was that Kaleb wanted him to collect? Well without Kaleb he wouldn't have known about the crown or the possible powers at his fingers. Still, no matter what he felt he owed to Kaleb he wasn't about to risk his neck, even a possibly immortal neck, for some god he didn't even worship and hadn't believed existed until but a few short hours ago.

'You think you can abandon me, ignore my will?'

The cold voice halted him and the horse both in their tracks on the edge of a thick set of woods. Claw like fingers of wood stretched out from the gloom, brush so tightly woven together that he doubted anyone could have entered the thickets without being scarred from the thorns.

"What?"

'You know who I am, you can remember that meeting, the way I helped you, called for you, brought you before me after the girl killed you. You're not having much in the way of luck are you Bevery?'

Gods.

'No, not gods, just one god.'

One god, Kaleb.

'You were expecting someone else?'

No, no he hadn't been, but how had Kaleb been able to hear his thoughts when he was so far away. Why had the horse stopped like that?

'My creature, it's very simple the horse is my creature, just as you are. You'll enter the castle and steal back the crown for me.'

Or what? What could he do to him? He was already dead.

'There are far worse things than death out there. Terrible fates, a hundred thousand glimpses at death. Your imp body could take so very much more than a human one could and still you wouldn't die.'

Interesting. He should have been afraid now. Kaleb was a god. He was just an imp. Why wasn't he afraid?

'Fear me!'

Why would he, or should he?

'I'm a god. I could destroy you!'

So do it already. Get on with it.

The horse trembled beneath his body, quivering as if his own life depended on Bevery's actions. Hm, odd. The fear had died, now he was no where near Kaleb, and close to the castle along with whatever protection it offered, he didn't fear the being. Why would that be?

"Because imps, demons, don't fall under the sway of gods unless they want to be there, or accept a bond. You didn't accept it, Kaleb never thought to offer you one." The voice that reached him was more a set of growls that words but he still heard it, understood the words behind the strange sounds.

"Who are you?" Bevery peered into the thicket, searching for the source of the words.

'Silence Hunter, silence! This matter is none of your concern. The imp is mine. Mine I tell you. I called him, summoned him. He is my instrument.'

Hunter?

"He might have been, if you had swallowed your pride and completed the ritual Kaleb. But you didn't. Foolish really. You had the chance of a weapon, a true weapon and blew it. Perhaps if you'd paid attention to what you were doing instead of dwelling on the delights your latest little toys have been offering you then maybe you wouldn't have screwed up." The more the man spoke the clearer his words became. If the being was indeed a man after all.

Bevery watched the shape move through the thicket, a mess of thorns and brushes that parted with ease as the being walked into view. Human shaped, dressed in furs, furs of all sorts, deer, wolf, bear all patched together in a hap hazard fashion.

'He's mine. You have no interest in the workings of humans, or my pleasures Hunter.'

"I take interest in whatever it pleases me to take interest in." Fang like teeth glinted against his lips. "And this amuses me."

Amusement. That's what he'd become.

"You could always become prey for the pack and I instead. Unlike Kaleb I do delight in hunting imps should they enter my domain or any area that catches my attention for a time."

"Master of the Hunt..."

"Yes, of course. Who else would I be? Look around you Bevery, Imp. A forest, the darkness, away from the beaten path. A place that exists anywhere I wish it to be at the time." He gestured towards the woods, then back to the road where the horse stood, unmoving but for the soft quivers that Bevery could still feel through his thighs.

'Don't try my patience, Hunter. You're going too far this time, interfering in my plans, my wishes.'

"And I would fear you why? If you really have a problem with me little Kaleb, come find me, come face the pack and I. We're always ready for a good hunt. Man flesh has lost it's interest to me, god flesh would be so much better. A thousand meals you could provide before I let you go again. How do you think your teeth would look as a trophy necklace? Or perhaps I could let you watch as I kept you prisoner within the home of the pack whilst all your petty little plans fell apart in your absence?" The soft mocking growls filled the air.

The gods hated each other? Warred? He'd never given the idea a moment's thought before now, yet here he found himself facing the idea head on. Hunter, the only god with no temples, who chased away those who wanted to worship him. Picking out lone men and women from time to time to act on his behalf for however long it pleased him to do so. Another myth come to life before his eyes.

Silence replaced the growls, leaving only the soft shiver of the horse beneath him, the beasts gentle snorts as they both waited for the next move to be made. Still he didn't fear, not Kaleb, nor Hunter.

'This isn't over between us, Hunter.'

"Of course it isn't, but this little section of your plans is. Find something else to keep you amused for now. The imp is warned, and will be twice over before I let him go on his way. Leave the castle alone. There's nothing there for you now. Nothing. That battle is some time away." One hand curled about the hilt of a wicked looking dagger that sat on Hunter's hip beneath the cloak of furs.

'I choose my battles, the time, the place, the reason.'

"Maybe you do most of the time, but I am telling you this time you will back off. My chosen resides in the castle. My chosen. Interfere in this and the pack will seek you out, no where exists on Erien that will permit you a place to hide from the pack on a hunt. You know that."

Chosen. No chosen of Hunter had been spoken of in a hundred years. And he or she was at the castle? All the more reason he needed to return. The chaos that would follow the knowledge would grant him the time he needed to ease back into good graces in the court.

"Go! Now Kaleb. Leave the imp be, leave the castle be!"

'For now, Hunter, just for now. Watch your back forest spawn. I'll be there when you least expect it.' The presence died with those words, fading not just from the back of Bevery's mind but from the air around him. Sent packing by the beast lord, the eternal hunter. A power play between the gods, not something he had expected to see, nor something he wanted to be a part of.

"Then I suggest you find another place to call home. The castle of the dragon throne is also off limits to you. Not just for now, but always. I won't tolerate imps getting in the middle of this." Hunter smiled, a calm dangerous look in his amber eyes. The smell that wrapped about the being was rank, heavy with rotting corpses, dried blood, wet earth. It clogged at his throat, threatening to cut off his air, then as quickly as he realized what he was smelling it was gone. No scent at all lingered behind.

"I'm a hunter, I can disguise my scent, by body, the trails left behind. All the better to capture and corner the prey I have taken an interest in, don't you think?" The fangs slid away from view, the furs changing, melding into a casual court dress of soft tunic and boots. "Any hunter can adapt to the situation, to those around them, meld into the background. You'd never see me coming until the moment my teeth ripped out your throat and my fingers closed about your center of power. Draining it, feeding until you had no choice but to follow me anywhere I wanted you to be."

Kaleb he had feared out of instinct, but this one, this hunter, he was learning to fear. "I understand. I won't... I mean I'll stay away from the castle. But where am I supposed to go?"

"Do I look like someone who cares where you go?" A feral smile ruled Hunters face, the glint in his eyes making it all too clear that there wasn't even a hint of tease within his words.

"No sir." Sir, was that what you called a god?

"Good, I'm glad we got that little matter cleared up." He'd gone from a beast of the forests to a well dressed courtier with near impeccable manners in a matter of a few moments. "You're an imp, learn about your kind. It might just save you a few problems in the coming moons."

"From where?"

"Human's keep knowledge in books, search out books, a wise one, someone learned. They'll be able to help you. Stay away from mages though. They tend to like to trap your kind for their own little spells. Never will understand mages. Strange beings." Hunter shrugged, then picked off a stray thread from the soft tunic he had created for himself. Even the growls, the slight lisp from his fangs had now vanished.

"Is... I mean is there a reason why you're dressed like that?" He couldn't imagine that would have worked well for hunting in the forests.

"I have someone I need to meet in person, Imp. Now be gone with you. The matter between us is done."

"Thank you." He swallowed hard, resettling himself on the horse, glancing around for a moment. "For dealing with Kaleb I mean."

"He was in my way, you're just a by product of that." Hunter shrugged. "One I have no further use for. Go. Now. Before you begin to annoy me."

Annoy him. Somehow, between Kaleb and Hunter the one that held the potential to frighten him more was Hunter.

"Yes sir, I'm going." He wasn't sure where he was going but anywhere that took him away from the possible line of fire where the Master of the Hunt was concerned.

"I'll destroy him. Hunt him down, unleash my own pack on him!" Kaleb snarled, lashing one clawed hand out, barely hearing the sound of the vase crashing to the floor. Not that he'd even been aware of some of the more delicate pieces around the castle had survived long enough to be at risk.

"My Lord?" Arinnana darted back from him, falling to the floor out of reach of the shards, head to the ground. She'd learned well. Belly, crawl, grovel, don't let the anger turn on her. She'd survive a little longer than some others had done at his feet. "What has happened, what may I do to ease your anger, to please you? Tell me, command me and it will be done."

"Hunter!" The snarl didn't ease from his voice. Of all of the gods and goddesses that walked the world of Erien that one was the least predictable. What could he do, there had to be some way of bringing the beast lord back to heel. Not that the creature had ever been at heel before. Lord of the forests, hunter, pack leader. No worshippers. How could he have any power yet be lacking in the source?

Another way.

Runes?

"Hunter, the Master of the Hunt? What could he do to annoy you my Lord? He's powerless, a beast, nothing more than the animals of the hunt to answer to him. He could never match your will."

Naïve child. Human's could be like that.

"Daughter, daughter, daughter. There are times I worry about your lack of understanding of such things. Yes, the Master of the Hunt has no human or Fae followers that we know of. No temples, no shrines, he wishes nothing to do with that side of life. But his power is without question. Even our Lord fears him." Guinelia leaned against the entrance of the door. "Forgive my interruption my Lord, the waif child is now resting, sedated of course. I would not want her wandering around the castle at this time. She might well try and test her blade against someone else. After all the trouble that we've gone to in bringing a few servants back into the castle I doubt you'd want some insane little human girl killing them off... not yet at least."

Guinelia, insane in more subtle ways than the very waif she spoke of. Amusing in some respects. "Over stepping your place again my pet." Arinnana bristled at the words, but remained silent, her nails almost scraping at the stone floor.

"If you believed that, my Lord I would already be dead." The older woman, her hair in rat tails from the lack of care, knotted in places, remained leaning against the door frame. "For now I amuse you. I have some measure of use to you. Should that change I know I'll die, no doubt in some terribly elaborate way, lots of blood and screaming perhaps?"

He should have been angry, even more so after his run in with Hunter, instead that anger slipped away, laughter bubbling at the back of his throat. "You do indeed have some uses little Guinelia. Not just as the mother of the one on her belly who seeks to over throw us both when she garners enough power. You truly don't care for your life. Interesting. So rare in humans. Madness yet retaining your intelligence. An interesting combination. Perhaps I should put you at the head of my armies when I gather them?"

A low snarl, barely swallowed, filtered from the woman on the floor.

"Ah yes, I know you my pet. I'm well aware of your motives. You want your prince as a mate, his line would be a good addition to my plans, but he's not the real focus of my desires is he?"

"I would never seek to over throw you my Lord." Arinnana protested, raising her head from the floor. "I know I could never match your power."

"Not yet, not unless you found yourself a partner, one whose power might match mine, or raise yours up enough to give me a good fight. Humans, always after the same thing. Well like your mother you have some use to me at this time, so your life is safe for a little longer." Mother against daughter, and the new waif to teach, to mold to his ways. One that wouldn't betray him as long as she believed him to be her father. An easy image to maintain.

"And Hunter, my Lord?" Arinnana tried to refocus his line of thought.

"He's prevented the Imp from entering the castle and freed him of his fear of me. An unfortunate incident, one that there will eventually be a reckoning of when the time is right. For now I need to focus on a new way of getting the crown. Hunter will be dealt with at another time. Perhaps with the right bait." Bait that even now slept in a drugged rest in another part of the castle...

"And Jeriah?"

Ah yes, it would eventually come back to the man that had wronged her, tried to take her pet prince away. "You forced his hand there pet. What follows from there is your own fault, but I would hazard a guess at your prince being safe for now at least."

"For now?" Anger flashed within her gaze, nails long broken dug against the edge of the stone. "He's mine. Mine my Lord. To be kept safe."

"Unless it pleases me to do otherwise." He smiled, watching the emotions tense against her shoulders, anger, frustration, the helplessness. Delicious. "And for now it pleases me to let him live."...

Chapter Fifteen

"Can we be tracked?" She nestled tightly against his chest, his arms wrapped tight about her waist as Orent flew through the clouds. "By Arinnana or others?"

"No, Orent would feel it. With the crown and the reason for the trip she's taken every precaution to hide our flight. Once we've landed we'll have only a few moments to enter the circle before we're sensed again if someone is looking for us." He tightened his grip around her waist, wishing that the flight could last forever. Too much going on around them. He would have nearly sold his soul in order to be able to enjoy a few quiet days together, like normal newly married couples had the chance of. Instead they were running around trying to figure out how to fix the crown. Wonderful.

'You have a beautiful woman in your arms, one that loves you and you're complaining?'

Great, all he needed, Orent and her love life tips.

'I'm not about to offer you tips snack. You've got to figure this one out on your own. Besides from here it doesn't look as though you're doing too bad. She's comfortable around you, is willing to take the risks involved in order to heal the breach between your family and the crown. Says a lot to me, but what would I know about human relationships?'

He would have punched Orent if A, she had been a man, and B it wouldn't have hurt him more than it would have hurt the dragon.

"How much longer before we get there?" Riana squirmed a little closer to him. She looked odd in the clothes she'd borrowed from him but odd in a good way. He was still trying to figure out why Orent had wanted her to pack a white dress in the pack. It didn't make sense. Though no doubt the dragon had a good reason. White would look good on Riana, of that he had no doubt.

'It's a ceremony Rhodan. You know how we dragons are with such things. The right trappings for the right event. Has to be done. Humor me on this.'

Like he had a choice.

"We should be there soon, before the moon reaches its zenith."

"Be a close thing, looks like there is a storm following us in."

'Not a storm, the power is gathering, called before we even arrive. Not sure why, something has alerted the stones. Just be thankful that for now Kaleb and his friends can't track us. Once we land you two are going to have to move fast. Riana you'll need to pull the dress on, and run to the center of the stones with the crown. The rest will come naturally to you.'

Would he be able to protect Riana?

'You won't be able to enter the circle at first, Rhodan. Maybe not for most of this. Your job is to stop anyone or anything else entering the circle whilst she heals the crown.'

"I thought I'd be there with her?"

"So did I." Fear touched Riana's words.

'I never said he would enter the circle with you from the very beginning. This is your task to carry out Riana. Yours. Not his. Not mine. Yours.'

"I don't think I like the sound of this." Riana protested. "Couldn't he enter the circle with me, from the start?"

"She's right, I don't like the sound of this either. It's too dangerous. Anything could happen to her." He could feel the knots in his throat, the tension that formed across his back, down into his thighs as he shifted his position on the back of the dragon.

'Trust me on this. I'm not about to put you two at risk unless there's a damn good reason, am I?' Orent rumbled beneath them, her voice pulling them closer somehow. No one could have doubted the love and care the great beast had for the two humans, even if she did still delight in calling him pet, snack and anything else she could get away with.

"Orent, is there no way he can enter the circle with me?"

'He has a task of his own to perform Riana of the Fae. One that the crown would prevent him from doing if he entered the circle at the wrong time. Instead of binding the line to the stone he might sever the link entirely if he entered too soon. Your power must be brought to focus on the crown and the stones that link dragon kind and his line.'

It didn't make a lot of sense, she wasn't of his line save by marriage, yet was supposed to be able to reform the bond. Something he was missing in all of this. Not that they'd had much in the way of spare time to find out the rest of the story. Cluiun had been right before they'd left the castle, children's takes could wait until after the deed was completed. Though it didn't stop him from wanting to bang his head against a convenient wall with the frustration the lack of knowledge threatened to cause.

Unless... what if she was pregnant? That would explain how she could bond the lines. She'd already be part of his family, carrying his blood. His child. He wasn't ready for that. Panic struck, cold chills wrapping about his spine. A father. Gods above and below. Children. What did you do with those things. They were noisy, smelly, messy at both ends at the same time.

He wasn't ready to be a father...

'You can stop that right now snackling. She's not pregnant. You're not that potent.'

He didn't know if he should be relieved or disappointed by the news. Not that he wanted children, but it would have been a feather in his cap to have become a father so soon. A small frown creased across his brow. Why wasn't she with child yet? They'd been together pretty much the past two nights. Well maybe not, there had been one night though, one very good night. Shouldn't have been enough?

'Complaining about having to put more work into it?'

No, why would he be, it wasn't exactly a task he had a problem with.

'Then let nature take its course. All things will happen when the time is right. With the stress her body is about to go through in the circle I doubt even a Fae child would be able to survive. Better that she isn't carrying a new life within her. The loss might well be more than she is ready to cope with on top of everything else she has already been through. Despite her gifts she is still very young.'

Women lost babies all the time, an unfortunate fact of the harshness of life. However he was more than a little grateful that he wouldn't have to face such a loss with her just yet. It might well happen eventually, but now... no now wasn't the time.

'Pray that the time never comes that you have to endure such a thing with her. I've heard, felt the pain of the ones that have lost their children. It hurts. Such a terrible loss, never fully heals. They carry it through out their lives.'

He'd never given it that much thought. Now he found himself dwelling on the problem.

'You've other things to be thinking about, like keeping her calm, focused. Keep her foremost in your mind. Don't let her fall emotionally. She needs to be steady during all of this. It will hurt. I won't lie, rebinding the crown will cause her a great deal of pain. She can either ride through it or surrender to it and be lost to us.'

His grip tightened that little more about her waist. Finding her only to loose her so soon was a fate he didn't even want to contemplate.

"I think I can see the stones." Riana murmured, her soft voice carried on the wind that lifted the dragon higher into the air. "I thought they would be further away, that we'd have a little more time before facing this."

"So did I love, so did I."

'We've got a little time yet. I want to circle and check the area before we land. There are enough things that might go wrong without adding laziness into the matter.'

The longer it was before they landed the more comfortable he would feel. Even then the moment would come too soon and he would be left, helpless, outside the circle watching his wife tossed to the winds of fate...

"Just what have you got planned?" Cluiun frowned as Simon vanished into a large closet in his room. "I'm not going to dress up as some court popinjay just to please fashion tastes and not be thrown out of the dance."

"Don't worry about it my dear naive fellow. It's not going to work that way. Black. Yes that's the color we need for you. Black with just a hint of scarlet in the right places. Leather, silk, suede would be over doing it though. Not sure where to put the scarlet but the color is needed. You can't go in there just dressed fully in such a dark color."

Cluiun smiled, rubbing one thumb down the scars that marred a path through his face. "I don't see why not. It would work out well. Most are looking to be the bright peacock in the middle of the ball. I'm happy enough to be the dark, mysterious type, threatening anyone who looks my way."

"You would be, brute. Quite happy to scowl and glower at the poor helpless court types. Well I think that might well work this time around. Have you thought about an eye patch?" Simon glanced out, dangling a scarlet silk eye patch from his fingers.

"I can see perfectly well, despite the scars."

"It was just a suggestion, a fashionable point you could make." Simon blew a kiss his way and darted back into the over large closet. "How did you get those anyway?"

"A wolf." If any other man had blown him a kiss he'd have punched him out.

"Ah and thus the name. I had wondered about that."

A smile formed across his lips. "Now I wouldn't have guessed that you'd have known the meaning of my name. Not many do."

"The Cluiun, the Wolf. Most might think that it was just an affection of yours, some strange name you picked up along the way. But it makes sense." For a moment the light heartedness slipped from Simon's voice. Those brief glimpses into something more than the court fop he tried to make others see. "Perhaps we can ... no no I think you're right, black. Full black."

The longer he spent around the odd man the more comfortable he became around him. "Aye, full black. Leather and I will agree to silk just to fit in to some degree with the court ways, but nothing more than that. I'm not about to appear to be someone that I'm not." If he gave Simon a free reign then he'd end up in a hot pink outfit with a dozen yellow rose or three.

"I think I have what you need now." Simon slipped back out into view, bringing a pair of pants, a top and vest with him. "This should work, and should fit you very well indeed. At least if I'm judging your size about right. You're such a big luscious boy. Do you work out?"

Would slapping him be a good idea?

Slapping? Since when did he think about slapping a man? Punching. Kicking, stabbing, or gutting. But slapping?

"What about scent?"

"Don't even think about it." He growled, taking the clothing from Simon's hands and turning to start changing.

"But it would complete the outfit." Simon protested, stomping one booted foot against the floor. "You really don't let me try anything new with you."

"You're pouting." He didn't look back as he pulled off the older clothes, slipping on the shirt, soft black silk that wrapped about his body in a smooth embrace.

"Of course I am." Simon plopped down on the edge of the bed. "I'd prefer it if I could dress you up, show off that body of yours. You really have got quite the … talent there." He could almost hear the hunger in Simon's voice, not the most comfortable of feeling. Not that he was going to bring it up right now, that would have given Simon further ammunition to play with. And he was used to men having special friends on board ship. Not the first time he'd been hit on, but hopefully it would be the last for a long time.

"Well I'm more interested in attracting Katrina's attention, then sparking off a decent fight with Haon." He tugged the leather breaches into place, tying them shut. "She strikes me as the sort that would be interested in the darker image, the dangerous bad apple."

Simon sniffed, looking over Cluiun with an indignant air. "Well you certainly fit that bill. Won't you even let me tie that hair back? I've got a nice wide black velvet ribbon that would make you look dashing."

"No, I don't think so." Ribbons, blah. He wasn't about to go that far. Not even to try and capture the attention of the woman in question. Not that he thought such a thing would be needed. The right words, a soft brush across the back of her neck, an invitation to dance. One thing you learned quickly on a ship was how to remain nimble. That made for a good dancer, at least as long as court hadn't invented some new form of dance that he was unfamiliar with. If so he'd just have to play it by ear.

Or persuade the band, no doubt there would be one, if only a few playing string instruments the harp or something of that nature, to play a tune he was more familiar with. A wild upbeat spin around the floor, something similar to the dances the gypsy people's still used. That would put a challenge down, turning her about in his arms, before Haon, using a beat that most men wouldn't be able to keep up with and one that would leave her wild in his arms.

Good.

"I think I'm about ready to face court, don't you?" He turned, smoothing down the leather vest over the silk. If this didn't do the trick nothing would.

"You might well be but of course you still need to wait. You have to be late to the dance you know."

"Whatever for?"

"Fashion dear boy, fashion."

Wind, she could feel it even with the heavier clothes as Orent circled the stones below. Even in the darkness she could see some movement, a glimmer of life nearby. Just who it might be she wasn't sure but that was just one of the risks that the dragon was checking for now.

Stones, a circle of thirteen stones, the number of moons in the year. Set out in a way that if a stone fell it would do so without touching it's partner on either side. Just like other circles she'd heard rumors of across Erien but had never seen before this night. Rumors, stories, she heard about them from all over the world. Tales carried to her father's home by bards, sailors and merchants. One day, she had promised herself that she would visit the stones she'd been told about. Never had she thought that she'd be doing it in such a manner though.

'Looks clear. I can see someone, but they're some distance away right now. Can't touch them though. I know it's a male. I know they are heading to the circle, but I daren't probe any further.'

It sounded almost as though the dragon was hiding something.

'Of course I am dear, I'm a dragon, it's my nature to hide a few things from humans. Doesn't do your kind a lot of good to be privy to everything going on. Poor little minds can't handle the strain.' The long drawn out sigh at the end of the great beast's words only left her swallowing a nervous chuckle. *'Yes I know, you're Fae or partially, not human, but the same applies.'*

Odd, Orent meant it.

'Yes, in this case I do.'

Why?

'You'll understand better when it's all done with. Just trust me. Trust me and hold onto your love for Rhodan. Onto the power you have, and remember that you have everything you need. Don't listen to the offers the crown tries to make to you, or the voices you'll hear.'

A frown creased her brow, the doubts raising their ugly heads at the back of her mind, only to be squashed by the warmth of Rhodan pressed against her back. Believe. She had to believe.

Even from the box she could feel the presence of the crown. A nagging sensation at the back of her mind, a pressure that demanded attention no matter how hard she tried to shut it out. It wanted her. Needed her. But she wasn't the one the crown was meant for. She had no idea what would happen if she gave into the push to open the box before it was time to, but it wasn't something she was willing to chance.

The small hint she'd been given back in the castle had been enough.

In silence the dragon landed outside the great stone circles, flicking her wings out in a soft motion before folding them along side her great body. *It's time children.'*

Soft music filled the low lit hall, a dozen couples mingled on the dance floor, in the middle of a room lined by long tables, comfortable chairs in the corners of the room, small gathering places for anyone who wanted to spend a little more in the way of intimate time with a chosen partner, or three. At the far end a string quartet provided the music that set the pace for the night. Three or four small groups settled around the room, but the largest group was the very one Cluiun had been hoping to see. Haon and his entourage. Complete with Katrina lingering on the outer edge of the group, still out of favor. Good.

Slow paces. Easy steps. Jumping straight into things wouldn't help and would look clumsy, obvious. Not a mistake he was about to make.

Several sets of gazes followed his path through the hall to a table that had been left almost empty. A large one, half lining the wall nearest the musicians, just a few people at the other end of it. Ideal. It provided a hint of privacy, the loner not seeking out any other to provide him with company. The mystery would grow with each passing moment as he sat there, leaning back from the table, eyes half lidded as he watched the room.

Haon, he knew the man was watching him. Two men facing off silently in a room that was only truly big enough for one of them. Hopefully the discomfort would grow before Cluiun made his move. The more uncomfortable Haon felt the easier it would be at the end of the night.

He glanced, slowly, about the room, taking in the dancers, the small groups of courtiers. No sign of the King, not unusual by all accounts. Such gatherings had become a meeting place for the young and upcoming power builders of the court. Not a place the older members would be seen dead at without good cause. No, the only ones here would be the very men and women he wanted to send the message to.

Katrina looked pale, drawn, as if she hadn't slept in over a week. Shadows lined beneath her eyes, a weariness marked each step she made across the hall on the rare occasions that she moved from the outer edge of the gaggle or women. They knew it, knew she had been pushed to one side and made no attempt to hide their disdain. It didn't matter what power and position she had within the court, Haon had marked her as no longer being in favor.

How long he watched the group he wasn't sure, a candle mark perhaps, or a little longer? By the time she moved across the room for the fourth time he was ready. The loneliness in her movements, the soft, furtive glances back towards Haon, the mocking giggles that followed her steps only added to his decision to move now.

"Can I get you a drink?" Not the smoothest line he'd ever come up with, but the woman was desperate enough for some sign of approval from anyone that it worked well. Relief washed across her face, a glimmer of a smile before her eyes narrowed and she glanced back towards the group in the corner.

"If it wouldn't be too much bother?" She half flinched, almost as though expecting this to be a trick, a foul little prank to show her just how much of a fool she'd been.

"Not at all my lady, not at all." He flashed a feral grin her way, almost feeling sorry that she had to be the one to bring Haon out of his safe area.

"Why would you want to get me a drink, I can easily summon a servant to fetch one for me." There it was, the hint of suspicion, the waiting for the joke to be played.

"Why not, I'm here anyway." He nodded towards the small bar area, ordering a mug of mead. "Wine, or perhaps something a little stronger?"

"Wine, please."

He leaned against the high table, smiling. Bars, dances, there were always places to spin a few lines, lead a woman or target out into the light before closing the trap. He'd not been at many private parties, but the presence of a drink area didn't surprise him, it made sense with the guests here. Easier on the servants.

"Is there something the matter, my Lady? You seem a little distracted. Shouldn't a woman like you be the belle of the ball, with a hundred partners wanting to spin you about the dance floor?"

Tension eased from her shoulders, the dress showing a little more cleavage that was suitable for a woman of her station. No, that wasn't fair either. It didn't suit her, be it because of her sense of sorrow, her lack of presence, the slump to her shoulders. If she stood up, held some measure of pride there it might have looked good. She'd let herself be dragged down by a man who enjoyed degrading women, using them for his own purposes.

Not something Haon would be able to do again if he had anything to do with it.

"I don't seem to be in favor at this moment... Cluiun isn't it?" She peered up at him, nervously meeting his gaze. Her eyes weren't as dark as he'd first assumed, nearer a slate grey left tired and wary by her time with the slime in the corner.

"Aye, the Cluiun, bold pirate and feared outlaw at your service my Lady Katrina. And yes I know your name, I make it a point to find out the names of the most attractive women in the court." He pressed the slender glass into her hand, bowing as he did so, brushing a soft kiss across her knuckles. "And you, dear lady, qualify without a doubt." Or she would have done if she had shaken herself off from Haon a few days earlier.

"You flatter me, Cluiun." She half smiled, stepping back a little as she glanced over towards the group in the corner then looked back at Cluiun. "Did they send you?"

"They?" He made a pointed look back at the same corner. "No, I'm my own man. At most I'm friends with the prince and his new bride, but no other."

"The prince... you mean Jeriah, no.. no of course not. You mean Rhodan. I'm sorry. I get flustered at times. Jeriah isn't a prince." She shook her head quickly, glancing back towards the corner, lowering her voice. "I'm sorry, please forget I said that."

"Said what?" He flashed a grin, stepping to her side and slipping an arm about her waist. "Discretion dear lady is a part of my trade."

"Yes, I imagine it is." Heat flushed along her cheeks, following quickly down her slender neck. Odd that, how she could be a little on the plump side but still have a slender neck. A delicate quality to her that might have shone under a different set of circumstances. "Tell me, do you dance Katrina?"

"Dance?"

"Yes, dance, spin across the floor in a flurry of silk and satin?"

For the first time a true smile claimed her features. "Yes, I dance, I just don't often get the chance to do so. I'd love to, if given the chance. I mean... I'm not trying to force the issue, or put you in an awkward situation."

"Now why would that be awkward? I brought the idea up." He turned, leading her across the dance floor back towards his table. "Why don't you set your drink down here and we can show this little gathering what a dance really is." He set his own drink down, then brushed the back of his knuckles across her cheek in a gentle caress. "That's if you would do me the honor?"

He knew the right words, even if he wasn't court born. Knew the game and could play it better than most. Just this once it felt wrong...

"Katrina!"

Interesting, it hadn't taken that long for Haon to bite.

"Yes?" She turned, shaking softly, the tremble barely hidden.

Haon stalked across the room, closing the distance between the three of them. "I thought you were just going to get a drink Katrina." He glanced pointedly towards the small group. "I was wondering what was keeping you."

"I asked the lady to dance." Cluiun answered before Katrina could. "Is there a problem with that, after all you don't appear to be lacking for company in your cozy little corner."

A low growl formed at the back of Haon's throat. "And if I want her back with me?"

"I would say that's the lady's choice, wouldn't you?" Good, push the possessive nature, make it seem as though the power was back in Katrina's hands. Where it belonged in the first place. "If you wish to return with him and back to standing in the corner, ignored then feel free to. However if you wish to dance with me I'd be more than willing to spin you around the floor."

"You're not welcome here, pirate. Your kind belongs locked up in the cells, waiting for the headsman. If you hadn't managed to wrangle your way in with that scum sucking princeling that's exactly where you'd be." Haon kept his voice low, but still loud enough that a neighboring table heard at least a hint of it.

"Ah, unlike you who prefers to prey on women, keep them dangling from your string to be tossed aside. Then gets defensive when a real man pays attention to one of your cast offs?" The words slashed through the air, sharper than any blade, cutting into both Haon and Katrina both. "Forgive me my Lady, but those outside his little circle are well aware of the games he plays. He's a coward. One that doesn't even have the nerve to face me head on, but seeks to order you back to the corner like the whipped puppy he believes you to be."

Even the music had now stopped, conversations dying away as the two men faced off in the room.

"Is that true?" Katrina spoke barely above a whisper.

"Stay out of this." Haon growled.

"I'd say I'm in the middle of this." She didn't move, for the first time in Cluiun couldn't guess how long, she grew a back bone.

"I said stay out of this woman, and I meant it."

"No, you're done telling me what to do."

Haon's hand lashed out, slicing through the air towards Katrina's face, barely stopped in time as Cluiun grabbed the man's wrist.

"I think you just went too far."...

Chapter Sixteen

A low hiss of air passed over head, sending him flattening to the ground before the air had finished brushing against his body. What in the name of all that was holy was going on? Dragon pass?

Jeriah pushed slowly back up to his feet, straining to see into the darkness as he heard the low passage of large wings above his head, circling once before landing some distance away. At the circle? Had to be.

Had fate actually turned his way?

If that was Orent, then Riana and Rhodan were with the beast. And if they were here then something of importance was going on. Something he could exploit. Good. Anger at the situation fueled something else, the drive to push forward, find a way to exact revenge. Riana and Rhodan in the same place and he'd be able to settle the score with both of them.

Wet, he hated the rain, worse still the cold. Arinnana, Rhodan, Riana, Justin, they were all to blame. That damn Cluiun as well. Simon, now that one would be of use once the others were dealt with. Offer him a constant supply of new fabrics and the man would come to his side. And that one missed very little. If anything. Especially about the court.

He could just about make them out in the rain, at the outline of the stones. The dragon and two figures, human figures. No sign of the Cluiun. No doubt that lazy creature was enjoying the fun of the court, drinking the place dry or attempting to. So that left him to deal with Riana and Rhodan alone. Easy enough to do. Kill Rhodan by holding the woman hostage.

No, there would be more to it than that. He had a few plans in mind, or ideas at least.

What about the dragon?

He faltered in his climb towards the stones at the thought. Orent would try and stop him, protect her prince, her bonded. He'd have to take it carefully. How though, that was the missing piece of the puzzle.

Dirt dug its way under his fingernails, the edge of a rock cutting into his knees, past the soft court style clothing. Not even the cloak offered him any further protection from the weather that lashed against his body.

By the time he reached the lip of the hill not a single part of his body had be saved from the cold, painful touch of the storm that even now turned from a mild rumble to a wild crack as lightening split open the sky...

"Riana, put the dress on." Orent called out, lifting one wing to shelter her during the change. "Ceremony. It's best we do things the way it was meant to be done. Hurry, we don't have much time left."

"I didn't realize we were on a deadline." She almost laughed, darting under the offered wing and taking the bag that Rhodan half threw at her. "Why do I need the dress?"

"It's Fae material, same cloth your mother would have worn for her wedding to your father. Important that we keep some things in line. The patterns. It's a little hard to explain now, but all things on Erien answer to a pattern of life, through the threads, the runes on the stones match the ones on your dress."

"There are runes on the dress? I didn't notice them." Rhodan darted under the wing, his fingers moving to her tunic, helping to pull it off.

"You wouldn't do pet, she won't be able to see them until she's in the circle. The stones will react to them. No one really knows what the runes do, but the link, the ability to wear them is rare. Fae of her line can, that's why the crown reacted to her the way it did."

More pieces of the puzzle.

"Wouldn't this be easier if you'd explained it before hand?" Rhodan gave voice to the question that she had held back on asking.

"No, it would have only left you both confused. I'll explain more later, you have my word on it. When you're both ready to understand."

That sounded like a brush off, but she already trusted the dragon to keep her word. It might not be immediately, but once the great beast knew they were ready to understand the explanations would come.

"Ready," she smoothed the dress down over her thighs, the leggings kicked off, her boots still in place.

"Good. Remember what I said Rhodan. Stay out of the circle until I tell you otherwise." Orent's voice rumbled through the air, rain bouncing from her wing as the two human's sheltered beneath it. "Time to step out into the rain, Riana of the Fae. Rhodan, draw your sword. You'll need it."

"My sword?" Rhodan frowned, pushing the box that held the crown into Riana's hands. "I don't see anyone I need to fight."

"You'll need it soon enough." Orent flicked her wing, sending a shower of rain drops back up into the air. "And I didn't say anything about fighting. Just for once in your life pet, do as I tell you to without asking a dozen questions."

Fear eased away as Riana stepped out from the shelter of the dragon. She should have been numb to the core with the pain she knew would come. Instead she held the box, a sense of calm wrapping about her body and soul alike, barely even feeling the rain as she stepped into the circle of tall, white stones.

"What! What are they doing?" Kaleb pushed up from the bed, abandoning the two women. "No. The crown. How dare they do this to me!"

"Do what?" Arinnana scrambled from the bed after him. "What's wrong my lord?"

"The crown, that Fae creature has taken the crown to one of the stone circles." Kaleb turned, looking around the room, seeking a target, any target. "Find me a human, a disposable one."

The need to destroy, rend, find a way to let his rage out in a way that would not ruin his plans was paramount. He could do that with something simple, a human, not one of his chosen this time. Sacrifice them to his anger.

The crown. It should have entered his possession. Not be taken to the circle, not run the risk of being reactivated like this.

Too late, he'd left it too late. If he'd known about the extent of Jeriah's greed. The crown, the chest, everything that was then wrapped up in the box, the plans the Fae woman had put into place so many years ago then there would have been a way of preventing all of this.

"Is there nothing that can be done?" Arinnana demanded as her mother darted out of the door. Even as mad as Guinelia was she left without questioning Kaleb. At least one of them had learned not to question him. Pity the daughter hadn't as yet. A few more lessons and she'd learn to wait until better times to inquire.

With a cold, cruel smile he reached out, tangling his fingers into Arinnana's hair, pulling her down to the ground on her belly at his feet. "When I feel the need to explain things to you I will, until then my slave you will remember to be silent and await my whim!"

Some days it didn't matter what happened, how well you planned everything things were still going to go completely wrong.

Rhodan could barely breathe as he watched her enter the circle of stones. Every part of him screamed to follow her, to dart through the rain and drag her back from the circle, pull her into his arms to protect her from the danger that would come.

'You have to trust her, and me in this.'

No smart remark, or jabbing nick name this time. Just the quiet reassurance that this was the right thing to do. Just stand back and watch the woman he loved, had come to love more than he had thought would be possible trigger a magic no one knew how to control. Let alone a Fae born woman newly come into her own powers. Wonderful. Rune magic. Who knew just what that thing could do?

'No one knows, not truly. There are a few bits and pieces that some of the mages have access to. The elder dragons have a little more in the way of information. The crown holds a piece of that magic, the stones a little more. My mother once told me that the stones themselves held the answer.'

More questions that he wanted to know the answers to.

His gaze moved fully to the woman, his wife, as she entered the circle of stones still clutching the box firmly in her hands. Strange. The rain didn't appear to be falling where she stood. The ground didn't even appear wet. How could that be?

A shadow moved at the edge of his line of sight. Something that shouldn't be there. What...

His hand tightened about the hilt of his sword.

"Whose there?" He took a step forward, keeping a firm grip on his sword, watching the darkness. He wanted to help Riana, be ready to pull her out when she needed it, or walk in at her call, but there was something else here. A figure in the night.

"Well well well, never thought I would find you and your new little bitch out here but I guess fate is finally smiling on me, isn't she?" Jeriah stumbled out into the clearing, shaking off the rain soaked cloak, his own sword, more like a slender child's sword, sat sheathed at his hip.

"What are you doing here?" Rhodan felt his jaw tighten. "This is no place for you. The business here is between Riana, Orent and myself, not the man who would be king in my place."

"Orent won't interfere in this." Jeriah straightened himself up, rolling back his shoulders as he took his place opposite Rhodan. "You should know the laws on this my cousin."

He did, that was the point. He'd been hoping Jeriah wouldn't remember. That the time for the fight could and would wait until Riana had finished. "Yes, I know the laws."

"So why don't we finish this... here and now, then I can spend some decent time with your bride when I'm done. She deserves a real man in her life, not a spoiled little prince who can't even be bothered to attend the duties he has been fortunate enough to be granted by a simple act of birth." Jeriah smirked, drawing the sword slowly from its sheath.

"Ignorant bastard. You've no idea just how much work I've put into my life, or anything else around me. You've sat back in the castle, waiting for a way to displace me, whispering lies in my father's ear whenever you've had the chance. Well it ends now." He shifted, easing his weight over onto the balls of his feet, gaze locking on the man that had become the bane of his life.

"Shall we take care of this now, or wait a little longer, throwing a few more insults at each other?"

"I've got a few more I could add to the discussion for even suggesting that my bonded would stoop to breaking the laws of man and dragon alike in this matter. I would not waste my fire on you, nor sully my teeth." Orent growled low from the side of the stones. "And no matter the outcome I would die before letting you lay one hand on Lady Xantriana of the Silver Woods."

"Time to dance then." Rhodan felt the tension ease as he faced off against Jeriah. No longer helpless to watch his wife in the circle he could do something to protect her, protect them both whilst she wove the magic neither of them could claim to understand.

"Are you insane?" Haon demanded, one hand moving to the sword that sat on his hip. Good, anger. Easy to force another to make mistakes when you got them angry. "Are you trying to get between myself and one of my women?"

"Your women?" Katrina almost screeched.

A flicker of movement at the door. Simon. He'd expected him to be here for some of this, just as long as he stayed out of fighting range.

"What else did you think you were? Now get back to where you belong." Haon grabbed for Katrina's arm, tugging free from the grip Cluiun had on him. If his words hadn't been enough to force the woman into a stunned silence, the painful grip on her arm did the trick. "And you, sea scum, back off. Now!"

"I'm not in the habit of taking orders. I'm more of the nature to give them." Anger turned to fury in Haon's eyes. "But if you think you're man enough to change my viewpoint on that feel free to step up and show me."

"Oh I think I can do that, but I won't be doing it alone."

Hands grabbed his arms from either side. He'd not even heard them clear the distance across the dance floor. Stupid. He hadn't thought the man would make such an open move with friends or his hired men in public. A crowd half gathering around him, blocking the majority of the incident from view of the servants. Of those that could see what was going on would any have the courage to call out for help? "Coward! Need others to do your fighting for you!"

"Now why would I sully my blade on a piece of scum like you?" Haon smiled, a cold calm calculated look in his gaze. "Not when I have friends who will happily assist me with the minor problem you've created."

"I'm a guest of the crown." Long shot but worth a try, if he could get them to loosen their grip on him for just a short while, long enough to kick free, grab his sword, he might be able to cause enough damage to alert the guard.

"Something we can rectify with your death. Without Rhodan here to back you up it can easily be explained that you had too much to drink, went wandering down to the docks and met with a nasty accident. Typical of your kind don't you think?"

"Here, sir? Or do we take him outside first?" A voice, a familiar one from the blow that had sent him into the darkness only a day ago, spoke from behind him. Not one of the ones holding him.

"No, not here. I wouldn't want to sully the castle with his blood. Drag him out to the docks where he belongs." Even now Cluiun could hear it, the attempt by the other man to appear better than he actually was. Hiding the pure slime that lived within his core. If no one else ever saw it, or heard it, he had. Though the way things were going he might well be taking that knowledge to his grave. Wonderful. He'd faced full blown storms, hunters, rivals and now was facing death from a bunch of power hungry court dregs. Not the type of death he'd actually had in mind.

Enough was enough.

Cluiun kicked out, his feet connecting with Haon's stomach. A growl of fury and pain sounding out even as at least two sets of hands thrust him to the ground. It was about to get messy.

Just enough force behind the kicks to send Haon stumbling backwards, not much chance for anything else though as a dozen sets of hands grabbed his legs, carrying him to the ground.

Where was Simon? He'd seen him just a short while ago. The man was a fop but not a coward. At least he hadn't thought him to be one.

"You made a mistake, Cluiun. You might have the odds in your favor on a ship, but dry land you're helpless. No crew, no extra knowledge to tip the balance. Alone, ship wrecked I believe would be the right term." Haon coughed for a moment, rubbing the kick marks that had left a set of imprints across his velvet tunic. "You should have stayed with your own kind, instead of stepping into my territory." The smile said it all, the warnings that Haon believed Cluiun should have heeded. Instead he'd pushed the lines, crossed the social barriers that had been forced into place.

"My dear boy, don't you think that someone might well, oh I don't know, tell Rhodan what you've tried to do to his friend?" The slow, comfortable drawl of the pink and purple dressed court fop carried through the small gathering.

"Stay out of it Simon. This doesn't concern you." Haon replied, barely even looking towards the well dressed man. "Back off or you'll find yourself joining him."

"Oh, I don't think so. Getting rid of one salt laden ocean traveler is one thing, trying to be shot of me in the same manner would raise a few objections. I mean where would the ladies be without my fashion sense?" Simon didn't even blink at the threats, instead of stepping away from the group he moved closer, the lazy look never leaving his face.

"Simon, you're pushing it. Get out!"

"In just a moment. If you're going to kill him I think I'd like to reclaim a few things from the brute first. Wouldn't want that silk to get blood on it, have you any idea just how difficult it is to clean off a silk shirt?" With each word Simon moved a little closer to the gathered men and women, his voice never loosing its soft, comfortable drawl. Neither fear nor hurry seemed to touch his words, despite the situation.

"I'm giving you one last warning, Simon." Haon turned, hands clenched at his sides as he faced the well court fixture. "I don't care just how many friends you've managed to gather together here, don't..."

The word tapered off in a soft, gurgling sound.

"You really shouldn't go around threatening people, dear boy. Not unless you're willing to face the consequences of your actions." The slender sword slipped free from Haon's body as silently as it had entered. Little more than a few drops of blood coating the steel, blood that Simon wiped from the blade with little thought.

No one moved. No one living at least, for the still stunned body of Haon crumpled to the ground, drops of blood flecking his lips as they moved in one last protest before a long, drawn out breath fled his dying form.

Then it came, a single scream, followed by a wail as a dozen women burst into tears.

"Oh my darlings, you really shouldn't cry wearing such make up, it will only ruin your skin." Simon turned, sheathing the sword that once again now appeared to be little more than just another one of his fashion statements. "And I do suggest that you boys let the dear man go. He really doesn't look too comfortable on the ground back there. Now off with you, let him up. Come along. I don't want to have to call the guards in here. Hard enough to explain why there's a dead body lying in the middle of the hall don't you think."...

The winds, why couldn't she feel the winds, or the rain? Both should have been leaving her dress coated against her body, chilling her to the core, instead she felt warm, as if the full light of the noon day sun now shone down on her instead of the moon light that left its soft caress against the tall stones. The box vibrated in her hands, the crown crying to be released from the confines of the smooth wood, it was alive, aware of the power that surrounded her, the box, the crown. Runes. She could feel them, warming her skin, feel them imprinted in the stones that towered above her, the same runes she wore on her dress.

Time. Why did she feel as though she'd been waiting her entire life for this moment in time?

'*Because you have.*'

Had she? Perhaps so. Instead of arguments, protests, she accepted it. For the first time in her life Riana accepted something without questions, without demands to know how it worked, or why she was meant to be here.

'*Open the box, let the crown know where it is.*'

Orent's voice? No, something else this time. Not the dragon, but still familiar, an old voice, powerful in a way she had never encountered before.

'*You know what to do, reform the bond. Blood calls to blood, and the power pulses through your veins with every beat of your heart. Don't give into the fear.*'

Fear. She didn't feel any fear, not yet, but that might change. She knew that now. Just as the pain would come if Orent was right about this.

The box opened in her hands, falling away as she grasped the crown in slender fingers, raising it into the air.

Lightening cracked the sky open above her.

A low rumble that claimed the air and ground both, nearly shaking her off balance as the blue white light snapped from stone, to stone, to stone.

Burning, her fingers burned as the light hit the crown in her grasp. Arching through her body until a scream tore from her lips. Gods. She hadn't thought it would be like this.

Had to hold onto it. Speak the words.

What words?

No one had told her what to say!

'*Because they have to come from you. Xantriana, you're the key, the child of the Fae to bring the dragon throne back to where it belongs. The runes, you can't control them, but you can guide them if only for this moment. Through the stones in the crown, through the runes on your dress. Listen to us. Listen to your own power.*'

Us? That's where it felt odd, the voice wasn't one, but many combined. The stones? The voices of the stones themselves?

For a moment she was aware of something else, movement beyond the stones, two figures almost dancing, but the lightening flashed through the night sky again, hitting her, the stones, the crown, turning blue in the moment it connected with her flesh. Pain. Rolling waves of pain that sought to loosen her grip on the crown. Tested her, seeking out a weakness to exploit. Some way of throwing her to the ground and giving her to the lightening.

No. Stronger than that. She was stronger. Fae born, mortal and immortal blood. Old lines, old power.

Fingers blackened under the fire that danced from the stones, lashing out at her. Pain she couldn't fight any longer, pushed too far. She couldn't keep hold of it, didn't dare to keep hold of it. Give up, she had to give up.

'And what of Rhodan if you do? What of the life together you hope for?'

Rhodan.

No. Couldn't loose him. Wouldn't loose him.

"Hear me!" The words where little more than a whisper, each breath a set of knives that clawed through her lungs. "Hear me and answer. The crown binds the land, the people, the dragons all together. A bond that was forged before most humans even knew about the dragons as little more than beasts that flew above them. A dangerous sight."

Not enough. She wasn't sure what the words were meant to do, or trigger, but it wasn't enough.

'Reach deep. Listen and reach deep.'

Reach deep for what?

No time for questions, just for answers.

"Forged in blood, forged in fear. Crowns and hearts, pain and honor."

'More.'

"What was shattered now make whole. What was sundered now will heal."

'More.'

"I have no more to give!" What did the voices want?

'Yes you do.'

Give what. Pain? She'd given enough of that in the last few moments. Just love left, and that belonged to Rhodan, didn't it?

"Love for the land, for his people, he's young, foolish, has made mistakes. Let the crown be healed, the bond re-formed between them. Give him, his people, this land, grant them all the chances they need. I have nothing left to offer you. Nothing but myself, and the love I feel for him. I don't know why I feel it, why I am here, why I was chosen, but please take what I offer, take it all if that's what you want, what you need."

Foolish words, nothing that really made sense to her, just a spilling of emotions from the heart.

'It's enough.'

Rolling pain washed through the circle in a blaze of light that rocked her to her knees. Darkness pulled her into the warm, comforting embrace, holding her close, the crown still clutched in her hands. His voice following her into the night, seeking to bring her back even as her mind fled without a second thought.

"Riana!"

Lightening tore his world in two, a fire that engulfed his wife, destroying life and hope in a heart beat only to return it as the light faded away leaving Riana crumpled on the ground.

"She's fine, and will be mine in just a few short moments." Jeriah snarled, lunging forward, the blade barely missing Rhodan's chest as he turned, slipping to one side in the near desperate move. He'd let himself be distracted.

"Like hell she will." Foolish to waste breath on Jeriah, he knew that and still did it anyway. Anger fueled his moves, the need to protect Riana, the drive to pull her out of the circle, cradle her in his arms. Jeriah wouldn't have her, even if she were dead he wouldn't defile her body with so much as a single breath.

He'd never thought Jeriah would have so much skill with a blade. His life had always been focused on court politics, not refining less courtly skills. Not that it mattered now.

Steel slid along steel, blades locking for a moment, Jeriah's breath warming his face. Rain slicked both men down, their hair wet, plastered against their faces, half blocking vision. He didn't feel the cold now, doubted his cousin did either. Just the beat of his heart, the burning of air in his throat, groans as the men separated, stumbling backwards from each other on ground left slick from the very rain that pelted them both.

"You never understood did you?" Jeriah wiped the water from his eyes. "Why I hated you, why I did everything in my power to be rid of you.

"Yes, I did. I just didn't care. I don't care now. So save the speeches." He lunged forward, closing the gap between them, sword thrusting into Jeriah's stomach with a fast, hard twist upwards. At least it saved him from having to listen to the other man's prattling excuses.

Shock claimed Jeriah's face, color fading, his eyes wide as his lips moved in a near silent protest.

"I'm done with you, cousin." He yanked the sword backwards, clearing it from his body, specks of vivid red staining the blade only to be washed away by the heavy rain. "But I'll be sure to tell my father of your final moments."

"Well done pet." Orent flicked out her wings, sending soft splatters of water across the clearing. "I don't know everything about human's but I don't believe he'll be getting up from that little encounter."

"Riana?" He didn't waste the time in checking Jeriah, his focus shifting instantly back to the woman in the center of the stones, A woman who didn't move, but lay there, hair spilled out around her on the ground...

Epilogue

Stones. A hundred stones moved around her in an endless circle. Lights, no longer painful, danced from one to the other, melting away their coverings, revealing faces. Faces she should have known, somehow she should have known them.

'*You did well child of the Fae.*'

Who…

'*Does it matter? No, I don't think it does. The crown is healed, the next steps are for you and he to take together. You and your children.*'

Children? They weren't ready to have children, not just yet.

'*In time though, and perhaps sooner than you think. You'll need them. Erien needs them not just Olain. This part of the journey is ended Xantriana of the Fae. We cannot tell you how much more there is to go, what tasks lay ahead, even we can't see that far into the future. Too many variables. Your kind tend to bring those into the picture with every new choice you make.*'

Her head throbbed, even in the darkness it hurt. That didn't feel right. Where you supposed to be able to feel pain when you died?

'*Dead, you're not dead child. Just asleep for a moment. The dead can't bring children into the world, nor spend time with the man they love. Can they?*' Humor, she'd not been expecting that. Not with everything she'd been through, they'd been through.

'*He's waiting for you, time to wake up child. Wake up.*'

If she hurt this much now, why would she want to wake up only to hurt even more?

'*Wake up, Riana.*'

Sleep, she wanted to sleep. Her eyes drifted closed fully, a chill seeping into her bones. No, waking up was just too hard to do right now. Maybe later. No more faces in the stones, or odd voices at the back of her mind. Just three days in bed, maybe four…

"Riana!"

"What?" She murmured, eyes opening slowly. What was he doing here?

"Gods, I thought I'd lost you." He cradled her in his arms, kneeling on the damp ground, half rocking her. "I turned around and saw you laying there, not moving, and I thought I'd lost you."

"Never." Tired, so very tired but still she reached out, brushing his cheek with her fingers. "I did it, Rhodan. Healed the crown. They told me."

"Who told you?" A frown creased his brow, a moment's concern, reaching for the crown. The stones almost glowed, no pain now, not for either of them. Just a simple, elegant crown. "I can hardly believe we went though this just because of a piece of metal to wear on my head sometime in the future. Seems strange now." He set it back in the box, closing the lid. "I don't need it now and it doesn't matter who told you it was healed, the clouds could have told you for all I care. You're safe now. Safe and I'm never letting you go."

His hands tangled in her hair, arching her closer to him, lips brushing over her own in a kiss that deepened, firing her to the very core of her being.

Is this what love meant, being held, protected, given enough room to take risks yourself only to be caught if you stumbled. She couldn't be sure, but if this was love, with everything that it entailed then perhaps, just perhaps being his wife wouldn't be such a bad thing after all.

"Maybe we should continue this elsewhere?" Rhodan whispered against her lips. "Though I might be persuaded to wait here a little longer if you're going to respond to every kiss like that."

"Well the rain isn't that bad." She smiled, heat claiming her cheeks as she leaned closer, seeking out his lips. "And I might ignore it for a while, to give us chance to recover, perhaps I need a little checking out? Make sure I'm fit to travel?"

'Humans. You're always picking the wrong time to start getting cozy. Forgetting about the poor dragon. Fly you here, take you there, eat that man, bite this one. Should put in for a reassignment. However, if you two have quite finished over there I really would like to get out of this rain.' Orent snorted, stretching out her wings. *'You can get on with your mating practices later. I'm wet, tired, cold and hungry and you two are beginning to look very appealing.'*...

So ends book two of The Erien Tales, Faeborn, but the tale is far from over. Look for further adventures in the next book of the Erien Tales: Through the Eyes of a Dragon, Orent's Tale.

To Moscow with Bony:
A Liverpool Man's Tale
Fredrick McCann

TERRI PRAY

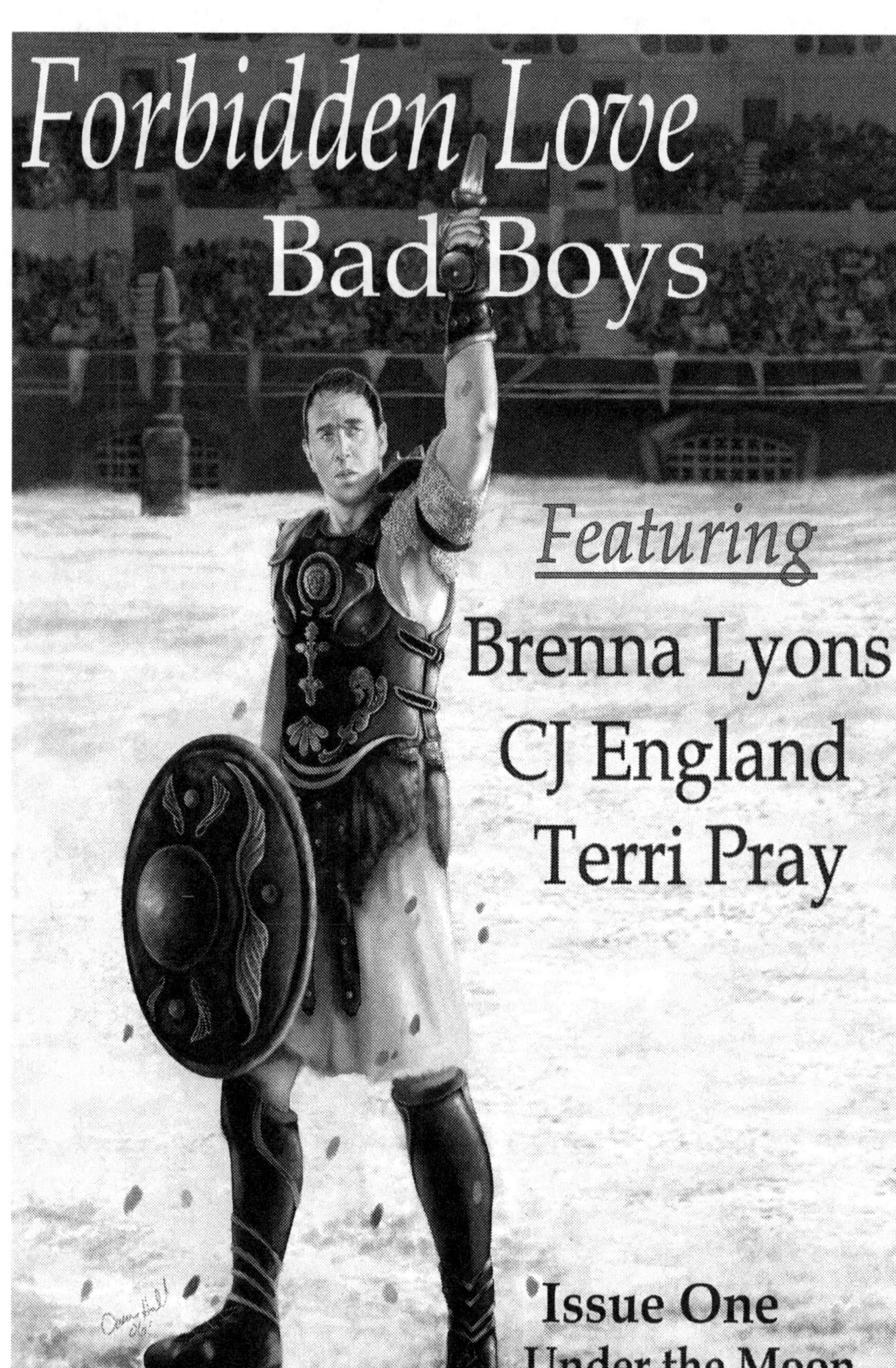

Forbidden Love
Bad Boys
Featuring
Brenna Lyons
CJ England
Terri Pray
Issue One
Under the Moon

Forbidden Love:
Wicked Women
Featuring
Brenna Lyons
Claudia Christian
Terri Pray
Under the Moon

Erien Tales
Book One:
The Dragon Prince
Terri Pray

Not So Noble
Tales
Terri Pray

To Moscow with Bony: An alternate history of a world without Waterloo, where Napoleon and Wellington march to Moscow. Follow what might have been if Napoleon's offer to work with the English and journey into Russia had been accepted. Told from the viewpoint of a Sergeant from Liverpool this Alternative History novel blends adventure, humor and military action in one tempting package. COMING SOON **FSW0003UTM To Moscow with Bony MSRP $18.00**

Astaria: Valhalla. A planet ruled by beauty, passion and violence, inhabited by a race of people bred for all three. A people constantly fighting their need to dominate or be dominated. Bound by strict codes of honor, family and blood. Two men, one woman, and the call of the sword. Can honor and passion co-exist? **FSW/UTM 001–Astaria Full color cover, B & W interior, 150 pages Softcover MSRP $15** Recommended for mature readers only.

Forbidden Love Issue 1 Bad Boys: Forbidden Love stands ready to bring you Bad Boys, Wicked Women, Assassins, Rogues, Bounty Hunters, Pirates, Wizard, Vampires and more. Are you ready to walk with werewolves? To dance with Vampires? Willing to face the wrath of your family and the scandal of your peers for one night with a Gladiator? Are you prepared to risk all in the name of glamour, power and perhaps even love? **Recommended for mature readers only. FSW601UTM Forbidden Love Issue 1 Bad Boys Color Cover, B&W interior illustration MSRP $16.00**

Forbidden Love Issue 2 Wicked Women: Debuting **Claudia Christian's, of Babylon 5 fame**, entry into the realm of women's fiction and from the wicked minds of Brenna Lyons, C.J England, Terri Pray, Sapphire Phelon, Under the Moon is proud to present tales of Wicked Women. From Pirates to Shape Shifters, these are women who will do whatever it takes to get the job done. They will use their bodies, their minds, their wits in order to win, regardless of the cost. Are you ready to face these dangerously wicked women? **Recommended for mature readers only. FSW601UTM Forbidden Love Issue 2 Wicked Women Color Cover, Color and B&W interior illustration MSRP $16.00**

Erien Tales 1: The Dragon Prince: The Dragon Prince is an adventure, romance and delightful fantasy. The Lady Orent adds humorous relief with her witty inner dialogue with the prince and an elegant element of fantasy to this tale of magic and romance. **FSW 2011–The Dragon Prince Full color cover, B&W interior, 96 pages Softcover MSRP $15**

Not so Noble Tales: Noble stories and high ideals have had their say, but now from the mind of Terri Pray come some not so Noble Tales. From glimpses of the world of Erien in Valiant the Not so Noble and A Man to Slay Dragons, to a peek into the mind of a serial killer. Meet a Bounty Hunter whose target is a Vampire that the rest of the Dark community would happily disavow any knowledge of, and find out just how hard it is to keep a job when you're dead. Step into the worlds of Terri Pray, but take care. You might just find you never wish to leave... **FSW 2010–Not So Noble Tales Full color cover, B&W interior, Softcover MSRP $15**

Available through http://www.genreconnections.com/shop